They all loved—

# THE GIRL FROM PETROVKA

**Joe**—a cynical American reporter who thought he had seen everything until the Russian girl entered his life and began tearing it up into confetti

**Kostya**—a Don Juan, Russian-style, whose bachelor flat was the nearest thing to a Playboy pad in Moscow

**The Minister**—who forgot about corn production and began sowing his wild oats

**Vladimir**—the serious young man who discovered that a woman could be more than a comrade worker

**And you, too, will fall in love with the most delightful heroine of this or any other year!**

# THE GIRL FROM PETROVKA

# The Girl From
# PETЯOVKA

## BY GEORGE FEIFER

AN AUTHORS GUILD BACKINPRINT.COM EDITION

*The Girl From Petrovka*

AN AUTHORS GUILD BACKINPRINT.COM EDITION
Published by iUniverse, Inc.

For information address:
iUniverse, Inc.
2021 Pine Lake Road, Suite 100
Lincoln, NE 68512
www.iuniverse.com

Originally published by Viking

Because of the dynamic nature of the Internet, any Web addresses
or links contained in this book may have changed
since publication and may no longer be valid.

This is a work of fiction. All of the characters, names, incidents, organizations,
and dialogue in this novel are either the products of the author's
imagination or are used fictitiously.

ISBN: 978-0-595-47602-2

Printed in the United States of America

# 1

☐ When I have some free time in the early afternoon and it's not unbearably cold, I often take a walk along Petrovka. It's not a ritual or anything symbolic, but simply a way to stretch my legs and absorb some sights and sounds of city life after a solitary morning's work and the winter sullenness that invades my office through the window. Petrovka starts just round the corner from the office and runs about half a mile almost due south, ending beside the Bolshoi Theatre at Sverdlov Square, near the very center of town.

The street has unpleasant connotations because of the dominant building at the near end—near to my office, that is. This is the notorious 'Number 38', headquarters of the Moscow Criminal Police. Number 38 is a large stone structure with the look of a mental hospital. It's carefully maintained and surrounded by a ten-foot iron fence—one of the few buildings of its age in Moscow with straight angles and a façade unblemished by peeling plaster. Outside, a cordon of armed policemen patrol in overcoats cut to the uppers of their boots; they wave black limousines through the gates from time to time and never smile. Muscovites don't say 'police headquarters' but simply 'Petrovka thirty-eight'—'he was whipped off to thirty-eight'—and there are disturbing rumors about interrogations in the basement. The captain of the guard (presumably three or four rotate the twenty-four-hour watch, but they all have the same gross features, like the town bullies of Gorky's youth) peers at each passer-by, and it's assumed someone's stationed behind the bars of a ground-floor window with a telescopic camera. For prudence, therefore, I always keep to the opposite sidewalk. I pass there almost every day, and years have convinced me that this is enough to make police superintendents, and most Soviet officials of any kind, suspicious.

I used to seethe at this need for caution—the stupidity of such things here, the hundred daily humiliations. Time trains you to swallow them. There are so many more abhorrent pressures to rail at when the railing mood comes on that petty irritations like these pass almost unnoticed. Besides, you learn not to complain about the major wrongs too—unless you're unhappy enough to court expulsion. I myself can't risk that now; I must remain in Moscow for at least three more years.

In any case, I avert my eyes almost instinctively when I pass the blank fortress now. You must be very brave, very angry or very foolish to pry into matters like police work here. Number 38 occupies almost a full block near Petrovka's northern end. Just below this the old thoroughfare takes on its own personality, and it's here, in the center, yet backwoods, of the city, that I love to wander. Petrovka at this point is an ancient, bustling shopping street, lined with former merchants' houses built at the turn of the century and peeling, sagging, rotting under a hundred layers of chalky yellow paint. On the ground floor, the weary old houses are now a jumble of offices, small shops and proletarian cafés. The floors above are given over to decrepit three-beds-to-a-room apartments. It is an urban Russian salad.

The pavements bordering the houses are as jammed as an Oriental bazaar; their pedestrian traffic spills out into the roadway, ignoring the railings erected specifically to prevent this, as well as the fierce whistles of policemen

6

who yearn to establish order. Fat old women in mountains of smocks and shawls are hawking greasy *pirozhki* and a bizarre assortment of books they can't read. A forty-minute line has formed for a truckload of pathetic chickens sold directly from their muddy crates: a professorial-looking gentleman is wrapping his in the morning's *Pravda* and stuffing it into his tattered briefcase. Stalls selling ice cream, foul-smelling soap, runty lemons (at the equivalent of two dollars each), theatre tickets and odd items of flimsy clothing obstruct the already impossibly crowded alleyways. Here as everywhere on Russia's back streets, the ordinary people, the anonymous masses, join in their daily, and eternal, struggle to acquire the necessities of life. The street is awash with bulging black overcoats colliding in a kind of human kinetic motion, bumping and jostling each other without resentment—without, one would swear, even feeling the contact.

The shops are shabby and battlescarred, with the look of worn, wooden Woolworths recovering from the depression. Inside, crowds ten to twenty deep are fighting toward the counters, resolved to buy sausage, panties, pencils, *anything* before supplies are exhausted. The salesgirls, school dropouts with crudely bleached hair, compete in demonstrating contempt for the supplicating customers.

Occasionally one jolts out of her studied indifference to abuse a customer. 'How do *I* know if this pen works. You're the one who wants to use it, not me. Get out your money or leave.'

Some of the shops have been modernized recently on what was presumed to be a Western model, but the signs are so primitive and metal fronts so amateurish that the effect is more pathetic than smart. Petrovka is what Petrovka was; the changes themselves, even those wrought by the Revolution, speak more than anything of the continuity of Russian life. The rag-tag, cosy spirit conveyed

7

in paintings of peasant markets in the seventeenth or eighteenth or nineteenth century—it does not matter which—is the spirit now.

This is why I take my walk on Petrovka and drift among its crowds. It is the heart and soul of Russia, the real Russia, not the mask I write about in my newspaper or Soviet journalists in theirs. I'm not a Soviet expert and still less a Slavophile; just a rather veteran Chicago reporter who was posted here almost three years ago because in my last year at night school—the year both America and Russia entered the Second World War—I had an impulse to study Russian and liked it enough to continue on my own. None of this was planned, any more than this assignment. Nor fated: at my first sight of Petrovka, I felt only pity for its impoverished people. But slowly I came to understand the street and love it, as if it were somehow mine.

I don't want to overstate this. At my age you veer too easily towards cynicism or sentimentality—and in Russia, curiously, sentimentality can be the greater danger. But something moves me in the spirit of Russia's vagrant, peeling streets, as in the spirit of her eroded river banks. They are slovenly but dearer than a mile of chrome. Despite the 'eastern-ness' and dirt, I feel an indefinable communion here with the mystery and meaning of the world.

This illustrates, I think, why a peasant loves his sliver of barren land. We all infuse with patriotism and emotion whatever we have or know, however humble—especially when humble. Something about Petrovka makes this phenomenon, or paradox, especially tangible. On this street more than any other, you are engulfed by an involuntary affection for the Motherland of sadness and misfortune. Oh backward, drunken, tortured Russia, said Gogol. How miserable you are—and how we love you!

But I'm far afield already. Rambling—as Petrovka rambles—is an occupational disease in Russia, perhaps caused by the pace of life and the geography: fields and forests without beginning or end. It's not Petrovka itself I want to write about but the person who introduced me to it. And to Moscow and Russia—the parts I'd believed no longer existed. Oktyabrina went with Petrovka like bread, as the Russians say, goes with salt. Although I'd lived literally next door for years before she appeared, it was through her eyes that I began to know and love it.

To begin, finally, at the beginning: how Oktyabrina appeared.

One morning in December, I was at my desk working on an article for the Sunday edition. The desk is a splintery old book-keeper's, but a dozen correspondents have added makeshift extensions to it over the years, and it now hogs most of the office. The office itself, is a converted bedroom of my apartment, which is in a large building inhabited exclusively by members of the 'foreign colony'. The apartment, in turn, is the whole of the Moscow Bureau of the Chicago —————, my generally agreeable employers.

It's decidedly humble as the apartments of Western correspondents go, and after my wife left for good, I spent two solid weeks pleading for new quarters before the Soviet agency that deals with foreigners. This was less for professional reasons than to escape from memories of a purposeless marriage that clung to this apartment. Which is all I need say about my former wife.

I never got the new apartment: my paper's Washington influence is considered slight and our requests go to the bottom of the list. I suppose I could wheedle a separate office in time, but the memories have left and I've had my fill of hardmouthed bureaucrats. And if I make a nuisance of myself, they'll probably assign me a full-time housekeeper—meaning a full-time domestic spy. Besides,

9

I've become accustomed to my office, even to the sourish smell of decaying Soviet newsprint. The bookshelves literally groan with yellowing *Pravdas* and *Izvestiyas* going back to 1944.

That morning, fresh coffee dispelled the newsprint smell. I was writing what my editor calls in 'in-depth backgrounder' about the average Muscovite's reaction to recent border clashes with China. The piece was going well. It was one of those rare political stories with room for tolerable honesty because public opinion fully supported the leadership, if not for the desired reasons. I'd managed to convey that the average Russian hates China and the very thought of seven hundred million Chinese, and to hint—cautiously, so as not to antagonize the Press Department—that the hatred had nothing whatever to do with 'distortions of Marxist-Leninist teachings', but sprouted from unadulterated racism.

I was rewriting the lead-in, planning an effective way to foreshadow my conclusions, when the telephone rang, just before noon. A seething voice bellowed from the other end.

'Volodya? Dammit, I *asked* you for someone!'

Scrambled and amplified by the sadistic Moscow telephone network, the roar made my ear throb. There was a pause, a cough, and a second throaty crescendo. This time I deciphered, 'Gimme Volodya Mitkin fast'.

I said it must be a wrong number. The man snarled 'mother-fucker' with heroic rage, but a quick chuckle began before the receiver crashed down.

I put out my cigarette, bundled up as quickly as I could in my coat, hat, scarf, gloves and boots, and left the building, nodding, I hoped casually, to the police sentry in the courtyard. Then I crossed the boulevard in the burning cold, and walked toward a back-street residential quarter. I was heading for an out-of-the-way telephone booth, that was certain not to be tapped. The wrong number had been a signal from Kostya Kostomarov: call him from a safe place immediately.

Kostya was my closest friend in Moscow—the closest friend of almost everyone who knew him. He was a clown, a libertine, a black-marketeer, an impossible cynic: someone you could trust. The all-American boy, he liked to call himself, raised on the vodka and tears of Mother Russia. He knew enough, as his friends put it, to send half the city to a labor colony for life: anyone who couldn't keep his exploits or guilt to himself spilled them out to Kostya Kostomarov.

'Hurry, c'mon over,' he croaked when I finally got through to him from a booth impregnated with urine. 'Specialties of the house and two bottles of Stolichnaya, some of it's left.' His words were slightly furry, the limit of his disability after consuming enough vodka to amaze even his Russian friends.

I said that I had a story to finish, but Kostya cut me short.

'Procrastination on the nourishment front would be the gravest mistake,' he warned. He'd just heard that the Kremlin was 'cooking up' a new agricultural reform. 'Which means that thinking people had better drop everything immediately and have a big lunch—before it's too late.'

'I'll see you later,' I answered. 'When I've worked up an appropriate appetite.'

'Do it here—I'm sympathetic about alcoholism.'

'And listen, stop using the wrong-number system for invitations to lunch. One of these days you're going to want it for something serious, and I'll have a stomach ache.'

'Oh my,' he whispered with mock chagrin. 'Still my worst pupil. I'm trying to provide you with needed practice in undercover maneuvers—and you simply miss the whole point.'

He then embarked on an old monologue with obvious relish. 'It's that dangerous free-world upbringing of yours. You must rid yourself of telephone-trusting and all former bad habits. It's called socialist re-education, remember? You happy-go-lucky alien types somehow can't adapt to our higher form of life.'

'Let's guess what you're adapting to. The fumes are choking me over the telephone.'

He chuckled again, but I overrode his interruption. 'Hide the bottles under the bed and pretend you can't find them. It's excellent practice in undercover maneuvers.'

'What you smell, my friend, happens to be perfume. Of the tapping operator. It's our latest hit for the world market—a new scent from virgin land wild flowers called "Brezhnev's Breath". Anyway, let's have a little celebration together. Today must be Lenin's birthday, first-day-of-school day, wrote-his-last-sermon day or something. When was he bar-mitzvahed, anyway?'

'It's going to be lose-my-last-job day if I don't finish this article. Stay put and I'll be there by three o'clock.'

'Right you are, Hemingway—but you work too hard. You don't care about your friends. No one's here and it's lonely. Leave now and you can be here in twenty minutes.'

'Save some fodder. Three o'clock.'

'And watch out for your tail, OK? You need the *practice.*'

Kostya lives a mile or so north of me in an old thieves' quarter called Marina's Grove. I took a trolley instead of my car: you develop the habit of keeping as quiet as possible about visits to Russian friends—which means not parking your special 'foreign journalist' license plates outside their doors. Besides, trolley 22 goes from my building almost directly to Kostya's. It was after two o'clock when I boarded an old one, whose joints clanged and groaned in the cold. Its windows were covered by an extravagant thickness of frost.

Half a dozen passengers were huddled on wooden seats in the unheated interior. I dropped four kopeks into the cash box and ripped off a paper ticket. The trolley had hardly found its momentum on the icy tracks when I saw the omen.

Tickets on Moscow busses and trolleys are identified by six figures. When—according to local superstition—the sum of the first three equals the sum of the second, the bearer will soon experience great good luck or a sharp change of fortune. In two years, I'd examined a thousand tickets with no luck. But the red numeral on this one leapt from the paper: 393393. The nonsense made me smile—but I've always had a superstitious streak.

# 2

☐ The 'Kostomarov Residence' looks like a survivor from the 1812 fire, with an exterior of logs and a pitted tin roof. Kostya lives on the top floor, in the former servants' quarters. The names of the four families that share his communal apartment are scrawled on greasy cards next to the doorbell.

I pulled the bell three times, Kostya's ring, and he was at the door in an instant, smelling of a night without sleep. He greeted me with a wink, but according to his 'house rules', we said nothing until reaching the safety of his room. Don't advertise your accent, Kostya had warned me before my first visit. One person in every communal apartment is on retainer to report unusual occurrences to the police.

Kostya kicked the door closed with a bare foot and led me quickly down the grimy corridor past the communal kitchen and rooms of other families to his own, a flyblown rectangle with just enough room to squeeze between the chest of drawers and the bed. The floor and shelves were crammed with a massive assortment of junk. There was a collection of rusted draftsman's tools, broken bits and pieces of several television sets and large rag dolls, a blackened piano keyboard, and four or five ancient car batteries from the garage where he worked— the hopeful beginnings of his own car. All this was covered with a medley of pots, pans and empty bottles—and,

14

in areas that hadn't recently been touched, a thick layer of dust. The once emerald walls were spattered with several decades of curdled grease.

'Hi, Zhoe buddy. You're just in time for our daily bread.'

'Hello yourself, Kostya. How's it going?'

'So-so. How the hell can it go?' He tossed my coat on the bed and gave my shoulders a quick rub-down with his ex-sailor's, -miner's, -boxer's hands. For some reason, he always pretended that I was approaching infirmity, although we were almost the same age. 'You look cold,' he said, casting about amidst the junk for a bottle that wasn't yet empty. 'A man of your age must keep his tank full. Keeps the mind clear and arteries open.'

Kostya handed me a large water glass and filled it to the brim with 'fuel', his code-word for vodka. For himself, he poured a clear liquid called spirit, a home-brew of ninety-nine per cent alcohol obtained from a 'certain source' on the nursing staff of a gynaecological hospital. It was murder to swallow.

'Chin-chin—to you and yours.'

'And to every one of us. Cheers.'

He tossed down his glass in a gulp and broke into a John Garfield grin. 'Great stuff,' he winked. 'Heals cuts and bruises from the inside—it's pure.'

He slipped off his trousers and black turtleneck, revealing a worn pair of swimming-trunks. Kostya liked to be at home in his bathing suit during the winter months; it encouraged him to daydream, he said, of everything he'd been deprived of by history, geography and fate. Hands on his still muscular stomach, he surveyed his treasured room with distinct pleasure—one of the few in the city enjoyed by a bachelor alone. On a two-burner hotplate—he preferred not to use the communal kitchen —he was cooking a cauldron of his famous borscht.

'*Nu* stranger,' he said, warming himself in the steam of

15

the soup. 'How is it you're avoiding me? You'll give me a complex—my labor productivity will suffer.'

'I've got to stay sober. You won't know it, but there's been lots of news lately. Work.'

'Rationalize the journalistic process and you'll have it licked. Like *Pravda*: it's a cinch to write a couple of weeks' news in advance. Anyway you're dying to tell: what *is* the latest from our planet?'

'Kosygin arrived in Berlin yesterday for a big ceremony. There's some speculation about why Suslov went with him. It's in preparation for the giant hundred and fiftieth year memorial for Karl Marx.'

'Are you serious? Who's Kosygin? Why should I know a character with a label like Marx? I've told you a hundred times—you Americans have your friends, we have ours.'

He poured a second round of drinks and fetched a fat herring from the improvised refrigerator between his double windows. 'My home's your home,' he pronounced, skinning the herring. 'Humble apologies for the temporary disorder. Be a good guest and consume that little glass.'

I handed him a packet of Gillettes from the Embassy commissary. Razor blades had disappeared from Moscow shops six weeks before, and he'd asked me, somewhat sheepishly, for something to shave with.

'Comments will not be tolerated under this roof,' he said with mock-irritation. 'No ideological subversion from a pawn of the monopoly-capitalistic press. My dear fellow, it's easy enough for you over there to make toiletries: you exploit the working class. Besides, who needs razor blades? The Soviet people scorn such invidious bourgeois enticements; we have sputniks. Soviet cosmonauts are dancing in space at a billion rubles a waltz— that thrills us deeply as we fondle our stubble. To hell with your imperialistic razor blades. Shut up.'

16

He examined the packet delightedly and cleared a place of honor on a steamer trunk.

'Upon reflection, I might be persuaded to accept them,' he said. 'You Westerners invest so much ego in your industrial products—it's my duty to avoid an international incident.'

'Many thanks, I'm so relieved. They've run out of Tampax. Need anything else in a hurry?'

'Not at the moment. Well yes, now that you mention it. I require some Italian sunglasses and a sky blue Cadillac. It would be an aesthetic incongruity to use Moscow's public transport with a Gillette shave.'

The room was warming up. Kostya inhaled a Camel and closed his eyes, spinning out his pleasure.

'Peace to one and all' he sighed. 'We're a very peaceful people anyway, we hate to fight. You've noticed the absence of duels on the streets of our glorious capital? Yet another accomplishment of Communism. You have to drop a glove to start a duel, after all. So you stand in line for a couple of hours to buy a pair—and by that time nobody remembers why he was angry.'

He sliced some dried mushrooms and tossed them into the soup together with spoonsful of sour cream. Then he threaded a tape of Ella Fitzgerald on his recorder and sang along with her, miming the lyrics he didn't understand.

'Appropriate appetite achieved,' I announced. 'No doubt there's a forceful reason why you didn't go to work today?'

'I happen to have an official chit,' he said with dignity. 'Stamps, seals, everything.'

'Not the witness role again,' I asked. Whenever he saw a traffic accident, Kostya always dropped everything and dashed to it. This required his appearance in court as a witness, which afforded at least one day off work in return for his hour of testimony.

17

'*Nyet*, this time I'm on the critical sick list. Strange and terrible pains in my duodenal tract—can't you see?'

Kostya grinned again and explained in exquisite detail how five slipped-in-the-bra rubles and a promise of a half-box of Tampax had induced a pretty young doctor to 'liberate' him for the day. 'What the hell, we'll just have to steel ourselves and wait one labor day more to reach Communism. . . . Come to think of it, what's the rush?'

He gulped another swig of spirit and lay back on the sagging, unmade bed. 'Anyway,' he added, 'I have to stick around today to feed the kid.'

'Who's the kid?'

'Just a lassie who's been visiting me.'

'I see. I don't suppose she's over twenty-one?'

'She's a vigintinerian, I think. Times are tough. Soon I'll be running an old-age home.'

'So you've got another one.' Kostya had literally hundreds. Some days half a dozen 'lassies' called on him between noon and midnight—he gave them two-hourly appointments. And he liked them young. He kept a clay jug under his chest-of-drawers into which they were all trained to pee. Serious trouble would descend if his neighbors in the apartment observed a procession of teenagers filing to the communal bathroom.

'Not exactly. I mean she's not on the first team. I'm just keeping an eye on her until she finds her feet.'

'I can imagine. Who is she then? What's her name?'

'Oktyabrina. She's a ballerina who came in from some provincial company to make her name. That's all anyone knows about her. She turned up a few weeks ago, tired and hungry.'

'Sounds right up your alley.'

'There's an exception to every rule, to borrow Lenin's saying. You'll understand when you see her. As a matter of fact, I was wondering. . . .'

He lit another Camel and let the thought die.

'As a matter of fact, I'm worried about her. Look, Zhoe, I know it's a bit tricky for you, but I was thinking maybe you could. . . .'

At that moment, the bell rang three times. Kostya threw on his trousers and sweater, and dashed towards the door. 'Zounds, if the neighbors see the likes of *her* traipsing in here, that's all I need.'

The girl who appeared in the doorway behind Kostya was not merely unlike any other in Moscow. She was outlandish enough for Greenwich Village or the King's Road. Her face oozed make-up: a runny pool of pancake, mascara and lipstick, all applied as if the object were to test the absorbency of skin. I had the impression that a childish ingenue hid behind the mask, but it could be no more than a guess. Only the absurdity of the smears and splotches kept them from being unsavory.

She followed Kostya into the room and succumbed to a profound shiver—which, having caught Kostya's worried glance, she tried to convert into a joyful hallelujah gesture.

'Aloha, Kostya precious. You're in that dreadful sweater again. I *told* you.'

She herself was wearing what must once have been an evening coat—a summer model, unlined. A patch near the pocket, apparently treated with a cleaning fluid, suggested the coat was blue silk. 'How do I look, angel? I purchased it from the most *inspiring* old woman. She wore it the evening she was seduced by Rasputin.'

She held her hands coyly beneath the threadbare velvet collar and executed a shaky pirouette before Kostya's fragment of a mirror. Something both comic and pathetic showed in the way she arched her neck and tilted her head. She'd probably seen a photograph of Audrey Hepburn in a movie magazine smuggled into Russia

19

years before and passed hand-to-hand by a hundred girl-friends.

'It's my being-seduced-despite-everything-by-powerful-men wrap,' she disclosed, stroking the coat. 'This morning it drove a victim wild, almost caused a *skandal* on Gorky Street. He runs an atomic factory or something in a place called Dubna. Demonstrated what they're working on out there at the moment, a hush-hush project he called radioactive love.'

Kostya shook his head and looked at me with pained yet delighted eyes. The girl sounded like a precocious pupil of his; the irreverent mention of Dubna, the nuclear research center near Moscow, pleased him visibly. For some reason, his curious friend produced a faint pang in me. My inclination to laugh was supplanted by a notion that I'd seen her before—long before, which made the notion impossible. But she too seemed to flash me a recognition signal.

Kostya registered our exchange of glances and cleared his throat. 'Zhoe,' he said gravely, 'I'd like to present the kid. Kid, this is my old friend Zhoe—I mean, my friend of old. Virtue's my mate and all that, but in a jam—say some kind of cell—I'd rather have Zhoe.'

Oktyabrina offered her hand from the tattered coat. Her fingers were frozen.

'You two provincials ought to get on famously,' Kostya continued. 'Zhoe's an imported product too. Transatlantic in fact—from America.'

'How marvelously exciting,' exclaimed Oktyabrina. 'I'm from the Kingdom of Tanganyika myself.' She curtsied to the floor and they both laughed.

'It's an expression,' Kostya explained. '"I'm from America" stands for something far-fetched, like outer space—no one takes it seriously.' He pierced the ends of a raw egg with a corkscrew and pushed it at Oktyabrina. 'Drink this, kid, you need some emergency protein.'

'Thanks loads, darling, but I'm not the slightest bit hungry. And I can only stay a second. I just dropped by to see if you need anything. You're absolutely certain you're OK?'

Her speech was something I'd never heard before, a kind of Russian version of a clever Brooklyn girl parodying herself. She had begun to flutter about the room, picking up things and peering into corners to determine, I guessed, if there were new additions to Kostya's stock of discarded, mislaid and forgotten cosmetics. Soon she discovered a bottle of something streaky and added a layer to her face. Then she sank into the bed, sighed profoundly and closed her eyes. A moment later she was up again.

'Ciao children, I'm off. Into the snowy wastes. The most *delicate* errand of mercy.'

'Where do you think you're going?' Kostya demanded.

'Really darling, don't even ask. Actually, I've got an urgent appointment with a certain terribly important official. He's a frightful Don Juan as well as a balletomane—I must decide *this minute* whether to mix business and pleasure.'

'Balls,' barked Kostya. 'Sit down and scrape off the lipstick. You're going to have a feed.'

Ignoring her feeble show of opposition, he forcibly removed her coat. Underneath were layers of ratty sweaters over a washed-out green dress. The outfit was consummated by a scarlet ribbon tied across the chest as a sash. Near its center over her snippet of a bust, was pinned a hand-cut oval: a yellowed photograph of a Victorian woman wearing a crown.

Oktyabrina observed my gape from the corner of her eye visibly pleased by her effect. 'I'm planning to do Odette next season,' she explained soberly, nodding down to the photograph. 'Swan Lake. I mean a ballerina worth

21

anything must *live* her parts day and night, don't you agree?'

'It sounds logical to me,' I said, encouraged that she'd finally said something that was open to an answer.

'I suppose you've seen Spesivtseva's Odette in Monte Carlo,' she said, apparently encouraged herself. 'And you're terribly sad when you remember the old days. I don't understand what's *happening* to ballet in this country.'

She paused to catch her breath and remove her boots, which had apparently been lacquered with nail polish. 'Swans,' she continued, 'are an ancient folk symbol for purity, as you probably know. Purity, grace and redemption—which is why the part is so crucial. The symbolism happens to come from the old Teutonic legend of the Swan Queen. That, as well as the legend's Slavic variations, was Tchaikovsky's inspiration.'

'And the Teutons took it from Marx of course—the father of all our culture,' Kostya broke in. 'Now stop that psychopathic chatter and sit down.'

Kostya quickly seated her on the trunk and hunted for his wooden ladle. Soon he divided the mellow borscht into three large serving bowls. Then he jumped up again. 'What a disgrace!' he exclaimed. 'I've actually served without napkins.' He hurriedly ripped up an old *Pravda* and offered the segments on his arm, bowing elegantly like the proprietor of a grand establishment. 'Your very own serviettes, my lords and ladies.'

Oktyabrina wanted to laugh, but was too busy attacking the soup. In the seconds between large, slurping spoonfuls, however, she managed to blurt out an announcement. 'A man marries for soup . . . a woman for meat . . . it's an old Russian saying.' Then she too jumped up, to search for her handbag. When she'd found it, she removed a sprig of dill from the bottom and sprinkled some into my bowl.

22

'Dill is important,' she confided. 'For masculine powers. No, Kostya darling, *you've* had enough of this particular herb.'

She returned to her own bowl with noises of effort and pleasure. It was her eyes, I realized as she wolfed down the steaming soup, that were her most intriguing feature. They were a kind of greyish green, a mongrel mixture, but so large compared to the bones of her face that they would have been breathtaking had she been beautiful. But she wasn't in fact beautiful, not even pretty in a conventional sense—certainly not by Kostya's milkmaid standards.

'Do you thrill to the dance?' she asked me when her bowl was empty but her mouth still full of fatty soup meat and black bread.

'Well, yes,' I said. 'I suppose I do like ballet. More than motor-cycle racing, for example.'

'How marvelous! Actually I only fall in love with men who are manly enough to appreciate the subtle things. An artist can never separate her loves from her art.'

'I watched a ballet once,' Kostya confessed, scenting an opportunity to introduce one of his World War II stories. The ballet had taken place on a battle-weary cruiser on which he was serving as a gunner's mate. After VE day, the ship was despatched to Dubrovnik on a triumphant good-will visit—but for fear the crew would be contaminated by alien ideas, only the Captain and three senior officers were permitted ashore. In sight of Croatian beauties waving from shore, the crew were soon in a bad way, even for sailors. 'Even for *Soviet* sailors. Ever hear of socialist masturbation? "All together now—*stroke.*" '

Frustration, the Adriatic sun and dashed hopes of a new deal after victory heated the crew's blood to danger level. At last the Captain sanctioned entertainment by local girls. The cruiser vibrated with excitement as a stage was improvised on the main deck. Finally the curtain was raised . . . on excerpts of *Giselle*, performed by an amateur ballet group.

'*Giselle*, would you believe it? *Giselle!* We all took a socialist oath never to see another ballet. Or talk to a ballerina. The kid's an exception because—well . . . she's OK. You won't rat on me, will you, kid?'

'Who did Giselle?' Oktyabrina asked impatiently. 'Did you all fall desperately in love with her?' Except for a gleam in her eyes, I'd have sworn that the point of the story had escaped her.

'Anyway, I'm glad I never got ashore,' said Kostya, 'never set foot on foreign soil and never will, thank God. Everybody I know is dying to swap ten years of his life for a weekend in Paris—and it's insanity. You go abroad, see what real civilisation is like and you're ruined forever. I don't want to find out I've been fooling myself all these years.'

'Poor precious,' purred Oktyabrina, casting a skinny arm around his shoulders. 'Some day I'm going to take you on tour with me. To Paris, Rome, everywhere. You'll be my distinguished elderly gentleman—I'll buy you a cape and a cane. We'll sit in the sun and I'll take care of you, all right?'

'Promise?'

'If you throw away that awful rotgut.'

Kostya's grin cut deep lines into his cheeks. He was more than ordinarily paternal with Oktyabrina, but she pretended not to notice and plunged into a lecture about Giselle. The crucial difficulty of the role, she explained, is the inversion of the plot line. 'The first act throbs with passion, but in the second, you're all cool and celestial. The dramatic tension is fantastically difficult to maintain.'

'I knew a boxer once who specialised in dramatic tension,' said Kostya. 'It was otherwise known as "taking a dive". He was the favourite of a certain commissar in Odessa. . . .'

But I stopped Kostya. It was time for me to leave: my China story had to be telegraphed from the central post office before five o'clock. I shrugged on all my outdoor paraphernalia before going to the door, in accordance with Kostya's principle of shaving every possible second from the time his guests spent in the corridor.

'Are you really American?' asked Oktyabrina, studying my rather ungainly boots. 'I thought Americans were so marvelously *dashing*.'

'He had a difficult childhood,' said Kostya. 'Hunger, exploitation, class struggle—life's sheer hell over there.'

The concern that spread over Oktyabrina's face looked like a schoolgirl's at the movies. 'Yes, but *please* don't worry,' she cooed. 'Because you're *here* now. A good friend is worth more than a hundred relatives—it's an old Russian saying.' She gazed into my eyes again, an obvious artifice to make me feel special—which nevertheless worked.

'You've got it all wrong again, kid,' sighed Kostya. ' "A rich father-in-law is better than a hundred hundred friends." *Or*: Whatever the prophets say, marry like Adzhubei.'

'Kostya, darling, give me back my dill. I'll speak to you anon.' She turned to me with an expression suggesting that Kostya's soul was lost, but there was still hope for mine.

'Has anyone shown you Moscow properly?' she asked. 'If you're an authentic foreigner, there's absolutely too much to see. I really must recommend myself as your . . . well, *guide*.'

I managed to stifle my smile. 'Thanks awfully, Oktyabrina. But I've been here just a bit too long for a guide.' She was an engaging creature, but it wasn't wise for someone of my age and in my position to become involved with a capricious child in Moscow. Perhaps that

25

was a pretext. After the divorce, I needed a period of no involvement with anyone.

'Hell, no. It's a brilliant idea,' exclaimed Kostya. 'Of course he needs a guide—he's just shy.' And before he hustled me down the corridor to the door, he'd arranged that Oktyabrina would telephone me when she was free and identify herself as 'Tanya'—the signal to meet exactly half an hour later at the fountain just below Petrovka, in Sverdlov Square.

## 3

□ The call came a few days later. The voice was a strained falsetto, perhaps caused by the excitement of the subterfuge, or, as it seemed, the sport of operating a public telephone alone.

'It's *me*, Mr Washington. You remember Tanya, your dear old friend. I'm calling you from inside a *telephone booth*. Just to see how you're getting on.'

Oktyabrina sounded even sillier without Kostya. Yet her voice, like her eyes, somehow made me feel more alive. On the other hand, perhaps it was simply the thought of a change—any kind of change. The choices of what to do in the evenings boiled down to bridge again with the how-terrible-Russia-is Embassy crowd or a love-thy-factory film show alone on the hard bench of some local theater. In early winter, Moscow can be dismally empty for a foreigner. I was getting used to living alone again, but the few unmarried journalists I knew spent too many evenings drinking and brooding.

I replaced the phone in a better mood and checked the latest copy on my agency wires. The major news was a cabinet crisis in Rome—and the very notion of Italy, with a Mediterranean climate and Latin temperament, seemed like fantasy. I tuned into Moscow Radio while I dressed: a stitcher in a clothing factory was sighing that she worked on each garment as if it were meant for her dear leader Lenin himself; it exhilarated her—and helped

27

her raise her productivity. I listened to the next story too —about an asbestos plant—because I didn't want to arrive early for the appointment. After a full twenty minutes, it was time to go.

I left the apartment feeling foolish excitement. A passing taxi had room for one more passenger and soon dropped me at Sverdlov Square. I wrapped my scarf tight, hurried the few yards to the fountain—and waited. The air was like iron. After five minutes, my toes were too numb to feel my own stamping.

It was still early evening but the square, the streets, the entire city center were virtually deserted. Most Muscovites seal themselves early into their rooms for the greedy winter night, as if fear of wolves-after-dark lingered in the folk subconscious—or perhaps the Building of Communism precluded anything so socially wasteful as night life. From time to time a furtive black overcoat slithered along a path leading to the dormant fountain. It was so cold that my watch seemed to have slowed down. I played the game of trying not to look at it for a predetermined number of minutes.

Oktyabrina arrived half an hour late, strolling. An oversized aquamarine caste mark decorated her forehead. My thoughts raced at the sight of her: what was I doing with this odd waif? Yet something pulled me towards her —something more than the wild contrast she presented to everything around her. She arched her back and deposited a kiss on my cheek.

'Aloha, darling. Are you frozen? Who sold you that funny little hat?'

'Hello, Oktyabrina. What on earth kept you? As a matter of fact, I'm half icicle.'

'I'm dreadfully sorry, darling. Just imagine: there I was, dashing to wonderful you, when I ran into two of the most superb weightlifters. It took *hours* to reconcile them—they almost came to blows over who'd seen me first. How's the world ever going to have peace and friendship if men can't even stop fighting over *me?*'

She sighed delightedly, and slipped her arm in mine. 'Isn't Moscow heavenly at night? The bustle everywhere. The traffic. All the *lights.*'

The 'traffic' was a handful of World War II surplus trucks rattling laboriously along the icy expanse of Marx Prospekt. The lights emanated from a buzzing, single-strand neon sign over a lopsided shop: 'GL RY TO THE SO IET P OP E!'

'It's super to see you again,' she continued. 'Kostya says I should hearken to you carefully and remember what you say. *You* might be the steadying influence I need.'

'Kostya's wonderful at ambiguous compliments. Now, then, what's my personal guide arranged to show me this evening? It might be pleasant to get indoors rather quickly.'

She tugged on my arm. 'The list begins brilliantly, with the National Café. Why that curious wince, Zhoseph? You'll positively *love* the National.'

It was simultaneously a dismal prospect and the inevitable choice. Moscow's range of 'nightspots' is limited to a handful of beseiged restaurants and cafés. Without coffee houses or pubs, not to speak of bars or cabarets, the object is always to find some place—any place, as a refuge from the cold. The National was as close as any.

We walked past several deserted government buildings to the inevitable cluster of pleading, would-be customers outside the café. When I finally convinced the doorman that I was a foreigner, he reluctantly slid back his stave and let us in. The blue-faced supplicants who'd been waiting for hours were sad but not angry: Russians have long been resigned to people with privileged status jumping every line and laying claim to every 'deficit' item.

29

The National Café looks out across Manyezh Square onto the Kremlin walls. It is a cavernous hall full of funereal furniture, neo-Victorian gilt and all the charm of a self-service cafeteria. As in Russian peasant huts, the windows are sealed shut for the winter, making the clammy heat inversely proportioned to the cold outside. The air reeks of acid perspiration and potatoes fried in suspect grease.

Despite all this, the National—helped by the absence of competition—was then enjoying a noisy vogue. It was recognized as the ultimate of Moscow swank and mecca of its *beau monde*: underground jazz enthusiasts, pimps and currency speculators; would-be-actresses and middle-aged officials in search of would-be actresses; sons and daughters of the bureaucratic elite who had read about Paris and hoped against hope that some day, somehow, the National would become a real café; assorted dandies whose achievement of eminence was attested by the wearing of black-market Western clothing. A young man of the last category shared our table: a handsome country lad with black curls and a big smile. He sported a mohair sweater of unmistakably non-Soviet make that sagged to his knees and made him drip sweat in the suffocating air. He grinned and loftily exhibited the Italian label.

'Wanna sell your shoes?' he whispered the moment we were settled. 'Your shirt? Socks? I don't suppose your girl friend's got some spare er . . . unmentionables? He had moved his chair almost flush with mine, and spoke in an earnest whisper.

'The underwear of his girl friend,' pronounced Oktyabrina with a significant glance at me, 'happens to be the creation of Moscow Cotton Factory Number 4. Fashioned, alas, by honest proletarian hands. In brief, you wouldn't want it.'

'Go on, you're kidding.' The boy could not believe that such a creature in such an outfit—she was wearing the green print dress again, but the sash was now pink—could be Russian.

'If you appreciate the finer things,' Oktyabrina added, 'I'll be happy to arrange a consultation at a later time. But please desist from all commercial propositions now. My escort and I'—she gazed at me again—'are here to celebrate a memorable beginning.'

The boy took the rebuff good-naturedly and insisted on pouring us some syrupy brandy from his carafe to toast our acquaintanceship. 'You're in films, aren't you?' he winked to Oktyabrina. 'Come on, admit it. All the big stars come here.' Throughout the next hour he contemplated the room and its occupants as if this were Sardi's after a première. From time to time he raised his glass with a flourish and pronounced, *'Blesk! Blazhenstvo!'*—This is heaven! Bliss!—in recognition of his good fortune. He made a benign and gentle drunk.

Oktyabrina's enjoyment was more active. She wriggled in her chair to indicate rapture and batted her eyes to suggest that I'd been extraordinarily gallant to arrange such a supper—even if my motive was seduction. Her enthusiasm was somehow infectious: for the first time I glimpsed what Muscovites see in the café. Much depends upon imagination.

When the waitress finally appeared, we ordered caviar. Oktyabrina commented on its 'procreative powers', then wolfed down her double portion and appropriated a spoonful of mine. Rubbery veal followed with potatoes in congealing grease. Oktyabrina ate with the intensity of a hamster, occasionally stuffing bread into her mouth with both hands; and in a volume out of all proportion to her size. She approached vodka respectfully, however, screwing up her face before her one and only sip and

31

swallowing it with a jerk and a glower, as if the act were her duty as a proper Russian.

'Isn't this the *gayest* place?' she bubbled. 'Let's drink this toast to dear, exciting Moscow.' She had begun to relax and the broad vowels of provincial Russia breached her affected Moscow accent.

'It's time to tell me about yourself, Oktyabrina. Who are you for a start?'

'You're such an endearing boy sometimes, one can't put into words who one *is*.'

'Just some facts, then. Like what you're doing in Moscow.'

'Zhoe darling, I'm simply useless at small talk. It's so petit-bourgeois.'

She lit a cigarette flamboyantly, choked on the first puff, and we both laughed.

'Do I trust you with everything, then?' she said. 'Move closer.' Then she launched herself on her autobiography with a curious excitement, as if in the third person.

She was born twenty years ago in Omsk, a small city in southwestern Siberia. She never knew her father: he was one of the earliest World War II aces, having downed fourteen Messerschmitts and Focke-Wulfs before being shot down himself and killed heroically in 1944. Her grandfather was a minor nobleman whose estate had been in Omsk Province. He was shot from the saddle while commanding a regiment of White cavalry during the Civil War.

'Didn't that cause the family hardship?' I asked.

'Nothing unimaginably ghastly. You see, my family was never very *political* as such; after all, Mama and Papa named me in honor of October. That *proves* they never took the Revolution personally.'

Her mother was guided by the family motto—Glory Forever in Aspiration—more, perhaps, than the noble side itself, even though she'd been born a peasant. Self-educated at first, she won her way into medical school to become a revered doctor and the senior surgeon in Omsk's leading clinical hospital. She died tragically in a room above her own ward, of yellow fever contracted from a patient.

'I adored Mama. She was a selfless heroine. And I was her only child. She used to say I generated so much love in her that armfuls were left over for a thousand patients.'

Oktyabrina, now eleven, was placed in an orphanage the day after her mother's death. The shock made her first years there disastrous; she was the only girl in the history of the orphanage to make eight escapes. The staff were patient: both her parents, after all, had died heroically in the Motherland's service. Oktyabrina was eventually assigned an individual tutor, a kind of personal commissar, in the hope of mitigating her influence on the other girls. Everyone despaired for her future. But she was destined to undergo a sudden metamorphosis.

Soon after her fourteenth birthday, a second-string ensemble of the Kiev Ballet visited Omsk, and the orphanage children were taken to a matinee as a May Day treat. The dancers were glorious; Oktyabrina was thunderstruck. The next day she applied for Omsk's primary school of ballet. She spent the rest of her adolescence working terribly hard in preparation for a magnificent career in the dance.

'You see, I always longed to be a ballerina. And I *am* going to be one, I'm going to . . . why are you smiling like that, you rat?'

'I'm not smiling, I'm listening. It's nice to hear someone like you talk.'

'Don't be a nasty old man, Zhoe darling. They always warned us in school about your type!'

33

'Flattery again. And when did you come to Moscow?'

'Let's see—almost eight entire *months* ago. Can you imagine being stuck in *Omsk* all your life? I mean, don't you think it's everybody's highest duty to *expand* to his absolute limit?'

I said I used to think exactly that. I might have said more, but the café was now too clangorous and hot for the simplest introspection.

'Inside, I felt a drive for expansion. My dancing required the influence of the capital. So I decided to come here to study.'

'You mean you were sent here to study.'

'Not exactly. What's the difference? Take the reins yourself and you'll arrive faster—it's an old Russian saying.'

'But what about the current rules?'

'Really, you'd think it was some sort of staggering achievement. This is a free country. You get on a train and in three days you're here.'

The thought that she might be serious stifled my laugh. 'But I always thought you can't stay in Moscow without documents. What about your *propiska?*'

She reached for my *café glacé*, appropriated the ice cream and slowly melted a large spoonful in her mouth. I was beginning to recognize her expression. She produced it when caught in something drolly mischievous, like a child confident its prank will provoke amusement rather than anger.

'What about the *propiska?*' I repeated.

'The truth is I'm *frightfully* busy these days, darling. I've been meaning to attend to it.'

'Oktyabrina!'

'Oktyabrina *da, propiska nyet*. The situation on the document's front is ah . . . fluid.'

'Perhaps you'd better crystallize it soon,' I said as gravely as I could. 'You can be sent out of Moscow to-

34

morrow, you know. You can even get two years in a labor camp—it's a crime.'

At this moment our table companion snapped out of his stupor. Suddenly the boy was lynx-eyed sober.

'Crime?' he hissed. 'That's a lie. There's nothing criminal here, try and prove it.' Oktyabrina required several minutes to quell his agitation.

'For God's sake, Comrade,' he pleaded to me under his breath. 'Pipe down and speak cleaner Russian. This place has ears. It's crawling with informers.'

'Where are they?' I asked, now whispering too.

'Everywhere, goddammit. They're assigned to strategic tables and sit around all evening in civvies, listening for hot conversations. They swarm to the National like flies to garbage.'

It was not the time to appreciate the humor of the boy's implied reflection on his café society. I cautiously examined the occupants of the neighboring tables, trying to remember whether we'd said anything incriminating.

'Relax,' murmured the boy, now reassuringly. 'You can always spot them anyway—it's a certain kind of face.' He nodded towards a dour man in a heavily padded suit. 'Besides, they give themselves away. Sit around all evening reading *Pravda* and splurging with two dishes of ice cream.'

Oktyabrina was much amused by our exchange. 'You two should swap lessons on the facts of life,' she laughed.

She insisted on lighting another cigarette to re-test her skill. This somehow led to another series of toasts. Had the waitress not disappeared for almost an hour, the lad would have spent his last kopek on more brandy.

As it was, the evening had slipped by so quickly that my watch now seemed to be racing. I had to admit that Oktyabrina was absorbing company. And to admire her determination in face of her childhood hardships. It explained a good deal about her, I realized. Behind costumes and makeup—now tacky in the heat—lay dedication and courage.

We left for the exit, where five or six stalwarts were still hoping against hope to 'climax' their 'evening' with at least a coffee, and stepped into the shock of the night air.

'A glorious, enchanting, truly memorable evening,' said Oktyabrina. 'Zhoe darling, you know how to make a woman positively bloom.'

I tried to think of how to thank her too. 'Let me take you home,' I offered. 'If you promise not to meet any weightlifters on the way.'

'Next time, Zhoe dearest. You're really a sweetheart. I just wish you wouldn't look so worried.'

'It's common sense. You know what can happen without a *propiska*. . . .'

'Nothing happens, silly. You just train yourself not to have anything to do with *them*. Keep out of offices and things and never sign anything. No one official knows you exist. . . . Anyway, documents are so tiresome. After my debut, *they'll* beg *me* to accept residence in Moscow.'

'I'm sure they will. But meantime, there's your school —you can't avoid signing things there.'

'Oh the school doesn't mind. That's its secret, actually: one hundred per cent dedication to art, with no bureaucratic insanity.'

'You're extremely lucky. What's this paradise called?'

She drew herself up. 'The Institute of Academic Dance.

We approached Sverdlov Square, which at that hour appeared to be under blackout. 'Look, Zhoe, I've got a super idea. Why don't you come to a rehearsal on Friday?'

'I'd love to. But a foreign journalist couldn't get permission to visit a barber shop by Friday.'

'No, no, you just come along with *my* permission. We're a nice, informal specialized institution—it's not the Bolshoi, after all.'

She aimed a kiss at my cheek. A minute later she was skipping ahead towards the bottom of Petrovka, her breath making dense clouds in the frigid night air.

## 4

□ It was even colder on the day of the rehearsal—one of those days when an entire nation postpones everything possible to stay in bed. But the memory of Oktyabrina's enthusiasm overcame my own inertia. I took the metro to the nearest station and plodded on by foot. Moscow street maps are virtually useless for details of these areas, and the sprinkling of passing workers I questioned shrugged their shoulders without allowing the cold to seep between their scarves; and without stopping. In that weather, everyone *had* to keep moving, even if he—abnormally—wanted to be polite.

Finally I found the street and number. It was indeed not the Bolshoi. It was an ancient, one story structure of crumbling red brick—a warehouse. And it was set on a cul-de-sac in Avtozavodakaya, a grimy, industrial section of town. I was certain I had the wrong address.

A woman as hoary and ravaged as the building was guarding the gate. She was enthroned on an old crate, her felt boots propped on a mound of dirty snow.

'Is there a ballet rehearsal inside, grandma?'

'*Nye znaiyu.* Don't know.'

'I'm looking for a dancing school.'

'*Shto?*'

'A dancing school. Young people. Music.'

Suddenly, inexplicably, she was venomous. 'Listen

grandpa, don't grandma *me*. I'll be drinking my tea—
with sugar—long after the like of you is stiff in his grave.
Limp home for your hot-water-bottle while there's still
time.'

'I was just wondering whether there's dancing instruction somewhere around here.'

'*Nichevo nye znaiyu. Ni-che-vo.*' She spat the shell of
a sunflower seed past my face.

I had started to investigate the adjoining building, a
crumbling, abandoned church, when feeble echoes of an
old piano playing ballet exercises escaped from the warehouse and crept across the snow. The old babushka instantly broke into the wail of a tragic peasant ballad—
which did not, however, quite drown out the piano. She
sang at the top of her voice while contemplating me
from the corner of her eyes, unmistakably supplicating
for my disappearance. I hurried back to her.

When I approached the gate again, she was crossing
herself furiously and bowing, as if I were a Cossack with
a knout. 'They're just having some games in there, Comrade Inspector. Children playing. I'm innocent, God in
his mercy knows it. You're from the police?'

Not immediately—for the old woman required considerable calming—she led me to a side door and into the
building. A glance disclosed that this was no ordinary
warehouse. It was an agitprop depository for some of the
mammoth stockpile of decorations which bedizen the
city on May Day and the Anniversary of the October
Revolution. Red flags, red banners, red posters, banners
with Lenin, banners with slogans, Presidium portraits,
Party icons, photographs of Lenin, mosaics of Lenin,
tinted paintings of Lenin—the whole panoply of Party
propaganda aids for pranking the streets was there. It was
all stacked helter-skelter from floor to ceiling as if abandoned prior to an evacuation of the city. In one corner

lay a thousand-odd portraits of Smiling Khruschev. They were roped off and labelled with handwritten signs: 'SUPERSEDED!! DO NOT USE!!'

The old woman clumped down a rotten stairway near the back of the building into a deep frozen basement. Signs, posters, banners, portraits of Lenin, socialist slogans, parts of Glory-to-Communism floats—again the paraphernalia reached to the ceiling. At last Grandma stopped and pointed. The 'Institute of Academic Dance' was a clearing of concrete, surrounded by giant portraits of Suslov and Brezhnev.

Oktyabrina was in the centre of the space and in dusty leotards, attempting an arabesque. She suspended it when she saw me and affected a sweeping curtain-call curtsey. The smirk on her face was enigmatic; was she actually stage-proud—*there?* She risked the arabesque again, teetered, then held it precariously, biting her lip. Her trembling could have been caused by her effort, or simply by the cold.

'*Ochen khroshow,*' wheezed a man who was evidently the teacher. 'Very good. Excellent!' He ran his cane up Oktyabrina's leg to her bottom and thrust it gently in. Oktyabrina removed it just as gently, smiling with an indulgence that did not quite disguise embarrassment. The teacher was a wizened creature, certainly over eighty, in a threadbare overcoat, bespattered ascot and over-large beret. Goateed, nicotined, hunched apparently by arthritis, he stood no more than a head taller than his cane.

A second pupil labored behind Oktyabrina: a tubby, prepubescent girl who chewed her fingers during the exercises. And in a dark corner under a papier-mâché sickle hovered a fat mother-hen of a woman, presumably her mother. The exercise bar was the frame of a lurid 'FORWARD TO THE VICTORY OF COMMUNISM!' poster. The music was not in fact produced by a piano but by a pre-revolutionary victrola. The sound horn was ruptured.

The teacher cranked the handle, maneuvered his feet into a loose compromise between first and third positions and fixed his gaze on Oktyabrina's tiny breasts. From time to time he pronounced, '*very* good, excellent', and hummed a measure or two of the music in a wheezing voice. This comprised the better part of his instruction. Several times he reminded the little fat girl to point her toes, and once explained to Oktyabrina that 'the meaning of this movement is expressed through the position of the pate'. There were elements—to be fair, more than trappings—of authentic instruction in his unlikely classroom. But even if the old man were once a genuine teacher, he no longer had the physical or mental powers to watch a class competently, not to speak of conducting one. Soon after I came he suffered a sharp diminution of energy. He alternated between striking a pose when announcing an exercise and drifting into a quasi-trance during its execution. Back hunched, eyes misted over, he failed to notice the steady souring of the music as the victrola's power ran down.

Reassured that I was neither detective nor government inspector, Grandma bragged about her part in the underground school. For her work as the Institute's lookout—'to keep the meddlers and art-lovers out'—the 'professor' paid her a ruble for every class. Life was hard, she sighed: God was in heaven, but on earth a body had to put some fat on its bones—and what's wrong with a little private enterprise, after all? Only quacks call it a cancer in the socialist system. Socialism is the salvation of the common people, but you can't bake bread without a little yeast.

She returned to her post, and I concentrated on Oktyabrina's efforts. After the initial embarrassment, her dancing no longer seemed awkward, but simply unformed. She was serious, industrious, zealous—but woefully untrained. As her meager limbs flailed, the flush of severe exertion never left her face, as if she were Pinocchio learning to walk. It was an unhappy demonstration that natural grace—which Oktyabrina did not lack—has little to do with the language of classical ballet.

The class lasted a full hour after I'd arrived. A series of simple exercises was climaxed by a brief solo by both pupils. The fat girl's effort was calamitous, but Oktyabrina ran through some elementary steps to a Chopin waltz and was nearly steady throughout. Evidently it was her show piece.

As Oktyabrina approached the 'finale' of her performance, the teacher revived. He approached me, twirling the knob of his cane between his hands and beaming.

'You came to observe our little Oktyabrina, I presume? I have the pleasure to report her progress is very gratifying.' His voice was unctuous, but suggested a measure of self-amusement. 'We're very hopeful for her; she's our very best pupil. . . . You don't, I suppose, have a filter cigarette?'

The fat girl's mother smothered her in kisses and bundled her away, slipping several bills into the teacher's deft hand as she passed. Oktyabrina unwrapped the ribbons of her shoes with a delight-in-exhaustion expression. When she had combed her hair, donned her layers of clothing and curtsied to the teacher—who was relacing his tattered spats with a length of old string—we made our way out of the warehouse and walked towards the metro together.

Sustaining a soft humming as we walked, Oktyabrina packed and repacked the ballet-shoes in her bag. She was obviously waiting for a comment from me, but I could think of nothing encouraging.

'I still have more work to do,' she declared at last. 'On

my hands. Hands are very important nowadays in places like Sadler's Wells.'

Finally her patience ran out. 'Don't be bashful. How much *did* you appreciate my work?'

My silence was uncomfortable. At last I thought of an escape.

'It was rather cold in there, wasn't it? The Institute seems to save substantially on heating bills.'

'Stiffness is indeed a major problem,' she said seriously. 'Go on.'

'That teacher of yours is quite a character. Seems to like poking people with his stick.'

'Is that all you have to say? I'm very sorry for you, Mister Narrow-Mind. It turns out you're a little man.'

'Oktyabrina dear, I'm not a critic. I only know it's a long hard road to become a ballerina. And if you have extra . . . well, inconveniences like that fellow and that place, all those Politburo types, you'll be worn out before you start. I think you're very . . . courageous.'

'*I* think condescension is unbearable. Snideness too, but neither even *graze* me. Because no one gets anywhere without obstacles. Mature people learn to make sacrifices for their art.'

'Art? The old man's certainly artful. But I wonder what he knows about art.' This was too strong; I regretted the words as soon as they emerged.

'If you're trying to say I put up with certain peccadillos from my ballet master, you're hardly revealing anything new. What you *are* doing is degrading yourself rather sadly. The first thing *sensitive* people learn is to make allowances for dedicated artists.'

'He's not an artist, Oktyabrina, and you know it. I *hope* you know it. I honestly wonder whether he knows a plié from a pirouette.'

'Bravo—the dilettante has exhibited his two highborn words.'

'Has he ever danced anywhere? *Seen* a proper ballet?'

'Evgeny Ignatievich, for your information, was once the most promising young character dancer in the Mariinsky. In its heyday. When an enraptured world turned up to be thrilled and uplifted.'

'What happened to his great promise? Why hasn't anybody heard of him?'

'Everybody who knows and loves the dance knows him perfectly well. It happens, however, that he was forced to leave the Mariinsky before he achieved supreme world acclaim.'

'The plot thickens.'

'His is a tragic story. I'm not going to tell it to a cynic. If you must know, when the Bolsheviks took over the Mariinsky Theater, they dismissed every male dancer with certain instincts towards other men. Evgeny Ignatievich was the greatest loss.'

From my memory of Soviet history, this was nonsense. If homosexuals had in fact been purged from the famous Imperial Company, it would have been only with Stalinism's flowering in the mid-1930s, after St Petersburg had become Leningrad and the Mariinsky Theater was renamed the Kirov. And when Oktyabrina's teacher would have been at least fifty.

Besides, his current behavior no more supported the story than Soviet history: he certainly didn't use his cane like a homosexual. He was obviously an old confidence trickster, but it wasn't clear whether Oktyabrina knew it. Her voice was hurt—but I thought I detected the faintest trace of irony too.

'Then he was blackballed from ever dancing again on a public stage. He was humiliated, hounded—a martyr to his art. The body and soul of genius mangled and wasted. It's an honest-to-God drama—a *tragedy*, do you understand?'

She ran out of breath. When she resumed, it was in a pleading tone.

'We're his only pupils, Natashinka and I. He doesn't even get a pension—lives on I-don't-know-what.'

'How much does he charge for the lessons?'

'Kopeks. It's three rubles an hour, if I remember correctly; four for rehearsals. He won't take more.'

'I don't believe it! Ulanova doesn't make four rubles an hour.'

She gazed at me, shaking her head. 'Please just don't bother to come to rehearsals any more. And let's not talk about this particular subject, all right? It's extremely disappointing, you know—an American making a big fuss over small change.'

She moved a demonstrative step away from me and we walked on in silence. Behind an old mill, we passed the driver of a cement truck fitting a tube from his fuel tank to that of a private car. It was the usual back-street barter: the truck driver supplying a quantity of fuel tapped from the state in exchange for a bottle of vodka. Oktyabrina observed the operation in fascination. Then she snuggled to my side again and took my arm. 'Listen,' she cooed, and by the time we'd reached the metro station, she had extracted a promise from me to supply Evgeny Ignatievich with my old clothes.

## 5

☐ A few days later Oktyabrina took me to 'her' bench on a quiet part of old Gogol Boulevard. She picked her way through the slush and ice with exaggerated caution, as if encountering them for the first time—but managed to slip half a dozen times nevertheless. After each near fall, she tightened her sparrow's grip on my arm and emitted a half-nervous, half-exhilarated giggle.

'Honestly, darling. I don't know how some women do it. I'm a mess when I have to walk somewhere without a strong man.'

It was a raw day but the wind had subsided. Oktyabrina and I had discussed kittens, camels, beards, veal goulash, and the correlation between fame and talent by the time we reached the boulevard. It is one of the finest in Moscow, with a touch of faded elegance, surrendering peacefully to inexorable decay. The strolling is done on a wide dirt path, a kind of old-fashioned promenade, with a strip of park on both sides. It's called 'gardens' in Russian, but that suggests something far too formal for the place itself: a tangle of boot-beaten paths and tumble-down benches.

Alongside the promenade, a dozen chubby children wrapped in furs and scarves were hard at work making snow pies with brightly painted toy shovels. When Oktyabrina was spied a chorus of happy squeals sounded as they all swarmed to her side. She produced two handfuls

46

of cheap candy from both pockets and distributed one to each child. They clutched the tiny prizes in oversized mittens and shoved their little, fur-bordered circles of open face forward for a kiss.

'Thank you, Aunty Oktyshka! Thank you, thank you —you brought the best kind! Come and see what we're making today.'

Oktyabrina broke into her curtain-call beam and petted the toddlers tugging at her skirt. One of the shrunken old grandmothers in charge of the children re-wrapped the black shawl around her head and blessed her with the traditional Orthodox movement. 'That's Oktyabrina Vladimirovna,' she revealed to a somewhat less withered companion. 'The lady from the theater.'

Oktyabrina's bench seemed to grow out of the trunk of a poplar on the edge of the promenade. She brushed the morning's snow from its sagging slats and curled up in a corner. 'Close your eyes and you can smell the snow,' she said, squeezing her eyelids shut and sniffing loudly. 'Plenty of snow, the crops will grow. It's an old Russian saying.'

An indescribable feeling of timelessness, boundlessness and peace pervades these places, as if you were somewhere on the steppe, far removed from a major city and the twentieth century. We watched the children playing, and I smoked several cigarettes. Oktyabrina began to chatter about herself in her usual way, and soon she was telling me the story of her first love. 'Every girl should tell her admirers how she was first seduced—if it was magnificent, of course. It sets a standard for them to aspire to.'

Oktyabrina's first time was excruciatingly beautiful. It happened in Omsk when she was a child of sixteen in pigtails and a school uniform. One morning, a note fell at her feet while she was on her way to school. It was in a bold, stylized script; '*I have been watching you from my*

47

*window. You are my muse, my dream. In the name of everything sacred in art, come to me this afternoon. . . .'*

The note was signed simply 'Dubnikov'. Fuller identification was unnecessary: Dubnikov was the leading man of the local theater, tall and dark, with a mane of wavy black hair and a deliciously frightening reputation; a latter-day Eugene Onegin. When Oktyabrina entered his room after school, his dark eyes blazed. He stood up from his desk, uncovered a pistol from under his papers, and raised it to his temple.

'I can remember his exact words to this very day. He said his love for me was slowly killing him and unless I accepted him, he was going to complete the process swiftly.'

Oktyabrina was certain that the gun wasn't loaded. Dubnikov fired a shot into the ceiling, causing a chunk of plaster to crash to the floor. An instant later, they raced for each other. The snow from Oktyabrina's collar melted on Dubnikov's bronzed face.

'I allowed him to take me, of course. It was all absolutely perfect from the first minute. We had a short but very passionate and beautiful affair—once he ripped out the telephone with his bare hands because it rang at an inappropriate moment. Of course he couldn't be seen with me publicly because of his position. But he dedicated stacks of poems to me and a story that can simply *never* be published. In the end, we were forced to terminate the liaison by mutual consent. It was absolutely destroying our concentration on our chosen careers.'

Oktyabrina cuddled herself beneath her layers of clothing and watched my reaction. 'I suppose you think sixteen's shockingly early to become somebody's mistress,' she prompted.

'Not really. Some girls are mature at sixteen—it depends.'

'Not that I could help myself anyway. You could say I was raped in a way.'

'You could, if you had to tell an abbreviated version.'

'Men are always so terribly demanding. The minute you don't give them what they want, they start fighting and shooting. You're not the violent type, are you, Zhoe?'

'Not ordinarily. But with someone like you, you know. . . .'

'Well, what do *you* think's better the first time—to be absolutely *forced* that way by some terrible power involving life or death, or to surrender after a long and desperate courtship by a brooding type?'

'You tell me—it's your story, after all.'

'I suppose that means you don't believe me. You needn't plaster that distrust all over your face, you know. It makes you look quite nasty.'

'Oh I believe *you* completely. It's just that something about Dubnikov doesn't ring true. I suspect he was actually a bastard behind that Romeo façade.'

This surprised Oktyabrina, but after a moment's thought the idea seemed to appeal to her. She scooped up a mitten-full of snow and blew it slowly into the air. 'As a matter of fact, you're absolutely right—how on earth did you make him out? He was the most terrible philanderer. . . . Can you imagine? He preyed on girls even younger than me.'

'And you parted after his trial on charges of corrupting minors—at which you testified in his defense as dictated by your noble instincts, but on the private understanding he'd never try to see you again.'

Oktyabrina threw her hands in the air. 'That's absolutely *marvelous*, Zhoe darling. I'm proud of you. You must write a forceful short story about it. It's bound to set the world ablaze and make you rich. When I'm a famous ballerina, of course.'

We both broke out laughing, and Oktyabrina snuggled as close as she could to me through my overcoat.

'You're not angry with me, are you, Zhoe? I mean when I tell you certain things.' Her voice was now very grave. 'Maybe the reason I like men so much is because I grew up an orphan.'

'Of course I'm not angry, Oktyabrina. But look here, you needn't make up stories—not for me, anyway. I used to concoct them myself. But then you realize you don't need them with people who like you. It's one of the nicer things about growing older.'

I believed this when I said it; I even felt a wave of contentment over having come this far in life and achieved this kind of understanding. But as I looked down at Oktyabrina, the opposite thought quickly intruded. One of the nicer things about being young, by contrast, was the ability to pretend that things are better than they are. It's an expression of still uneroded optimism about yourself and human nature. I missed that now.

The best thing about Oktyabrina was the way she used her own pretense. Her imagination seemed to work at several layers above and below the surface of her tales.

Oktyabrina raised her mitten to my nose and applied a playful tweak. Her lips seemed to compress into a hint of a kiss.

'What a beautiful *oration*,' she murmured. 'Not making up stories with the people who like you. I've never even *begun* to think of life that way.'

'On second thoughts, perhaps you shouldn't take my word on things like this. . . .'

'But do you really *like* me, Zhoe? Aren't I too terribly young?'

'No, you're not too young. Nobody's too young.'

She looked at me again with her innocent expression. 'You're a wonderful man—a kind of very special man, are you aware of that? And because you are—and if you

50

really *really* like me—I'll make a pact with you. From now on, we'll tell each other absolutely everything. The whole truth, without fear or favor—OK?'

She sighed happily and rested her head on my shoulder. A one-legged man had sat down near me and was feeding a flock of pigeons with a loaf of fresh bread. We stayed on the bench enjoying the peace until the cold produced a sharp shiver in Oktyabrina.

When we left, she identified all the girls among the little bundles of fur and gave them extra candies.

'It's only fair,' she explained. 'Boys get all the advantages in life anyway.'

Despite the pact, weeks passed before I had pieced together even an outline of the 'whole truth' about Oktyabrina. She did not deliberately conceal the major headaches—where she lived, what she did—but simply dismissed them, as if talking about such things would be uncouth. The essential facts revealed themselves slowly, therefore, during 'trial trysts' on Gogol Boulevard and Petrovka.

From the orthodox Soviet standpoint, the most important was that she had no job. Nor, as her conversation made amply clear, any intention of seeking one. This was an outrage to socialist morality: 'He Who Doth Not Work, Neither Shall He Eat' is still the first commandment of Soviet citizenship. And not only of morality, but also law: new decrees had been enacted not long ago, giving lower courts authority to exile 'parasites', in the official language, to hard labor in Siberia. Since then a powerful campaign had been mounted to rid Moscow of parasites and hooligans.

Despite this, it was hard to picture her working at a real job, even if she'd wanted to. And even if permitted —which, under the circumstances, was highly improbable.

To get a proper job, she would have needed a valid labor book. And for the labor book, the prime prerequisite was a *propiska*: police permission, stamped in Russians' identity papers, to live at a specified address in a specified city. There was extremely scant hope that she could ever procure one for Moscow; to move into the capital from anywhere else, a Russian must be officially invited, almost always for a skill vital to defense, research or other high-priority state requirements. An important position, in other words, can yield its own Moscow *propiska*. But without it, you can't even apply for an ordinary job.

In short, Oktyabrina was caught up in one of the vicious circles that the Soviet bureaucracy forges, seemingly better than it does anything else. With the difference that this circle served a practical objective.

The conditions of life and supply of consumer goods are so much better in Moscow than in the provinces that if the interdictions were lifted, half the Soviet Union's rural population would be selling their cows and mattresses and riding, hitching or walking to the capital within a week. It was precisely to exclude people like Oktyabrina—even hardworking families eager for a better life—that the cumbersome rules 'closing' Moscow were devised.

In time, I stopped reminding Oktyabrina about the danger of living as a kind of un-person. Thousands of drifters do manage to live almost permanently in the capital, simply by avoiding all contact with everything official—especially, of course, with the police.

Oktyabrina apparently managed as well as anyone, although she hadn't been 'underground' long enough to learn the more sophisticated tricks. On the other hand, the simplicity of her life helped her avoid unwelcome encounters. Lessons and rehearsals occupied her three or four mornings a week, and the effort and cold so exhausted her that she rested at home, inventing outfits and sponge-bathing from an iron tub, during most of the afternoons.

The sponge-bath was both indispensable and adventurous. The water was heated on an encrusted, turn-of-the-century stove whenever the landlord left to play dominoes—out of doors!—with his pals in the courtyard of a nearby recreation center. The sponge was a real one, one of Oktyabrina's prized possessions—but she had to carry it with her when she went out. If she left it at home the landlord sniffed it for dampness, and denounced her until spittle formed on his lips because she had wasted his gas.

All this took place in what she called 'Domolinart'— short for 'Young Intellectuals' and Artists' Club'. This was a pathetic copy of imposing official establishments like the Writers', Composers' and Cinema Workers' Clubs, which are all located in large buildings nearby, with special restaurants, closed cinemas and other privileges for their chosen members. Domolinart was a room above the corner of Stoleshnikov Lane and Petrovka. Strictly speaking, Oktyabrina's quarters were not this room, but a three-by-eight corner of it, behind a tattered curtain rigged around her cot.

The room itself belonged to a former railway pensioner whose most exciting moment in life was seeing a train which had been traveled on by Lenin! He rented out one corner of his room to Oktyabrina and the opposite one to another un-person, a shy young man called Leonid, a former graduate student who was trying to stay in Moscow somehow after expulsion from a physics institute. Oktyabrina talked wistfully of his gentleness and melancholy.

I saw Leonid only once during these days—a shaggy head of dark hair and glasses with one broken lens were what stood out about him—because I visited the room only once. It was on Railway Workers' Day when the old pensioner had gone to a mass meeting and was certain not to return until late afternoon. Nevertheless, Oktyabrina was categorically forbidden to entertain visitors, and she rushed me in and out of the room in a minute.

Which was more than I cared to stay. The room was as depressing as any I've seen. Everything in it exemplified that combination of cheapness, neglect and pure grime that drove tens of millions of Europe's poor to steerage passages for the New World. Oktyabrina had once tried to relieve the gloom by buying patterned red-and-chartreuse curtains in a shop on Petrovka. But the old man came home unexpectedly as she was hanging them, found her tip-toeing on a chair, and ordered her to get back in her corner, and keep her rags to herself.

No doubt he later regretted this: although he was indifferent to curtains, their being free would have given him satisfaction. For he was as stingy as he was testy. And as mercenary: he paid the standard three or four rubles a month for his state-assigned room, and charged Oktyabrina and Leonid twenty-five each for their prized and illegally sublet corners. This fifty rubles nearly doubled his pension, but he still breakfasted and supped on black bread, onions and tea, treating himself to only one full meal daily of heavy soup and kasha.

As for Oktyabrina, the twenty-five rubles for rent, although exorbitant, was a drop in the sea. Her expenses for cosmetics—she insisted on Western brands, obtained almost entirely on the black market—and for pop clothes, of which she was the first and perhaps still the only devotee in Moscow, were obviously very substantial. It could not have cost her less than 150 rubles a month to live, more than the wages of a skilled engineer.

I mention money not because it played a normal part in Oktyabrina's life—ten-ruble notes often parachuted from her pockets like so much used Kleenex—but because the source of it was part, at least, of the elusive whole truth. Oktyabrina was kept. The man was never referred to by name, but by title: 'The Minister'. 'The Minister gets furious when I'm late,' Oktyabrina would say, dashing from one of our brief afternoon walks. 'The Minister's depressed, poor dear. He tried to drive his car without the chauffeur and the motor came apart.' 'The Minister's wife issued an ultimatum last night: she gets a Persian lamb by New Year's Eve or he sleeps in the kitchen—on the floor.'

Kostya never met him, but had formed a clear idea about his character. 'He's the Marxist-Leninist version of a sugar-daddy. Keeps his girls according to socialist principles: without giving them enough to eat. Your typical Minister.'

As I understood it, however, the Minister was not in fact that, but Chairman of one of the Ministry of Agriculture's myriad research commissions or First Secretary of one of its even more multitudinous departments. Still, he was a senior official, the kind I would have given a great deal to interview professionally—a vain wish, because bureaucrats of that rank are unapproachable even by Soviet journalists. For some reason, presumably Byzantine in origin, even agricultural officials live and work in a remote corridors-of-power world, hidden away in carefully guarded office buildings and behind thick white curtains across the rear windows of their cars.

The Minister's car sported these very curtains and a 'MOS' license plate, indicating it was an official government vehicle. I first saw it parked in front of Oktyabrina's lodging house the evening I took her to *Uncle Vanya* at a small theater just off Petrovka and walked her home after the amateurish but moving performance. It was the only vehicle in sight, an immaculate black Volga whose running motor generated a great cloud of frozen exhaust. Oktyabrina froze too when she saw it. Then she clutched me, stepping up on my boots.

'Oh my God. He's here. Zhoe darling, *disappear*.' She found her feet again and pushed me with both hands against my chest. 'Round the corner—*quick*.'

But before I could disappear, before I realized why I ought to, the car had begun to back up and was almost upon us. The man who emerged from the back seat was large and loose, with Groucho Marx eyebrows and a moustache longer than his lips. He caught the sleeve of his Persian lamb-collared overcoat on the door handle, entrapped the arm further in his urgent efforts to disengage it, succeeded at last, and duck-walked towards us with a fleshy smile. Oktyabrina waved to him with one hand; with the other, she continued to push me away.

'Run along now, Uncle Vanya, it's time you got some rest.' This was meant for me but almost shouted in the Minister's direction.

Even now, I'm still embarrassed by Moscow's unwritten code of bad etiquette. A foreigner's overriding responsibility to avoid casting suspicion on his Russian friends accounts for one of the cardinal rules:. if when in the company of a Russian friend he encounters one of *his* friends accidentally, you disappear at once. In this case, the Minister's position reinforced the obligation. I backed away to the corner and went the long way home.

# 6

☐ 'Are you Jewish, Zhoe?'

'What's that, another expression?'

'No really—are you?'

'Not that I know of. What makes you ask?'

Because you're nice. You don't get angry.'

It was early the following afternoon; we were entering Sverdlov Square from the bottom of Petrovka. Over the columns of the Bolshoi Theatre, gigantic portraits of Marx, Engels, Lenin and Brezhnev were being mounted in preparation for the evening's celebration of an obscure revolutionary anniversary.

Oktyabrina gingerly slipped her arm under mine. The sight of the sun after three weeks had infected everyone with a touch of childish exuberance. A woman laborer in overalls and a cotton quilt jacket was chasing her work partner, an identically dressed man, with a broom. Both fell giggling into a snowbank.

Oktyabrina giggled with them briefly, but caught herself short. 'I knew a Jew once,' she said seriously. 'In Omsk. He never told anyone but me he was Jewish. He was the sweetest little man with about four hairs on his head and very, very good hands.'

An old peasant couple stopped us for directions to GUM. When they'd moved off, Oktyabrina continued.

'Actually it was this man more than any other who taught me to develop my mind. I think Moishe Issakovich wanted me urgently, but he always sublimated his desire in the most creative way possible: by converting it into an *artistic* assault on my *mind*. Even when I was compelled to ignore him as a man, he never, never got angry.'

'I got the message about Omsk some time ago, Comrade Circe. I'm rather more interested in the company you're presently keeping.'

'I was coming to that, Zhoe darling. You *aren't* terribly cross, are you? Because I just can't help myself. The Minister's so madly jealous.'

'That's nothing I can't achieve if I tried.'

'He actually suffers with it, the poor dear. I simply can't let him see me with another man. Even when it's ineffably pure—like you and me, I mean.'

She paused again, straightened her hat—a home-made sombrero—and nodded grandly to a startled passer-by. 'The Minister's not Jewish either,' she said slowly. 'But he looks it, so it's almost the same thing. I heard a man call him a dirty Jew at the airport. There ought to be a pill or something to make funny-looking people more romantic.'

'He looks well enough off with that coat and car. At his age, that's a pleasant compensation. How long have you known him?'

'All my life, practically. He says *his* conscious life started when the clouds parted to reveal me.'

'Of course. How long have you know him?'

'He was on the train when I came to Moscow. Invited me to share his first-class compartment and insisted I accept all kinds of sweet things. He's really terribly cuddly when you give him a little respect.'

'He must have a couple of divisions of office staff to take care of that. What does he do to rate that Volga? I mean his title on the door.'

'He masterminds some kind of vegetable strategy, I

think. Mostly it's all kinds of meetings and absolute *stacks* of paperwork. That's probably what infatuates me most about him: he's always crushed by work. I don't think people would describe it as sheer love . . . I'm hungry. Want something delicious?'

She stopped at an ice-cream cart run by an exceptionally old *babushka* and bought us each a cup of the most expensive brand. Then we slowly walked back to my car and drove to the Novodyevichy Monastery ('New Monastery of the Virgin'), which is on a quiet bank of the river, two miles or so upstream from the Kremlin. The monastery is bordered by a cemetery where Russia's elite have been buried for centuries. Solitary flowers and sprigs of pine adorned the graves of Gogol and Chekhov, but the largest bouquet lay at the plain marble tombstone of Nadezhda Alliluyeva, Stalin's first wife. The sadness of her suicide corresponded to the monastery's mood—even its very name. Boris Godunov was elected Lord Protector there in the sixteenth century, and something of the spirit of those hard days imbued the grounds. Oktyabrina and I were both very moved.

Novodyevichy was my selection. After our false start, we'd returned to the idea of seeing Moscow together properly. Dropping the pretense of Oktyabrina playing guide, we concentrated on visiting celebrated landmarks. Oktyabrina or I chose a new one every other day or so from an old Tsarist guidebook she'd found in a second-hand shop. We both attacked the project earnestly, partly, I suppose, because neither had anything more pressing to do most afternoons. It was soon much more than a way to pass the time.

The best places were the oldest ones, and the powdery guidebook was a rich source of finds. I remember visits to crypts, crumbling cathedrals, places where Peter the Great slept, estates of Tsarist nobles. One day we drove to a village called Tsaritsino, where Catherine the Great

59

had ordered a palace in bizarre Moorish-cum-Gothic style, only to abandon it in mid-construction. The gloomy skeleton still stands, together with the ruin of something called the Temple of Love, which of course captivated Oktyabrina. Next was an outing to a splendid eighteenth-century estate called Arkhangelskoye, which was once owned by Prince Yussupov, Rasputin's assassin. This was enough to make it bewitching, even without its Pushkin-like charm.

Oktyabrina herself was an essential part of the outings: she gave familiar sights the freshness of new eyes. Although I was the supposedly observant journalist, it was usually she who noticed the icon-like quality of the faces in a fresco, the Minister's moustache on an old portrait, the angle of a broken statue which complemented the angle of a medieval arch. I never admired her more than at these creative moments. She would fling out her finger to designate the spot and blurt out her observation. Then she glowed—partly, I think, because she sensed a communion with me in these discoveries.

This was her positive side as a sightseer. Her negative side generated singular complications. The first problem was usually Oktyabrina's power of concentration—which fell rather short of proverbial Russian endurance.

The first forty minutes usually went well. But then she became hungry. Or thirsty. *Acutely* thirsty, acutely tired or acutely in need of a bathroom. She was crying out for relief with a well of reproach in her eyes. Unless her needs were satisfied almost instantly, she whimpered from genuine physical distress.

She could not use a public toilet because the filth and odor made her retch. She hated cafeterias and the grim little snack-bars called 'buffets' because cheap food—and there is hardly any cheaper—upset her even when she was ravenous. Yet waiting the necessary hour or so outside a restaurant was torture. Her metabolism and fastidiousness, coupled with the dearth of consumer services, kept her on the brink of crisis, like a diabetic inexperienced in regulating his system.

Her interests also made her a rather dangerous companion. Oktyabrina was attracted to museums and landmarks principally because they told a 'life story'. What interested her most about famous people were the intimate details of their private lives. I learned to stand a discreet distance away when I sensed this interest arising, for Soviet landmarks are meant to be shrines of Education and Reverence, and their intoning guides do not value questions about love affairs and décolletage.

She coaxed me several times to the Lenin Museum on Red Square. It was one of her favorites, partly because its location made it convenient for thawing-out during long walks. Although the rooms are stuffed with the same mass-produced Leniniana displayed in a hundred provincial Lenin Museums, the oil paintings here are original and represent a fortune in canvas alone. Lenin thinking, Lenin writing, Lenin reading, Lenin *haranguing the grateful crowd.* . . . The tableaux are so immense and so reverent that you feel overwhelmed, if not impressed.

But what attracted Oktyabrina was the room where Lenin's childhood is traced with appropriate veneration. She was fond of young Volodya, the plump, adorable and obviously pampered child in his party dress and blond curls. She visited this room a dozen times until an incident in January made us *personae non gratae* throughout the museum.

The incident is inexplicable without an appreciation of Lenin's place in Soviet orthodoxy—and the faith of the Russian masses. Lenin is not a man, not a mortal politician or philosopher, but Marx reborn and redeemed in the sacrament of revolution: the saviour of mankind. 'Lenin Is More Alive Than The Living!' All the fundamentalist fervor of the Orthodox Church is lavished upon him in

61

daily liturgies of praise and devotion; and since the state conducts the stupendous operation, his image literally cannot be avoided for more than an hour.

The Central Lenin Museum is this religion's holy of holies. Squads of guides recite incantations on their tours; each one is followed by a cluster of peasants who have entered the museum for an hour of reverence on their trips to Moscow. Smelling powerfully of onions and old clothes, they devour the sermons, perhaps just because they've already heard them thousands of times.

Oktyabrina was oblivious to all this; what interested her was Lenin's *life story*. She plied the guides for information about adorable little Volodya and his transition to adolescence. They tolerated her questions about Lenin's disconcerting lisp. They managed to control themselves when she mentioned his premature baldness. ('The trouble probably started when he lost his hair and got lonely, the poor man.') But late one afternoon when the second floor was unusually packed with worshipful peasants, Oktyabrina raised the question that intrigued her most: Why did Lenin take so long to marry his girlfriend, Krupskaya?

'I mean, was it really just platonic all those years when they were hatching the Revolution? Or did they respond to things better as man and mistress, because that way it was marvelously thrilling?'

The guide's mouth went slack. He backed towards a mammoth painting—Our Leader Inspiring the Workers of Petrograd—and gazed up at Lenin's sunlit face, imploring forgiveness for the stunning disgrace. The peasants, by contrast, wanted not forgiveness but revenge. After a moment of stupefied silence, they advanced on Oktyabrina with a collective growl, and her big eyes narrowed with the approaching danger. 'Excuse me, I have an engagement now,' she spluttered. She dashed from the room, through the corridor, down the stairs, and out.

I overtook her in the cobblestoned expanse of Red Square, where she was alternately trembling and laughing. We hurried into GUM for warmth, and drifted among the surging crowds for the tranquilising effect. After an ice-cream and more dalliance, I returned to the museum's cloakroom for our coats.

After that, we confined ourselves to the landmarks of Old Russia. Oktyabrina missed the child Volodya, but begged me not to worry since 'actually I'm beginning to see the whole country's a kind of Lenin Museum.'

The building in which I saw the Minister again is not strictly speaking a landmark, but ought to be—all the more because of its present sorry function. It is a fine eighteenth-century mansion near the Kremlin that once belonged to Prince Volkonsky, Tolstoy's maternal grandfather, who figures prominently in *War and Peace*. There is a charming Renaissance courtyard, a handsome entrance, a splendid staircase crowned by a lavish mirror —all in perfect proportion and suffering from a chronic malaise. For the building is now a Foreign Ministry 'reception hall', used for the elaborately staged and totally un-newsworthy press conferences to which foreign reporters are invited six or seven times a year.

The conference that morning was devoted to tractors and fertilizer production: a 'new' campaign to cure the country's ailing agriculture. Its strategy was apparently devised after the full damage wrecked by the deposed Mr Khrushchev had become clear. Nevertheless, production targets were again being raised to those of his discredited campaigns several years before. This glaring inconsistency was concealed under a torrent of statistics, sophistry, soaring harvest predictions, promises for 1980, comparisons with Tsarist misery and hosannas for socialist achievements that managed not to mention the Khrushchev plans at all. Or the fact that eggs had again disap-

63

peared from Moscow and the countryside was returning to a diet of bread and potatoes. It was not a press conference as known anywhere else but a succession of punctilious re-statements of an official declaration in the morning's *Pravda*.

I gazed at the filigree moulding on the wall behind the official table and imagined how the Volkonskys, not to speak of Tolstoy himself, would have blanched at hearing this bastardized tongue, Sovietese, spoken in their drawing-room. At the table sat the Minister of Agriculture and a brigade of serge-suited subordinates, all arranged in a row at the front table behind microphones, a Chaplinesque parody of mediocrity, self-importance and stocky bureaucratism. Oktyabrina's Minister was behind a pile of charts near the far end of the table, roughly twenty places from the dais.

As the leading officials droned on, I debated whether to speak to him. Under ordinary circumstances, I wouldn't have considered it seriously. The rules for foreign journalists are explicit and categorical: no interview may be attempted with any Soviet citizen except with the express approval of the Foreign Ministry's Press Department. Of course it's easy enough, and only marginally risky, to ask questions of someone on a street. But no one would dream of approaching even the lowest official without permission—which, after an interval of many weeks is customarily denied, without explanation.

But in the Minister's case, curiosity was again undermining my caution. And something about his expression, as he stared towards the ceiling, made him seem approachable. He was wearing a clip-on tie that had come unsnapped, and drawing heavily on Bulgarian cigarettes. His eyes were as dark as his hair and had a soulful glow, from the reflection of the chandeliers. From time to time, he snapped out of his reverie and gossiped with his neighbors at the table—who were paying as little attention to the speeches as was the audience. Finally the last peroration dragged to its end, someone announced the press conference was over, and the Minister and his fifty-odd colleagues got up happily and shook hands all around, while the journalists closed their pads on a quarter of a page of useless notes. The Minister gathered his unused charts and left the room with a look of slight puzzlement. I gathered my courage and stopped him in the corridor, on his way to the toilet.

My hunch proved right. He had to rush off immediately to deliver a report about the press conference at an agricultural institute, but promptly agreed to meet me that very afternoon. He was surprised, naturally enough, by the way I introduced myself, but more than anything, he seemed flattered. I think I understood what Oktyabrina saw in him: the painful shyness of a confirmed introvert. And the pain of waiting while he forced forth his words was equally embarrassing. He had a wracking, eye-fluttering stutter.

'F-f-f-fine. I'll p-p-pick y-you up a-a-at...' and distressing seconds passed before he named a place to meet.

Outside, the mansion's courtyard was jammed with pompous Chaika and Zim limousines, the drivers waiting in the cold for their bosses, the Ministry's upper strata. The Minister's Volga wasn't there, nor in the hierarchical line of cars belonging to the next-to-upper strata parked at the curb outside the building. But just as I entered my own car a block away, I happened to see the driver. He drove up swiftly in the Volga, screeched to a stop, and pocketed a ruble from a passenger whom he'd been taxiing 'on the left', as the Russians say, while supposedly waiting for the Minister.

# 7

☐ There is a certain kind of Russian who is unable not to
bare his soul to a stranger on the slightest provocation.
Spend twenty minutes with him and you are more than
his friend; you are his long-lost brother, a fellow member
of the human family, oppressed by the world's burdens
and your own propensity to sin. He is revealing himself,
flaying himself, confessing his secret fears, intimate de-
sires and darkest thoughts. No matter how weak and
tainted his inner self, he knows you will understand.

It is not always an agreeable quality: however endearing their artlessness, Russians, like anyone else, can
have dreary intimate thoughts and wearisome souls. In
any case, these observations do not apply precisely to the
Minister because he was not Russian but Armenian: born
and raised in the ancient, sacred capital of Yerevan. And
the solvent that dissolved his inhibitions to expose his soul
was not vodka but cognac: five-star 'Jubilee', the best
Armenian brand.

His report at the institute had gone badly; he was tired
and depressed. He greeted me like an old friend and
plunged quickly into confession. His tone was matter-
of-fact, his principal themes incompetence and irresolu-
tion. We started drinking in his car, which was parked in
an alleyway so the driver could join in. The first bottle
was downed from a cloudy water glass kept in the glove
compartment for that purpose; the second went down di-

rect. When it was dark, a band of urchins began pelting the car with snowballs, but none of us managed to get out and repulse them. By that time, we were tearfully maudlin, hopelessly drunk.

I remember a few things about the evening. The driver climbed into the back seat and seized every opportunity for solemn handshaking with the Minister, whacking me rather painfully in the stomach, for I was sitting in the middle. The Minister talked about his cousin in Los Angeles, an Armenian boy who had become a millionaire in the dry-cleaning business, a *success*. Someone turned the radio on somehow and following upon some searingly patriotic hymns, there was a melodrama about the birth of the first Soviet tank. While stretching over the seat in an attempt to shut it off, the Minister spilled a large pool of cognac on the upholstery. The car reeked of sweet grapes. The driver was extremely annoyed, and it took him some time to re-establish his pose of admiring deference towards his superior.

I think there was food at some point. A policeman patrolling a railroad station snack-bar looking for drunks demanded our papers quite late at night, and saluted nervously when, after minutes of fumbling, the Minister produced a cardboard document from inside his coat. The counter girl plunked three hunks of smelly fried fish on scraps of paper for us. Before we could eat it, the driver accused her of tipping the scale with her finger to double the price of the fish. The policeman returned for more explanations.

The Minister had long been trying to tell a joke, but was constantly interrupted by someone or something, often himself. Finally he shepherded us back to the car and started from the beginning again. The story was about a proud new Second Lieutenant just assigned to his first post, guarding the Motherland with a border division in East Germany. He was a model soldier in every way, except for a thumping stutter. On the first evening, he assembled his platoon and carefully rehearsed the sentries' arrangements.

'A-a-and re-re-remember, m-men,' he repeated. 'The p-p-password is, the p-password is B-b-blue B-b-boy. B-blue b-boy.' He drew a deep breath and rallied. 'B-but if th-there's no a-a-answer r-r-right a-a-away, d-d-don't sh-sh-sh-shoot. D-d-don't sh-shoot—it m-m-may b-b-be *m-m-me*.'

Something ruthless as well as ingratiating sounded in the driver's roaring laughter. Perhaps sensing this, he told a joke of his own, directed at himself. What's the transitional period, he asked us, from socialism to Communism? We dutifully said we did not know.

'The transitional period from socialism to Communism,' he repeated. '*Alcoholism!*' He tipped his bottle to his lips.

The driver's physical stamina approached the heroic. Miraculously, he piloted the car without mishap—although he'd reverted to vodka, as any upstanding Russian proletarian would have, and downed half a bottle alone. Somehow, he found his way to my building. Before I got out, he had begun to promise the Minister that he'd never sign a denunciation about the evening. He would never report a single thing about me—not even that we'd met.

'They can cut me up into little pieces—I won't know anything. Anyway, this American's the good type!' Then he began confessing to the Minister that he was paid—kopeks!—to spy on him. Not spy on him exactly, but keep an eye on him; and from a fat organization like the KGB, the money was insulting. 'It's a gross case of exploiting the workers—as usual.'

The Minister failed to react because the news was stale; the driver, he informed me, made this confession every time they drowned sorrows together. He told the driver he knew perfectly well he was under-paid, both for driving and the 'other thing', and assured him again that he would never denounce *him* for stealing gas and the Volga's spare parts. Or for lifting certain sacks of experimental corn seed from a laboratory and shipping them to his village.

The driver, nearly weeping now, said it wasn't really stealing—it was for the private plots of his hungry relatives on a sad collective farm. And wasn't it terrible anyway, he continued, that he and the Minister had got themselves hooked into agriculture instead of something *profitable* like stockings or sweaters.

'For God's sake,' the driver continued, hoarse with suspect sincerity. 'I grew up on a farm, I *know* it's hopeless. The only way to solve the agricultural problem is to smash every collective farm fast, and have every man for himself.'

At that moment every man in the car was far from for himself, but overwhelmed by the troubles of the others. We sat in a kind of stupor, gazing at a clanging snow-removal machine and night-crew of women wielding battered shovels and brooms. The snowflakes made a steady patter hitting the windshield. Finally we got out, shook hands all around, threw our arms round each other in a close embrace of overcoats and paunches, and pumped hands again vigorously. As always on that kind of night, there was a feeling of sublime comradeship, utter understanding. I was making my way to the door when the Minister lurched forward to present me with a symbol of all this—his clip-on tie. I gave him a packet of Gillettes.

After that, I saw the Minister often. Each time, he added new details to the unhappy tale of his life. The final injury was that even this story was ordinary: it lacked the makings of genuine tragedy—which the Minister might have achieved had he not been 'f-f-fated to b-be th-the m-man in the m-m-middle, n-not f-fish or m-m-meat'.

It started in a sun-baked hut on what was then the outskirts of sleepy, dirty Yerevan. The Minister, twelfth of thirteen children, was an awkward and withdrawn boy, struck by the stutter on his first day of school. But in school he was befriended by the physics teacher, a kindly man who owned a real camera and lent the Minister back copies of the new Soviet photography magazine. This gift would sustain him in all his solitary hours. He was not yet ten years old when his passion for films sired a hunger to create. While his fellow pupils talked of soccer and girls, he was consumed by thoughts of his adult mission: translating his own truths for the cinema.

In Yerevan's donkey lanes of the 1920s, film was a new world, an unprecedented vehicle for artistic enrichment and enlightenment. And in the Soviet Union as in no other country, this vehicle would bring truth and beauty to the masses who had so little of either—to the children of forgotten people, like the Minister himself. He was going to be a director, Eisenstein's first Armenian disciple. He was destined to make honest and memorable revolutionary films. His ragseller parents gave him to know that he was a special boy whose aspirations would be fulfilled, precisely because they were so exalted. Even now his daydreams were scenes from his own abortive scripts.

But fate was already mocking him. By the time the Minister finished secondary school, the Eisenstein era had ended, the estire Soviet artistic world had been 'Stalinized', and the only films produced were sterile potboilers glorifying Five-Year-Plan, Motherland and Leader. After a paralyzing crisis of conscience, he resolved to abandon his calling. On the morning of his twentieth birthday, his application papers to Moscow's Film Institute were burned in an outhouse. The act required supreme resoluteness—'w-w-which p-p-perhaps explains why s-so l-l-little r-remained f-for f-f-future years'.

After the bitter decision, there was a shortlived, tragicomic attempt to transfer his creative impulses to the violin. Then he tried his hand at half a dozen unskilled jobs in as many factories and warehouses. The war descended, and the Minister survived six years of it in and around Vladivostok; he was officially a medical corpsman and actually a General's flunkey. Back home, *faute de mieux,* he entered the local agricultural college, 'wh-which t-t-took anyone w-w-who c-could wr-wr-write his n-name and w-w-wasn't a t-t-total sp-spastic'.

After graduation, his career was a series of minor administrative billets in obscure provincial offices, befitting an above-average product of a third-rate institution. But in 1956, Khrushchev assumed full command of Party and state and he, the Minister, was summoned to Moscow. Khrushchev plucked him from obscurity, as he plucked so many other old cronies and new hopefuls, and made him a kind of Knight of the Order of the Socialist Economy. For he had written his undergraduate thesis on the advantages of corn as livestock fodder, and Khrushchev had a vision that corn and corn alone was the panacea for Soviet agriculture. The Minister was made a standard-bearer in the race to overtake the West.

Corn gave the Minister a Moscow *propiska,* together with a comfortable apartment in a Ministry building and all the prestige and relative riches of an established government post. But the memory of his childhood dreams of artistic creativity and the accompanying ache of remorse increased in proportion to his advance up the ministerial hierarchy. 'They g-give you a car and a fat salary, a-all k-kinds of privileges—t-together with a terrific sense of g-guilt.'

The Minister seemed less unhappy at plying a trade in which he had no real interest than having become accidentally a considerable success at it. He couldn't make up his mind how to react to this: resign once and for all, or work even harder to justify his privileges. In fact, he did the latter. He was always rushing from one conference to the next, fumbling in transit with a briefcase that swelled daily with ever more reports. But none of the meetings he attended, resolutions he signed, decisions he approved —*nothing he did all day* changed a single thing on a single farm. His job was a Dante-esque ordeal of perpetual bureaucracy; his working day a vicious cycle of more and more meetings—that is, of squandered time.

To make things worse, his wife loved the life. She had been a year ahead of him at Yerevan's agricultural institute; they met during a field seminar on silage. After graduation she worked as a dairy technician—in other words, cow-barn boss. When the Minister was called to Moscow, she decided it was unseemly for a wife of ministerial rank to soil her now-manicured hands with work.

Moreover, the moment she sampled lady-of-leisure life, she discovered that she was not only made for it but appreciated its subtlest refinements. She acquired a taste for chocolates, liqueurs and canasta, which she played most afternoons with the wives of the Minister's ministerial superiors. Soon she, like they, had hired a domestic for the cleaning—having developed a loathing for dirt and all other reminders of farms—and was collecting bits and pieces of an imported wardrobe. If the Minister, as she reminded him every morning when he brought in the tea, would only behave like a normal human being with certain people at certain parties, he too might go abroad next year to some kind of conference, and bring her back a proper outfit—*co-ordinated* with *matching coat and dress*—like the wives at the Ministry of Heavy Industry were wearing.

It was his lack of refuge that disturbed the Minister

72

most. His home was no more his castle than his work was a source of pride. The bitterest pill was the use made of him by three of the Minister of Agriculture's highest aides. They operated large tracts of Ministry land, officially set aside for experimental soil control, as private hunting parks for themselves and their cronies. The Minister had been designated to deal with the necessary paper work, making him an accomplice in a fraud he especially despised.

Almost every time he told his story, the Minister quoted a passage from Tolstoy's *Death of Ivan Ilyich* about a certain Tsarist privy councillor who was a 's-s-superfluous m-m-member of v-various s-s-s-superfluous in-in-institutions'. Such men are 'obviously unfit to hold any responsible position, and therefore posts are specially created for them, which though fictitious, carry salaries of from six to ten thousand rubles that are not fictitious and in receipt of which they live on to a great old age'.

'You can't improve on Tolstoy for delineation of character,' he stuttered. 'The point is, some of those p-privy councillors probably wanted to do s-something meaningful with their lives, and s-simply didn't know how. Oh, w-what's the use of b-boring *you?*'

At this point I would try to calm the Minister. This wasn't as improbable as his station in life might have made it seem, for most Russians—apparently Armenians too—have a broad childish streak. Sometimes this manifests itself in simplicity and artlessness; at other times in a very embarrassing inferiority complex, even, or especially, on the part of the bureaucratic elite. The Minister would wait for my words, as if I had something important to tell him about how to arrange his life. And when it turned out to be something trite and unhelpful, he pressed my arm and smiled, as if I'd been trying to be kind by showing him I too could be banal.

What I usually talked about was my two post-college

73

years in a cold-water Chicago tenement. Under the influence of an inspiring seminar in American literature, I'd decided to become a writer and was at work on my first novel. It was the low point of my life, for reasons involved with a pretense that it was the high point. I wore a trench coat and black polo-neck sweater; I waited for people to ask what I did, and answered 'I write' with overtones of melodrama and nonchalance. All the necessary props were there to enhance the romantic figure I fancied myself, including a girl friend: my first real companion, as well as lover. She was a kind of ingenue—too innocent to recognize that anxieties about my manhood and place in the world forced me to be unkind. When she went to live with a professor twice my age, I was actually young enough—insensitive enough and deranged enough—to feel relief instead of grief. When the bubble burst, and I found I had nothing to say, I stayed in bed for weeks. Finally I was well enough to win a job on a four-page weekly.

The Minister would listen in a kind of reverie. Once his notes fell from his knees onto the floor. 'Very few of our contemporaries fulfilled our own notions of our own promise,' I said. 'Perhaps this will sound terribly callous; I know Stalinism caused unimaginable suffering. But in a way, it relieved some other people of bitter disappointment—of discovering their own limitations, I mean. I think I'd have welcomed some kind of external tragedy to let me drop writing without facing my lack of talent. Well, maybe not. . . .'

The Minister would shift in his chair and put his floppy hand on mine.

'Anyway,' I continued, to lead us away from our awkward introspection, 'anyway, the trouble with our century is that we all encountered magnificent, inspiring literature in our youth. This fooled us into believing we should be able to produce art of the same level—like a

Sunday tennis player watching world champions in a stadium. It looks so easy that he runs home for his racket to do it himself.'

By contrast, Oktyabrina—when she was with us—said little. She would lift the tip of the Minister's moustache and peck five quick kisses on the corners of his lips. The Minister's heavy-set face immediately flushed with affection and relief. The five kisses were a kind of ritual, followed by loud sighs, romping squeezes and a standard fragment of dialogue.

'Is it going to be all right, my dauntless one?' Oktyabrina would ask.

'B-but I t-told you f-f-from the f-first m-moment on the t-train. It's g-g-going to be perfect.' Then it was the Minister's turn: 'Is it g-g-going to be a-a-all r-right, my p-princess?'

'It's going to be *super*.'

'When?' they shouted together.

'Now!' they shouted louder. Then they embraced clumsily but enthusiastically—the Minister seemed puzzled about where to position his long, loose arms—and Oktyabrina rubbed her cheek on the fur of his overcoat and laughed a real laugh.

She was calmer with the Minister than I'd seen her before. On Sundays, we often went on an outing to the woods north of Moscow, and I think the silent, melancholy countryside calmed her too. As soon as we crossed the city limits, she was like a country girl romping up the lane to her village after years away, and rejoicing when she hears the bark of her old dog.

The Minister had the use of a well-equipped dacha in a huge, high-fenced government reserve, but we went instead to a tiny room of an unpainted cottage he'd rented privately from a peasant family. It was agreed that should we encounter one of the Minister's colleagues, Oktyabrina would be presented as *my* friend, and I as a

75

journalist from one of the 'democratic' countries—East Germany, say, or Poland.

But, in fact, we never did meet anyone we knew. And for my part, I told no one in the Western colony about those days, even though from a journalist's standpoint, a close association with someone like the Minister would have been considered a major coup. My western colleagues would never have believed that nothing the Minister said was newsworthy in any way.

Our Sundays had a pattern. We would meet in the morning to buy provisions, usually in 'Food Store No. 1', a wildly incongruous emporium built by a pre-revolutionary entrepreneur in the style of a brothel for robber barons. The garish interior was always packed from wall to ornate wall with resolute workers amassing the week's provisions, and we'd all stand in four or five separate lines at counters and cashiers to expedite the convoluted shopping process.

On the way out of town, the Minister would stop for gas at an ancient, one-pump garage, serving himself in the Soviet manner. While he fumbled with the filthy hose, a large woman in a greasy jacket—the manager—shouted insults at him, together with every other customer in sight. The Minister could have avoided all this, as well as the hour-long line of cars at the pump, by instructing the driver to fill up in the Volga's regular government garage. In fact, he could have avoided the whole hard shopping grind, and saved himself considerable money too, by buying his provisions in the special shops for high officials.

But the Minister liked everything to be on a do-it-yourself basis. Much of the day's meaning for him lay precisely in the ritual of 'r-r-rubbing in with r-r-real l-life'. 'O S-sacred S-s-simplicity,' he liked to pronounce as he fumbled, now dirty-handed, with the car keys, promising himself he was going to track down the quotation as soon as he was a bit less busy.

Unfortunately, do-it-yourself also meant the Minister liked to 't-take the h-h-helm' of the Volga and do all the driving. Once we simply left the road—and this was in the light of midday, when the asphalt happened to be dry and ice-free. Incredibly, he failed to notice that all conversation ceased every time a truck passed us or we approached an oncoming car. What saved us was his notion of speed, which he seemed to tailor to the era of the Grapes of Wrath villages along the way.

Finally we arrived at our own village, a typical settlement of ramshackle houses strung out along the main road. The Minister's cottage stood alone, just below the woods. We unloaded the provisions, tied on our snowshoes, and set out on the day's highlight, called the Long Walk. The landscape was neither distinguished nor decorative; just a slightly rolling tract of snow-covered farmland with a blotch of a duck pond and the usual drifting paths and rotting fences. Still, it managed to convey an overwhelming beauty and sadness. A disused church, now serving as a grain storehouse, stood exactly where it had to, at the crown of the rise above the village. A landscape painter would know what this means, for that humble scene somehow inspired sublime feelings, like a work of art.

Our route took us to the top of the rise and into the woods, which smelled sharply of snow and evergreens. We followed animal tracks where they crossed the snowed-over paths, and the Minister and I fed Oktyabrina's tingling curiosity about the terror of being alone and lost in a Siberian forest. Even with snowshoes it was hard going over the unbroken paths, but the unspoken rule was to be thoroughly chilled and famished before returning to the cottage.

We always bought enough sausage, pickles, cheese and sprats for hors d'oeuvres for six people, but almost everything disappeared before it was properly set out on the little table. Then we each made our own portions of shashlik on the wood-burning stove in the corner, and for dessert, I supplied something exotic like chocolate bars or tinned pineapple from the American Embassy commissary. My little treats provoked the usual questions about life in the fairy-tale West, especially in Hollywood. I never knew whether to paint the West gloriously, to satisfy their expectations, or dismally, to soothe their hurt at knowing they'd never see it for themselves. Besides, I myself had actually forgotten what life 'on the outside' was like; it was beginning to seem almost as mythical to me as to Oktyabrina and the Minister. And how to explain to them that they would not have been happier or felt closer to the important things anywhere else than in that creaking cottage?

After the last glass of brandy, the Minister perused some papers, apologizing that the work load increased with the approach of the planting season. By this time, it would have been inexcusable to break the tacit ban on shop talk and ask him exactly what he did. But he himself volunteered that his principal job was running a research laboratory specializing in corn. And he continued to muse about his fate. 'It's funny when you think of it,' he stuttered one afternoon. 'This whole system we h-have. The Russians took over Armenia. The B-Bolsheviks took over R-Russia. All these violent changes. Without them, I s-sometimes wonder what I would have b-been?'

After the meal we would venture into the fields again if the light was good. This was when the Minister photographed Oktyabrina with his 8mm movie camera, an excellent Japanese model that he'd been brought by a traveling colleague. He posed her with painstaking attention to detail and a natural sense of composition. Following his directions, Oktyabrina pulled at branches, disappeared down trails, sat on tree stumps looking elated or pensive —sequences she performed with great earnestness and, I thought, surprising grace.

This was usually the end of the day, for the Minister had to plan for the protracted drive back, and dared not be late: eight o'clock was starting time for his wife's regular Sunday soiree. One evening after we'd returned to Moscow and the Minister had dropped us off, Oktyabrina confided to me that she occasionally considered abandoning ballet. But she always mastered the temptation—for the Minister's sake more than her own. 'He's counting on me to make good. Because of his own artistic disappointment, of course. It's a terrific pressure, actually. I can't let him down.'

She spent almost an hour that evening dipping into a stack of popular pamphlets with titles like *Further Triumphs of Collectivized Agriculture* and *The People's New Five-Year Plan and the Farm*. This was part of her campaign to 'read what the Minister reads' so that she would 'understand what the Minister understands and suffer what the Minister suffers. As his alter ego, I can *hardly* do anything less.' But the pamphlets—cheap adulation of Soviet agriculture that managed to be simultaneously vainglorious, heavy and hollow—defied reading for more than a page at a time. Oktyabrina salved her conscience by dashing to a kiosk, whenever she saw one, to buy the latest issue of an equally impossible magazine called *Farm Life*. She carried a copy with her religiously, and spoke in a language I couldn't decipher to the photographs of the milking herds.

# 8

☐ The plans to celebrate the Minister's birthday were laid days in advance, pondered, rehearsed, and revised half a dozen times. In the end, Oktyabrina decided to give him an 'intimate reception' at home in Domolinart. The food and drink were to be supplied by the maître d'hotel of an Armenian restaurant called the Ararat, and paid for from the sale of some of Oktyabrina's better cosmetics. It was to be excellent value because the maître d'hotel ran his 'take-out' service on supplies filched from the restaurant. The railway pensioner was bribed with two bottles of vodka to stay with friends for the evening. Oktyabrina herself paced about her room, squinting to visualize the arrangements in her mind's eye. It was to be her first venture as a hostess and it required a supreme effort of self-control not to tell the Minister all about his own surprise.

At the last minute, however, there was a frantic change of plans. The maître d'hotel informed us apologetically that he could not deliver the food to Oktyabrina's room. An investigation by a team of People's Controllers had been sprung on him, and certain irregularities discovered: watered wine, reduced portions, and soup without the required ounces of meat. Unless he was able to place a bribe quickly, he was in danger of being arrested for embezzlement and speculation—his second rap. He returned Oktyabrina's sixty rubles and, deeply regretting that the money would go to the state instead of into the fund for his new dacha, he suggested the party be transferred to the Ararat itself. The least he could do, he said, was to reserve us a good table, ensure the bugging equipment was on the blink, and assign us waiters who weren't informers.

Oktyabrina was deeply disappointed. The *intimacy* she'd been designing was all *in ruins*, and she might *never* have another chance to be a real *hostess*.

The evening went surprisingly well nevertheless. We had the table of honor, which stood in a pseudo-oriental alcove with an oil painting of radiant Armenian girls driving muscular Russian tractors and a potted palm of matching taste. It was so hideously pretentious that the combined effect was somehow homey. The Minister had been told he was wanted at the restaurant for consultation about the preparation of a traditional Armenian stew. When the unmistakable swish-clump of his galoshes resounded along the cracked tile floor, everyone fell silent and straightened in his chair. At the sight of the table, the Minister blinked; for the first five minutes, he remained quietly bewildered. The more he thought about things after this, the deeper he was moved. He reached across the table and touched Oktyabrina's hair with shaky fingers. Several large tumblers of cognac steadied his hands without dulling his emotion. He kept declaring that he didn't deserve the honor, and dabbing freely at his cheeks.

To everyone's surprise and relief, the Minister and Kostya took an immediate liking to one another. As his birthday present, Kostya gave him a pair of handsome morocco gloves—which were more than symbolic because they had obviously cost at least a week's salary at some black market source. 'In the old days,' said Kostya as he presented them to the Minister, 'when people wanted to imply a man was a Don Juan, they'd say he

81

changed his women like gloves. Well, socialism's cleansed us of our nasty old bourgeois habits. Now a comment like that is the highest compliment to a man's fidelity—because we change our gloves once a decade, if we're lucky. . . . Anyway, I'm sure we don't want to pursue this . . . er particular subject with this evening's guest of honor. But we do all want to wish him what he bestows upon others: long years of tranquility. And of happiness and health.'

Beaming and blushing, the Minister gazed fondly at Oktyabrina, and whispered something into her ear while trying on his present. Then Kostya launched into a genuinely choice selection of suggestive political jokes and the Minister laughed so hard that he developed hiccups and pleaded for respite.

Kostya complied for a time, which gave everyone a chance to compliment Oktyabrina extravagantly on her skill with the arrangements. The clamor of soup being slurped, particularly from the corner occupied by Evgeny Ignatievich and Oktyabrina's favourite lady from Gogol Boulevard, testified eloquently to the enjoyment of the victuals. Then Kostya stood again and proposed an elaborate, highly elegant toast to the Minister's future, wishing him long life and as many devoted and admiring friends forever as were gathered there at that 'humble' table.

The Minister responded in the same spirit despite the stutter. Then, surprised and delighted by his own recklessness, he asked our indulgence to a joke of his own. It was an extremely stale one about members of a rich collective farm dreaming of Communism: they would all have a private airplane in which they could fly to America for potatoes. Everyone roared although—or perhaps because—we'd all heard the story a dozen times before. 'Of c-course I'm corny,' the Minister said in my ear, 'but try to explain that to these l-lovely chaps.'

82

The party gathered momentum as it progressed. The usual screeching of waitresses and cooks resounded from the kitchen: who worked harder than whom; whose mother was a stupid cow. But the supreme informality only made everyone more relaxed. The maître d'hotel was charmed by Oktyabrina in her lacy pinafore, and dragged a chair to our table to join us. Perhaps sensing the days until his arrest were numbered, he ordered more food and drink at the restaurant's expense. Evgeny Ignatievich assured us he could not remember a more successful evening, even during the heyday of St Petersburg salons. He was absolutely enchanted by Kostya's girls, two rather pretty, if unwashed, assistants in a neighboring dairy he'd picked up on his way to the Ararat. The girls were somewhat dumbfounded by the lavishness in which they suddenly found themselves. Between bursts of giggling and attempts to hide their sour-smelling working smocks, they kept whispering to one another, presumably about how to respond to Evgeny Ignatievich's persistent under-the-table exploration of their legs. Oktyabrina hardly had time to notice: her eyes kept darting from glass to plate; she flurried about making certain that neither was empty for a second. In between, she tried hard to keep a conversation alive between the Minister's aide, a silent type, and the Gogol Boulevard woman who'd called her 'the lady from the theater'.

The restaurant itself was in excellent spirits. The band produced a non-stop medley of apparently wildly popular Armenian songs. It was a bizarre ensemble of trombones, violins and ancient Armenian stringed instruments. The musicians were correspondingly diverse: sweating, shirt-sleeved young men, clearly dashing in their own image, cheek-by-jowl with middle-aged women with enormous arms and moustaches. Together they played so deafeningly that you had to shout into your neighbor's ear to ask for the salt. Most of the diners at neighboring tables were singing; none pretended to be sober. At one point a man stood up on a chair, clapped for silence, and made a public declaration of love for his frowzy but delighted wife. A group of extremely swarthy, conspiratorial-looking men in black market nylon shirts, probably black marketeers themselves, sent their respects to our table, together with four bottles of native wine they insisted we sampled. Then, hearing an American was present, they inquired whether it was true that Franklin Roosevelt had Armenian blood. I sensed it would do no good to disappoint them, and the gift of a fifty cent coin managed to distract them into a flurry of entrepreneurial deliberations.

Even Leonid was drawn out of his depression. He had arrived late and drank a surprising amount for someone of his age and his intellectual bent. He was wearing a clean white shirt and patterned tie that Oktyabrina had given him. The Minister said if he wanted his hair cut, he would send around a mowing brigade of Communist labor to give him an estimate—but joking apart, his generation was the hope of us all, and he prayed they wouldn't abandon their ideals.

When his turn came, Leonid offered a joke based on his own background and inside professional knowledge. Who invented the X-ray? he asked us. No, not Roentgen —not any German, in fact. Or Englishman, Frenchman or American. In the late seventeenth century, no one else but a certain Ivan Ivanovich, an upstanding Volga mu-zhik who was serving his statutory twenty-five years in the army. Rumors reached him that his wife was distrib-uting her favors to one and all back in their village. He wrote her a letter through the battalion scribe: 'Dear Masha. You can't fool me with your goings-on. You fat bitch, I see right through you.' The letter had recently turned up in an archive, and Leonid's former physics Institute was in the process of preparing a paper on this

84

incontrovertible proof of the precursor of the X-ray. *I see right through you*: Mother Russia was first again, as always.

There was only one awkward moment all evening, caused by Kostya's pointed and somewhat crass joke about a KGB bureaucrat. A fleeting interval of embarrassed silence was ended by Kostya's suggestion that everyone dance to escape his 'big clumsy trap'.

Dancing to that music—and in our incongruous pairs —was something to be seen. The black marketeers came over to invite Kostya's girls, but they dissuaded outsiders because by that time the birthday party had developed a kind of family reunion warmth. Free of ballet's restrictions, Oktyabrina was wonderfully light on her feet.

We all left together when the restaurant closed after eleven o'clock. For the first time, a smell of spring was in the air, blown into our faces by a wet wind. We walked down to the river and listened to the happy sound of ice breaking up as it flowed past swiftly in the dark. When the familiar Kremlin chimes struck midnight, everyone congratulated the Minister heartily again and thanked Oktyabrina with considerable ceremoniousness. It was only then she revealed that her own birthday was 'not far hence'. There was a chorus of 'ohs' and 'ahs', and befitting pressure to make her divulge the date; but she held fast to her refusal. She was not, she said modestly, going to spoil *this* glorious birthday now with thoughts of another one, belonging to someone so manifestly less deserving. . . .

A policeman approached to peruse our little group, but was impressed enough by its respectability actually to lift his hand to the Minister in a kind of salute. Soon after this, Evgeny Ignatievich gallantly offered to accompany the elderly lady home to Gogol Boulevard, and the rest of our group strolled along the quay for a while, playing a traditional game called 'Frankness'. Anyone was allowed to ask anyone else any kind of question, and the answer, on one's honor, had to be scrupulously honest. The Minister's aide, who had hardly said anything all evening except in a private conversation with Leonid, was the last subject—or victim, as he called it. It was discovered rather quickly that he had been celibate for almost a year, not by his own choosing. Kostya then arranged that he 'borrow' one of the dairy girls, with her giggling permission, for the night, provided he give her taxi money to get to work in the morning. And exhilarated by the change of weather, he invited us all to another intimate reception in his room the following Saturday. It was to be the first of his 'pre-May-Day celebrations' combined with a 'coming-out party' for a crew of girls he'd recently met who worked in a candy factory.

Less than a week later, the Minister got his bad news. In connection with the new chemical fertilizer crusade, the Ministry had been subjected to another radical reorganization. The Minister's entire research laboratory was to be liquidated by the end of the financial quarter, and the staff reassigned to 'actual field production' on laggard farms, meaning plowing and weeding in stony northern latitudes. It was the standard treatment for junior agricultural medicine men who had failed to work a miracle cure. The Minister himself had been ordered to a teaching job in Saratov, a provincial city on the Volga.

Our last drowning-sorrows fling took place the following evening, with the vodka and cognac augmented by a fifth of bourbon so that I could swallow my full share. But instead of getting drunk, I was car-sick. My sense of loss was compounded by how much I'd disliked and distrusted the Minister before I'd met him, a few weeks ago.

The Minister himself took the blow calmly. Corn, he explained, had fallen from favor years ago, together with

Khrushchev; ever since '*that* p-poor dreamer's' over-throw, he'd known that his own Moscow days were num-bered. He sounded more relieved than hurt when he told Oktyabrina and me the details. 'Just think. All that g-good land plowed up and p-p-planted in c-corn w-when it really should have been l-left in gr-grasses and p-pasture. M-millions of acres turned to d-dust bowls. As if I needed a c-colossal tragedy l-like *this* in my l-life.' He smiled apologetically and lowered his eyes.

Oktyabrina, on the other hand, was frantic with dis-tress. '*Oi, mamachka, mamachka,*' she wailed, and fell into the Minister's perplexed arms, rending her hair. It was a gesture-for-gesture duplication of the scene in every Soviet war film where the wife, mother or sweet-heart is informed that her man, the smooth-cheeked sol-dier with plans to be a nuclear scientist, has been killed at the front.

But the truth is that Russian women do take personal loss with this gushing emotion. Oktyabrina's instincts told her that the Minister would come to grief. Appar-ently she interpreted his reassignment as a kind of crimi-nal sentence; all that day she talked about the 'calamity' and kept referring to Saratov as 'Siberia', as if the Minis-ter were being sent into exile with hard labor. 'I'm not in-terested in geography and require no cosy consoling,' she snapped. 'That man's gentleness cannot *take* another chilling. He'll never be the same again.'

But she slowly allowed herself to be convinced by the Minister that his new post was in fact a gratifying pro-motion which he couldn't reasonably turn down. They exchanged elaborate promises about long, daily letters and week-end trips to Moscow—Saratov was only twelve hours away by train, after all, and 'r-remember what traveling by r-rail m-means to us both'. Oktyabrina was to be given the Minister's office plants to look after be-cause he would clearly soon be returning permanently to

87

Moscow where he'd need them again. 'If t-there's one c-certainty at all in the M-Ministry, it's that n-nothing is final.' The research laboratory would be resurrected one day, even Khrushchev might be rehabilitated. The Ministry and its roulette wheel were eternal; 'Only the l-l-land suffers in the l-l-long run. . . .'

By the following day, Oktyabrina was enumerating the advantages of the temporary Saratov assignment. Moscow wasn't really *good* for the Minister, after all; he needed a *change* and a *rest*. This way they could spend whole *weekends* together, and in between he would get back to research. He could invent some new kind of marvelous plant, a hundred times better than corn. When his Lenin Prize was presented, everyone would feel terribly ashamed about the way he'd been wronged. . . .

As for herself, she was going to dedicate herself more than ever to *work*. 'This might be just what I've needed all along, don't you think, Zhoe darling? I mean, now I'll have a *higher* motive for becoming a success. Because if things somehow don't work out brilliantly for the Minister in his lab, I could bring him back to Moscow as my personal impresario.' She said this quite flatly, while devouring the last of a huge chunk of halvah for quick energy. She was exhausted and famished, having just cleaned up her corner of Domolinart and carried down back issues of *Farm Life* for transfer to the Minister.

On the morning of his departure, however, she was emphatically sullen. She wore little make-up except for white powder and grey semicircles under her eyes, and her principal adornment was a velvet armband of a mulberry color, presumably to signify mourning. She insisted on going to the station to watch the Minister board the train. This turned out to be physically difficult as well as psychologically tense because the funeral of an Artillery Marshal had caused a massive diversion of traffic. As usual on these occasions, main thoroughfares were sealed off without notice, and hundreds of thousands of unsuspecting people, we included, had to wait over an hour while the Wagnerian ceremony ran its course. Luckily for the people caught on the street, the temperature that morning was only a degree or so below freezing. But the delay spoiled Oktyabrina's plan to hide a book of Volga folklore in the Minister's compartment before he'd arrived at the station.

In the end, we literally saw him off, but without saying goodbye. When he found his train, his wife was the first thing in sight—a smaller woman than we'd expected, who was wearing an Austro-Hungarian kind of hat and carrying a parrot in a pink-painted birdcage. She was giving orders to a porter, a conductor and the Minister's driver in a way that discouraged us from approaching. Instead, Oktyabrina and I watched from the opposite platform. She'd hardly said a word to me all morning, except to mutter acidly about the funeral, as if I were somehow at fault. 'And this is the miserable send-off the Minister gets,' she mused, 'after all *his* heroic labors.'

The train was bedecked with little red plaques testifying that its crew were members of a Brigade of Communist Labor. The Minister settled his wife in a first-class compartment and then reappeared, sweaty and flustered, on the platform. He was wearing a cloth cap I hadn't seen before, apparently a new acquisition for country life. It made him look like a veteran Chicago cabbie.

When the first warning whistle sounded, the driver embraced him and whispered something into his ear; then the two men waited side by side for the next warning, obviously uncomfortable because they had nothing further to say. Finally, the Minister boarded, the doors were closed and the immensely long train pulled out, quickly disappearing into an underpass. Oktyabrina gazed in its direction for a long moment and sighed profoundly; the end of an era.

89

Within a few minutes, I was aware not only of the Minister's absence, but also the vacuum he'd left between Oktyabrina and me. For weeks we'd hardly seen each other without his company or talk of him; I realized we were almost strangers again. And although the Minister himself wouldn't have believed it, he had a certain ease that made his relationship with Oktyabrina entirely unselfconscious. I found myself wondering what to say.

'Let's go to the country, Oktyabrina. For a picnic or something.'

'Not today, thank you. I have . . . an engagement.'

We started back down the empty platform, walking in an aimless half step. And no longer together: Oktyabrina was now yards behind me, with a glaring every-person-is-alone-in-the-world expression. When we reached the waiting-room, she sat down on a bench amidst a horde of peasants and their bundles of potatoes, chickens and rags.

'You needn't wait for me all the time,' she muttered. 'I can quite well take care of myself—in my own country.'

'Of course you can. I wanted company for lunch.'

'Can't you see I must be in solitude now? Have your high and mighty lunch—while the Minister's delivered to his fate.'

'Please call me when you feel better.'

'This is a grievous tragedy. I cannot be expected to rally soon.'

I set down the plastic carryall bag containing her leotards and paraphernalia and walked towards the exit at the far end of the waiting-room. After the loss of the Minister's support, Oktyabrina's demonstration of independence was transparent enough, and fully understandable. What puzzled me was my own rather childish uncertainty about how to behave. Was I meant to assume the Minister's role? What *was* his role?

Just inside the exit to the street I saw a magazine I wanted at a kiosk and joined the short line at the counter.

Before my turn came, the sounds of a swelling commotion echoed through the hall. It was a typical Russian *skandal*, with a dozen participants squawking indignantly at each other in place of a real fight—and above the other shouts rang Oktyabrina's newly arrogant voice. It was delivering a long tirade I couldn't make out at that distance, except that it wobbled with outrage. I hurried back to the bench. A crowd had gathered around it, relishing the action. In the center, Oktyabrina was face-to-chest with a large policeman. He was sweating in the heat of his uniform overcoat, and his expression was slowly changing, like a cop's in a silent film: first dumbfounded, then scandalized, finally furious.

'Will you leave her alone or will you not?' Oktyabrina screeched at him. 'She's a poor, ordinary person. Working class—just like yourself.'

The policeman slowly opened his mouth, but apparently had not yet composed a response.

'She's your *comrade*, for God's sake,' Oktyabrina continued, 'if you could understand anything. Aren't you *ashamed?*'

Oktyabrina's 'poor, ordinary person' was a matronly woman in a fur-collared coat, distinctly better groomed than average. The spectators—who from time to time supported Oktyabrina with cautiously quick and spontaneously dispersed remarks—informed me *sotto voce* that the matronly woman was an old-time speculator who often operated in this railroad station. This time she had been peddling black-market slips from a suitcase when the policeman spied her and made an arrest. It had happened directly in front of Oktyabrina's bench.

'You just *have* to show off your authority, don't you? All of you. Arrest people—close down laboratories. Ruin people's lives.'

The policeman slowly recovered from his shock. He ordered everyone to move back, gripped Oktyabrina by

91

the wrist and pronounced her arrested. Just then, the spry old speculator saw her chance. She bent down as if to fasten her boots, satisfied herself that the policeman hadn't noticed the movement, and slipped nimbly through the crowd. Soon she was outside it, and scampering towards the exit. Only now did the policeman catch sight of her. He looked back to Oktyabrina, his second catch, frenziedly weighed his choice, and started in pursuit of the old woman, freeing Oktyabrina's wrist. But the crowd closed ranks, and he lost more minutes struggling through. Someone brushed the cap from his head. By the time he recovered it, the woman had made a clean escape.

At the same time, Oktyabrina dashed the opposite way, towards the emergency exit. She was struggling with the illicit suitcase as well as her own plastic bag, but saw me as she emerged from the crowd.

'Hello again, Zhoe darling,' she panted happily, handing me the suitcase and bag. 'Can you manage with both these little things? They're the most wonderful crinoline slips. Meet you outside in a minute—I'm simply *starved*.'

# 9

☐ At lunch, Oktyabrina began questioning me about my apartment. It had occurred to her that it was time to pay me a call, 'just to see how a bard of current events actually lives'. On the heels of her triumph in the station, it was futile to impress her with the risk. Not one (sober) Russian in a hundred will visit an apartment in the foreign colony; at the very least, it means an entry about him in a big black book. But Oktyabrina did promise solemnly not to draw attention to herself as we entered, and her costume gave her a fair chance of being taken for a foreigner, provided she kept mum.

In one sense, precautions like this are useless, together with any and all conspiratorial safeguards observed with Russian friends. Kostya and I, for example, realized that the KGB had known about us for years. By now they surely knew about my friendship with Oktyabrina. Still, there is always a pressure to be as careful as you can, if only for the relief of taking some kind of action in face of the danger. And perhaps a larger benefit accrues too: one reason why a few Russians see Westerners without interference may be their observance of certain discretional rules.

Oktyabrina rehearsed her part. I parked the car in the lot behind my building and we emerged laughing, according to the script. Oktyabrina nodded in vigorous agreement at my steady stream of booming English; she understood nothing of course, but managed to control her giggle. When we approached the sentry in the court-yard, she held her breath and strode past with a passable imitation of nonchalance. In the safety of the lift, her triumphant grin unfolded: she *knew* she could dupe another silly policeman, and I had to admit I thought she had.

'Not bad for a dancer, my beauty. Perhaps you should act.'

'Zhoe darling, *you* stole the show. You can really *talk* that funny noise.'

Oktyabrina entered the apartment with a symbolic ballet leap and another sigh: the beginning of an era?

'You *will* offer your caller a Coca-Cola, won't you Zhoe darling? I've heard absolutely everything about its devastatingly decadent effects.'

'Throw your coat anywhere. One can of Pepsi coming right up.'

She sniffed her glass suspiciously before proposing a toast. 'To dearest Zhoseph and his wonderful maturity. There's scant peace in a home'—she winked knowingly 'where the hen clucks and the cock remains silent'.

The apartment was in its usual disorder, but it swept Oktyabrina's breath away, despite her efforts to appear blasé. She trod back and forth from room to room, feeling her way into corners and cupboards like a cat in a new home. Did I really live here *all alone?* It was a little lunatic wasn't it?—all these *rooms* for one person. She fingered the sheets on the bed, tested the water in the bidet, and stretched out tentatively on the old davenport in the living-room.

'Does it look absolutely incongruous to see me hereabouts? I can just picture all the women you've seduced, on this very divan. Not that I blame them—it's kind of *romantic* here. All this *space!*'

More than anything, she was dazzled by the bathroom's 'romance', which was actually a cheerless

94

reminder of the hasty departure of one of my predecessors from the apartment. Near the middle of his assignment, he contracted a severe case of a common professional disease: an obsessional craving for something to remind him of real luxury. One of his projects was to have the bathroom wallpapered in crimson velvet imported from Helsinki. The job was completed just before he left Russia suffering from a minor breakdown. This was several years ago. Since then, the velvet had torn away in critical spots making it more tacky than most of the furniture and carpets left behind by other correspondents. But Oktyabrina crept around the room, stroking the walls and oohing.

'Zhoe darling, it expresses a side of you I hardly even imagined. What absolute *perfection!* I simply wouldn't change a *thing.*' She paused to let her glad tidings sink in. 'But you simply must do something about the kitchen. It's going to be *crawling* soon.'

She scrubbed the stove furiously, expressing increasing concern about my eating habits and the condition of the apartment. Her point was restated in reflections about older men who live alone; they needed someone *understanding* to look after them, and wasn't it *scandalous* that nowadays you could never find a housekeeper with a *heart?* There was a certain mature man in Omsk—my age—who lived alone and was absolutely *lost* until she joined him—although no one would believe they never actually had an affair. . . .

Suddenly she spied a pair of cockroaches on the floor, creeping with the cheeky sluggishness bred in infested cities. Oktyabrina swooped down with her fingers and disposed of them without a break in her narrative.

She never officially moved in. Towards the middle of the evening, she would pull herself up, yawning, and return to Domolinart. When we walked back together we would pass groups of students celebrating spring with guitars. They winked at Oktyabrina and me, assuming we were lovers. Neither of us minded this; it was a nice touch to our unspoken understanding not to initiate any sexual approach. Each of us had our own reasons for avoiding even talk of a physical relationship, although the divorce's effects weren't going to keep me numb forever.

During the day, Oktyabrina encamped on the davenport, and surrounded herself with a growing assortment of junk. From time to time, she'd make a quick survey of 'her' corner of the room, as if guarding a claim to squatter's rights. Soon little piles of underwear, knick-knacks and cosmetics marked the boundary of her territory.

She usually arrived in mid-morning with a scrap of news or gossip. She disappeared into the bathroom almost immediately for lengthy stints of washing hair, sweaters and underwear. Ivory Flakes enchanted her almost as much as the wallpaper, and when the door was locked for hours without the toilet flushing, I think she was contemplating herself in the full-length mirror. One morning, she brought me a glass of tea at my desk and hovered over it until I was fully distracted.

'Drink, Zhoe darling, you must be positively *dying* of thirst. A good glass of tea makes a writer's pen free. . . . Do you have a lover at the moment?'

'What?'

'You *are* such an adorable prude. I asked you whether you're involved in a current entanglement.'

'My sweetest, this household has only one serious rule. In case you've forgotten: please let me concentrate until lunch. It pays the rent.'

'Well, I think it's marvelously *convenient*. Just think: we can both have a nice little intermission from that sort of thing. Don't be angry, darling, but you look as if you need some recuperation. Foreigners just aren't made for our Russian winter.'

The next day a battered cardboard suitcase made an appearance near the head of the davenport. When its lid was up, it appeared to contain a collection of old clothing, but I was sworn never to open it myself. The following morning, the Minister's plants were transferred too, and stood on the floor beyond the knick-knacks because Oktyabrina couldn't make up her mind *exactly* where they belonged.

A happily uneventful week passed. The plan was to call Oktyabrina 'Marina' because my apartment was certainly bugged. But everything was so untroubled that we forgot our own subterfuge by the end of the first day. When we did remember after that, it provoked giggles and a happy sense of triumph.

Our routine was simple and relaxed. I did my morning's work in the office as usual, or pressed on with my reading in Russian when there were no urgent stories. Oktyabrina, her enthusiasm for ballet tapering rapidly, would stretch out in the living room, 'slimming' her 'literary backlog'. This meant leafing through whatever Soviet magazines were lying about and trying her hand at the puzzles quaintly called *crossvord* in Russian. She rarely completed more than four or five entries before exhaling with great weariness and turning to a fresh puzzle. Yet I was often interrupted by urgent requests: 'Who wrote "The Teaching of Marx is Invincible Because It is True"? Five letters—starting with Ж —I think.'

But her favourite occupation was browsing through back issues of *Life* and *Look*. She devoted herself to this for hours, sometimes putting a magazine she'd just perused on the bottom of a pile, to be returned to yet again. Although she couldn't decipher a word of the text, she loved the photographs and was positively transfixed by the advertisements, especially for Westinghouse kitchens and stunning ladies admiring General Motors cars. By the end of the week, she was no longer tearing off her reading glasses and hiding them under the pillow every time I walked into the room. The frames were plain beige plastic—the only 'square' Soviet thing she owned, no doubt because glasses can't be bought privately or made at home. They magnified her eyes even more, making her a caricature of the pretty young thing in the boudoir comedy who affects spectacles to fool her father.

In the afternoon, we often went sightseeing. Although it was still cold, dauntless spring grew stronger almost daily, encouraging the hope that justice exists in the world. Despite the terrible odds, relief and redemption were approaching. Old women were clearing the cotton wadding from the outer windows of their rooms, preparing for the magic day when they'd be flung open to the streets. The water of melting snow cascaded down broken drainpipes and along sidewalks; pedestrians were splashed to the hip in muddy slush. But the lifting of winter's siege had an irrepressibly uplifting effect on everyone.

When Oktyabrina took a box of cookies with her to blunt her recurrent hunger, our walks often extended to several hours. We were both pleased when no special itinerary suggested itself: this meant a stroll along the regular route, Petrovka. The old street felt cosy in early spring despite the slush, vast puddles and smell of wet decay. The crowds were larger than ever.

I grew accustomed to the sights of Petrovka. In clothing shops with floorboards almost worn through, there would be a melee around a rear counter signifying a batch of cotton socks that elsewhere would be discarded as rejects. The entrance to an old department store was always so packed that the last woman to join the line yards away would lower her shoulder to drive against the last back. The jostled woman would not complain—wouldn't even turn around. She would be too busy driving against the back in front of her.

But the street was always full of more important sights. The lines on the faces of the women who worked the stalls, and the stoop of their backs, bent by ponderous clothes and heavier burdens. The bundles of tightly wrapped laundry carried by women shoppers—which, on closer inspection, proved to be infants, miraculously alive and breathing in their winter swaddling. The façades of the grander buildings, encrusted with sculptures, pillars, pediments and porticos, a typical blend of pretentiousness and decay, part Greek, part Roman, and all the more Russian for their labored imitation of the West. The steamy, sweaty basement cafeterias where weary shoppers compete for mess-kit utensils of bent aluminium, or rip off hunks of unidentifiable meat with impatient teeth because the last wobbly knives were stolen months ago and not replaced. The smell of diesel exhaust, tar, bitter tobacco, antiseptic cleaner and sour, sweat-soaked wool: the unmistakable smell of Russian industry and earth. The girl friends linking arms and waists and the men friends sneaking gulps of vodka and baring souls in tiny clearings on the sidewalk. The intensity of physical and emotional contact which nourishes the human spirit despite—or because—of the elements that are hostile to it. The understanding of why Russia always was and will be a land of hardship and suffering—and of compassion for those who endure hardship and suffering.

Sometimes we walked up one side of the street and down the other, then reversed the order for a second trip. At other times we walked on to where Petrovka becomes Coach Row Street and then Red Proletariat Street both, despite their names, slices of the same life, with the same bad asphalt and sagging houses. But most often, we lingered in and around the lower part of Petrovka itself, investigating its jumble of shops and savoring the primordial Russian flavor. Oktyabrina studied fabrics and trin-

99

kets with the diligence of a comparison buyer, but it was the street itself that moved her—moved us both.

'Tired but happy, they returned home,' Oktyabrina would say after our walk, mocking the cliché of Russian travel stories and simultaneously emphasizing the idea of 'home sweet home'—my house was also hers. She would make directly for the davenport, collapse on it, and cover her legs with an old blanket to which she'd pinned some pink satin. It was nice to see her there, in spite of the added disorder. After years of occupancy by bachelor correspondents and then my wife's departure, the apartment had become hollow. I couldn't help thinking that neither 'older men' nor 'younger girls' should live alone.

'I don't have to be a super-star overnight, do I, Zhoe darling,' she said late one evening while postponing her return to Domolinart. 'I can be happy if I just get on the stage some day and bring some little glow into people's lives.'

She herself glowed so brightly when I asked her for help with a Russian word or gave her something like a pair of old cuff-links—with a story, of course, about their romantic origin—that I sometimes invented questions for the sake of her reaction. For her part, Oktyabrina produced a dozen questions to my one: why are typewriter keys covered with glass? in what State was I born in America? how much does nail-polish cost in France? I jotted down the queries for several successive days in an attempt to unravel her train of associations. Nothing fitted, except that questions about shoes and books seemed to be followed or preceded by thoughts about children.

And that curiosity about the mechanics of sex hovered in the wings, although rarely expressed itself explicitly. One morning she found a diaphragm lying, in its case, on a high-up kitchen shelf. I'd seen it there myself a month before, but had then conveniently forgotten its existence.

It was my wife's—she was fond of leaving it on the bathroom sink whenever we had visitors. Oktyabrina approached my desk, examining the open case as if it contained something fascinatingly nasty, like a centipede.

'Zhoe precious, what on earth is *this?*'

She could not have known. A few diaphragms are sold in Russia, but their quality is crude and the idea is almost unknown. When the Bolshoi Ballet first traveled to New York and made the discovery of American technology, nine-tenths of the corps—according to an interpreter I know—dashed to doctors to be fitted up.

'What on earth is what? Oh, that's a . . . a . . .' But I didn't even know the Russian word.

Oktyabrina was now holding the diaphragm itself between two fingers and at arm's length. Having scrutinized me meaningfully, she dropped the device into my wastepaper basket.

'Whatever it is, it has an *odor*,' she announced. 'I *will* bottle you those pickles, Zhoe darling—but Mother Russia will be blasphemed if you cover the jars with *that.*'

Then something paradoxical happened. At this moment, I think for the first time, it struck me that Oktyabrina would soon be a flesh-and-blood woman. Somehow her girl-next-door innocence awakened me to something very different underneath. The thought dissolved quickly and we went to a movie together in place of our walk, to enliven the drizzly afternoon. It was a sublimely bad Soviet-counterspies-smash-imperialist-agents adventure, during which we annoyed the audience considerably by groaning during the most 'heroic' scenes. Films like this were one of our private jokes, together with a particularly silly-sentimental song for Pioneers, which Oktyabrina had sung throughout her childhood. The melody was so infectious that we returned to it four or five times a day.

Let there always be glee
Let there always be glee
Let there always be Mama
Let there always be ME!'

A few days later, I was scanning a new book in the living-room when she emerged from the bathroom and her daily hour-long soak in the tub. A small towel covered her from armpits to knees. There was something terribly fragile about her with a face of scrubbed pink instead of the usual layers of make-up. Her shoulders were so thin and her waif's eyes so trusting that I got up and kissed her before I realized why. She smelled of soap and hair, like a little girl before going to bed.

A surge of happiness swept over me. I had made the gesture; a barrier was broken.

As I stepped back to my chair, Oktyabrina's face screwed up as if in pain. She uttered a wail and began crying in long, looping sobs.

'For goodness sake, what's the matter?' I asked.

'You too,' she blubbered.

'Me too what?'

'*You too*. Every man's always grabbing for the same thing. Just because I'm unclad—I don't *want* to be kissed all the time.'

I didn't believe her. Who could take offense at such a gesture? At someone who'd never grabbed anything, who offered her only protection, with no strings attached?

'You're all some kind of . . . *machines*. You don't know what it's *like* to be kissed all the time.'

'What are you talking about? *I* don't try and kiss you all the time.'

'No no no. Just the first time I'm easy prey.'

It was then that I realized the depth of her fear. I'd

been a Platonic dud with her—glad of the company of someone sexually undemanding, but wondering nevertheless how and when to apologize for my paralysis. And now it turned out she really needed to be left alone: virginity so shone through her bravado that I couldn't even talk seriously about these things with her. But why was I so hurt? Why was I sorry to see her fumbling with a shirt to cover her shoulders, and, after it was on, to sense a defeat for us both?

'For goodness sake, Oktyabrina, snap out of it. There are kisses and kisses. Can't you tell what kind that was?'

She studied me from her corner of the room. 'Kisses and kisses,' she murmured. 'Then the dark-haired Ruslan bent slowly over the fair Ludmilla, still sleeping in her deathly paleness. He *kissed* her with aching sweetness, and the spell was broken. . . .'

'I was just trying to say "hello". And let me tell you: for my own reasons, I'm no threat to you.'

The sobbing subsided slowly, like a child's who is appeased after a fall. 'I know, I know that of course,' she mumbled at last. 'It's just that . . . I happen to have a very infectious cold, if you must know everything. I didn't want you to catch it—Westerners are such easy prey.'

She retreated to the bathroom in a gay saunter, returning a few minutes later in sloppy trousers and an oversized sweater. The glass of tea she presented me was thick with sugar. As I sipped it, she pronounced a declamation.

'I do love you very much, Zhoe dearest. I want you to know that for ever and ever. But there is also love and love—do you understand?' She adjusted the cushions on my chair and leaned over precariously to place a musical kiss on my cheek. The telephone rang again, and when I returned to the living-room, she was curled up on the

103

floor next to the chair. Her hand was running back and forth over the carpet in a large arc, as if through thick grass.

'Zhoe, listen to me carefully. I don't know you very well yet, but I'll tell you something very few people understand. Every woman really needs three men in her life, do you understand? Every woman needs a lover, a husband and a father. Sometimes the three are combined in one person, but that's tragically rare. Anyway, *I've* always pictured journalists as fathers. I suppose it's because they have to write things they dislike for the sake of the state—it's like protecting your family by sacrificing something cherished of your own, I think it's frantically noble. . . . To tell you the absolute truth, of the three sides, it's the fatherly one women need most. . . .'

During the next few days, she was extremely attentive. She arrived in the morning with bottles of yoghurt and buttermilk for my lunch; a man of my age and sedentary occupation couldn't be too careful. When the gas man came to read the meter, she directed him to check all the fittings on the stove and hot water heaters, all of which she insisted on overseeing because 'you can't trust repairmen'. By this time, the sentries in the courtyard were giving her their little respect-for-foreigners nod when she came and went. I don't think we fooled them—or their bosses; despite their policemen's uniforms, they actually work for the KGB. But they rarely stop someone they're used to seeing. And there is always the chance that one shift assumed another made the report on her. At least that was our hope.

The next time she had a bath, she talked about it, by way of describing her new Polish pine salts, for an hour in advance. I didn't ask whether this was meant to warn me or to indicate the earlier incident had been forgotten. She emerged from the bathroom wrapped from neck to toe in my bath-robe, with the towel wrapped around her head. She marched into the office with her arms folded, imitating a sîrdar—but I was less certain than ever about who she really was.

It was when she was in the tub that afternoon that I got up and looked through some of her things. They had spilled from her open handbag on the floor next to the davenport, and a small pool of cream was leaking onto the carpet. I screwed the lid back onto its jar and then, to my own embarrassment, began investigating. Among handkerchiefs smeared with lipstick, flattened tubes and old bus tickets, I saw her 'passport'.

'Passport' is in quotes because it's a document for internal identification, rather than foreign travel; every Soviet citizen is supposed to carry his at all times, something like 'papers' in an occupied country. I know of nothing expressly secret about them, but this was the first one I'd seen. It was in an olive drab binding embossed with the Soviet state emblem; slightly smaller than an ordinary passport and quite dirty and frayed. Inside, there was a photograph of Oktyabrina: a skinny adolescent in a woven peasant blouse. It was a head-and-shoulders view only, but you pictured the rest as a farm kid in bare feet. The following information was listed on the first page:

1. *Surname, given name and patronymic:* Matveyeva Oktyabrina Vladimirovna.
2. *Date and place of birth:* 14 April 1950. Village of Nikolaiyevka, Omsk Province.
3. *Nationality:* Russian.
4. *Party affiliation:* Not a member of the Party.
5. *Social status:* School pupil.
6. *Military status:* Not obligated to serve.

All the following pages were empty, but the last one bore a police stamp showing she was registered to live at a certain street address in the village of Nikolaiyevka. It was true, then, that she had no Moscow *propiska*. But what did Nikolaiyevka mean when she'd talked about her native city of Omsk? I looked for it in my atlas without success. Then I searched on the large wall map of the Soviet Union in the corridor. Finally I found a tiny dot, several kilometers northeast of Omsk. Perhaps it had later been incorporated within the city limits.

It was only much later that I awoke to the other discrepancy. According to the passport, she was not twenty at all, but had barely turned eighteen!

The other disquieting matter was the disappearance of cigarettes. I noticed it only when my consumption had mounted to three cartons a week. Still, I often give packs as tips, and it never would have occurred to me that Oktyabrina was involved until I noticed her inspecting me one morning when I opened my drawer and discovered only two packs were left. I then tried an experiment: I bought the usual three cartons and kept track of my consumption. Sure enough, a small but steady depletion was unaccounted for. One day it was one pack, the next day two; they were taken from the middle of a carton so their absence would be inconspicuous.

It was a trivial loss. I buy cigarettes in the hard-currency store at duty-free prices: two dollars a carton—one of the foreign colony's thousand privileges. And Oktyabrina's coveting them was understandable: a pack of Camels provides considerable prestige and even more actual barter value among 'underground' contacts. I would have supplied her with all she wanted, of course—and did give her a few packs whenever she asked. But it was unsettling to have genial domesticity at one level and senseless petty theft at another.

We were driving to a movie early one evening when I raised the matter cautiously. I pretended to have forgotten my cigarettes and asked Oktyabrina if she happened to have a Western one.

'Anything for you, Zhoe darling. I adore the way your forehead scrunches up when you drive.' As usual, she was extremely pleased with the prospect of an evening 'out'. She had opened her handbag and begun searching for the cigarettes before she realized what producing a pack of Camels would mean. The handbag snapped shut.

'I was mistaken. Sorry.'

'Have a look in your pockets, will you, sweet? Maybe there's an old pack. I'm desperate.'

'Why do you imagine cigarettes would appear in my pockets? *I* don't indulge in common habits. Certainly not on the *street*. . . . Sweetheart, what is it? I happen not to carry cigarettes for my men, is that a crime?'

No cigarettes were missing during the next few days. Then the leakage started again, but never more than one packet at a time. Oktyabrina often blinked—it could not quite be called a wink—when she saw me open a new pack. And when Gelda appeared, she conspicuously presented her with two full cartons.

# 10

☐ The whole course of Oktyabrina's involvement with Gelda was set by how and where they met. It happened during the opening gush of a rainstorm. No April showers mood obtained because in Russia—testimony to its pinched warm season—'May thunderstorms' occupy that place in spring's song and verse. This was a prosaic, chilling rain, pouring down, as the Russians say, as if from a bucket.

Oktyabrina and I were strolling up Petrovka, talking about why I divorced and whether parents should drink in front of their children. The downpour struck suddenly. In the clownish moments before feeling soaked, we sang a chorus of 'Let there always be sunshine. . . .' Then Oktyabrina's mascara washed down her cheeks like ink in a sink.

'*Refuge*, Zhoe. No rain without clouds, no tears without sadness—and I need both like a whale needs an umbrella.'

We were alongside a long, low building with sharply sagging windows and chipping ochrey paint: refuge had to be taken in one of its four or five ground-floor shops. A sign tacked to the corner of the building announced its impending demolition and replacement by a sleek skyscraper. The sign was almost illegible with age, for the demolition had been scheduled for years before; it was now part of the landscape, like the faded poster above it:

Lenin haranguing a massive crowd of workers at the Putilov works in St Petersburg.

The crowds in the downpour that afternoon were almost as dense. Oktyabrina chose the door with the least resistance, above which a sign read 'Secondhand Bookstore No 44'. Inside, there was a murkiness caused by the dust of powdering paper and city soot.

Oktyabrina blotted her mascara with my handkerchief. When my eyes adjusted, I saw walls stuffed with old books from floor to lofty ceiling. Every millimeter was crammed, causing the old shelves to bend radically under their burdens. Lenin was inside too: as in every bookstore, new and used, throughout the country, the most prominent department was devoted to politics—principally works by and about Vladimir Ilyich. But in this decaying shop at least, he provided some much needed decoration. Plaster busts and full-color portraits of him were everywhere, accompanied by well-known citations on decaying crimson banners about the inevitable victory of Communism, the wisdom of the working class and importance of reading books.

A tight knot of shoppers and employees were engaged in one of those shouting matches without which no shop can function. I followed Oktyabrina around it and found myself staring into the eyes of the cashier. This was not accidental: she had looked up from her work and was examining us with a rapt gaze which seemed to combine hostility and defensiveness, passivity and aggression.

Even at first glance, this strange girl was commanding in spite—or because—of her appearance. She was inside the cashier's booth, sitting on a stool that had been augmented by several thick volumes to raise her to normal height. Black hair, matted and streaked with grey, clung like mattress stuffing to her oily, pitted cheeks. But everything was redeemed by the eyes—which went quizzical when they shifted back from me to Oktyabrina. It was the first time I understood the lyric paeans to solid, coal-black 'Russian' eyes.

I couldn't make out Oktyabrina's air-sent message to her. It was followed by quick strides to the booth, the opening of its door and the whispering of a quip into the girl's ear. When she dismounted from her stool, ignoring the line of customers at her window, she proved to be almost a head shorter than Oktyabrina. This meant that Oktyabrina's presentation of a soggy paper-flower necklace from her own neck to the girl's formed a downward movement—although she somehow managed to create the impression of looking up, as if the girl were the General.

Gelda was with us every minute of the next four days, except when she worked. This subtracted only a few hours, since we met on a Thursday and Gelda took the following afternoon off to lengthen the weekend. She and Oktyabrina closeted themselves in my bedroom for hours, chattering like maiden aunts. When the door finally opened, the exhaust was a heavy vapor of smoke, moist exhalation and feminine odors.

Gelda told me nothing of their conversation, hinting at confidences that would be revealed in good time. But during meals and Oktyabrina's brief absences, we had our own spirited exchange. I soon knew more about her background than Oktyabrina's.

Books drew us quickly together. I owned some novels that are wildly prized by Moscow intellectuals: emigré editions of great Russian writers—Nabokov, Pasternak, Zamyatin, Bulgakov—that are taboo in Russia. Gelda's curiosity about my shelves swelled to intense excitement when she spied these titles. When I gave her several, she gushed with gratitude, as if they were priceless first editions.

For her part, she quickly compiled a list of books for

me which, while not prohibited, are so long out of print and so rare as to be virtually non-existent. She was eager to introduce me to a body of literature hardly known outside intellectual circles but which, she promised, described aspects of Russia better than the great masters. She offered to find some of the books themselves for me, and give me the first of them on Monday.

'Geldechka, you *promised!*' Oktyabrina was annoyed by the digression to literature. 'You're *not* going to work on Monday. We're going to buy you an *outfit*. In the latest pastels.'

'Yeah,' replied Gelda. 'Pastels will work wonders for me—like a haircut helps a hanged man.'

But Gelda and I would have cottoned on to each other even without the 'contraband' of books. She was articulate and intelligent, and when she talked about herself, which was whenever she was asked, she wove each episode of her life into a kind of capsule chapter of Russian history. Her only reluctance in this was prompted by characteristic misgiving: it was too narrow; she should be talking about the human condition. Otherwise, her attitude towards herself was entirely straightforward— meaning, under the circumstances, incurably fatalistic. Her voice was often disagreeably nasal, but lacked the faintest hint of self-pity or shame.

Gelda was only four years older than Oktyabrina, but like the offspring of most prominent intellectual families under Stalin, she had been exposed to an abundance of 'life' (meaning, as usual, death) at an early age, and become middle-aged, like Europe's post-war novelists, while still an adolescent. Adolescence was some ten years ago; now her matted hair and bony cheeks gave her the look of a forgotten actress, eking out her twilight years in bilious poverty.

Acting once ran in her family. Gelda's namesake was a paternal aunt who had been a character actress in the

111

Moscow Art Theater just before and after the Revolution. Another aunt designed costumes for the Bolshoi. In fact, her entire family were minor celebrities in Moscow's artistic intellectual elite. Now Gelda was the only survivor except for an elderly uncle, and two cousins who worked in an upholstery factory near Kiev.

The family was destroyed because it was Jewish, liberal and recklessly outspoken. Gelda's father, a talented editor, was shot as a 'rootless cosmopolitan' in 1950. In keeping with contemporary protocol, no one was informed of the execution: the man was simply dragged away, fumbling for his glasses, after a knock on the door at two a.m.—and was never heard from again. Gelda's mother, an Estonian cellist, went mad soon after this and took to submerging her hands, together with Gelda's, in a cauldron of scalding chicken soup at dinner-times on Sundays.

The mother spent two years trekking from prison to prison seeking news of her husband, even though his fate was painfully obvious to everyone. She caused acute embarrassment and sometimes panic by talking obsessively about the case to relatives and friends. In whispers, they begged her to forget her husband and think of a new life. Soon people avoided her entirely. It was cruel, but in Stalin's last mad years the risk to oneself and one's own family of associating with this woman was too great.

The hands-submerging ritual continued, despite Gelda's variety of attempted escapes at the first scent of chicken soup from their apartment's communal kitchen. Gelda's mother also continued to play the cello, but her dementia deepened. After years, a neighbor in the apartment could no longer endure the querulous hag and her daughter's Sunday whimpers. She reported Gelda's mother, a medical investigation was launched, and the woman was committed. By that time, Gelda was nine, and abnormally short. The medical investigators also concluded that she was both mentally and socially retarded, but did not know that she had already absorbed more literature than many of her school-teachers. Compulsive reading in the bad basement light had already weakened her eyes.

She was also fat, unclean and ugly in a way that children can be only when severe deprivation affects them before they can understand its cause, encouraging them to attribute the guilt to themselves. As so often, the guilt had physical effects: Gelda was 'a lump of rashes' and sickly obesity. The great watery weight evaporated during adolescence, and she was now almost gaunt, existing principally on canned cod livers, a hard-to-find delicacy, and *prostokvasha*, a thick, refreshing soured milk. She also chain-smoked *papirosi*, the cigarettes with the long cardboard holder usually associated with the clenched, brownish teeth of a truck driver.

What had not changed from youth was Gelda's personality. She belonged to the category of deprived children who react with a kind of involuntary magnanimity, together with occasional belligerence, and spend much of their lives effacing themselves and indulging in inordinate generosity to others. Gelda was always the 'easy' one: the girl in her class of whom any favor or unpleasant errand could be demanded, and who volunteered when not asked. This was so ingrained in her character that she preferred not to use her lunch break at the bookshop—except to see Oktyabrina and me—but to give extra time to one of the salesgirls. She called them 'the children', and looked almost like their mother, although in fact most of them were roughly the same age as she.

The salesgirls, in turn, were a godsend to Gelda's need for self-sacrifice: except for an elderly lady with long service, they were all relative newcomers with no special knowledge of books, and needed frequent coaching and reminding. Gelda herself had worked in the shop for almost six years, ever since her graduation from a vocational high school. She knew every phase of its operation far better than the manager, a Party functionary with a green suit and stuffed-animal mentality, who had been given this sinecure of a job after an ignominious failure as director of a small bottle works. Without Gelda's managerial help, especially in keeping the books (his early attempts at embezzlement had got him into an impossible tangle), he faced certain downgrading again.

In contrast to the manager too, Gelda had read literally thousands of the books that passed through the store. She was the only member of the staff permitted to take them home, a grave violation of the rules about the protection of state property. Her current book was always open at her side, even in the cashier's booth. Yet like most members of the intelligentsia, she never laid eyes on a newspaper: the turgid style and moralizing repelled her, even when there were no recognizable distortions or lies. She enjoyed taunting the manager by flourishing a torn page of *Pravda* when marching to the toilet—its intended function, in the perpetual absence of toilet paper, was obvious. The manager himself always pondered *Pravda*'s every word searching for clues to shifts in the Party line.

Despite this, and despite the total disparity of their life styles, the manager and Gelda had achieved a relatively smooth working rapport. The only serious trouble came when Gelda fell into one of her terrible moods. Gelda even introduced Oktyabrina to the manager, and he volunteered that he might 'do something for the little girl' when his luck changed and he got another plum job. (He was now angling for the management of a railroad depot that handled imported consumer goods.) The offer

114

to help Oktyabrina was prompted by less than pure chivalry: the manager carried a not-so-secret torch for the oily-cheeked Gelda and often tried to coax her into his cubby-hole of an office for what she called a 'quick sniff and the usual three minutes of pawing'.

The extraordinary thing about Gelda was that despite everything, she was attractive to men. A significant percentage who entered the bookshop, especially the rougher-looking types, took stock of her in the way that indicates desire. Something about her, if only the attraction of 'ugly beauty', was stubbornly sexy. But Gelda herself looked at no man unless he sported a moustache—and if it turned out to be thin, short, wispy or limp, she rarely looked twice. Her obsession with moustaches was overpowering, and she happily succumbed to it. Her last important lover had, as she put it, a 'Serbian smuggler's one'. She showed me his photograph. It was badly blurred, but the moustache was indeed thick and black—I would have said Mexican rather than Serbian—and the man himself was correspondingly dark and powerful-looking.

They met in a line for suitcases at the East German shop. The man remarked that a good suitcase was an essential refinement of life. But before they'd reached the counter Gelda enticed him to her cramped attic room. He told her he taught acting in the Shchukin Academy, one of Moscow's best known drama schools. Through her old family contacts, Gelda learned that her man had nothing to do with the Academy—where she felt he might have been a janitor, for she herself had quickly determined that he knew nothing whatever about drama and little about school. Soon after this, she discovered his real occupation, for objects began disappearing from her room in order of their value. The transistor radio, the long-playing records, the horn comb (one of the last of

115

her mother's mementos), finally the box of talcum powder. . . .

Still, Gelda clung to him, leaving him to his profession when she left for work in the morning. After work, she bought him supper and arranged for the evening's entertainment, usually a band concert or sporting event—never the theater because he refused to 'mix professional obligations with pleasure'. Gelda saw through everything and dismissed everything for the sake of the moustache and the special things he did with it. The Serbian was the most compelling love of her life.

When he finally disappeared, it was with every object in the room except the furniture. He even took the wormy wooden frame in which her father's photograph had stood, leaving the yellowed photograph itself on the bare, badly-stained mattress of the bed.

Gelda's attractiveness to men and her own attraction to moustaches were not her only curious qualities. She kept a handsome aquarium in her room, only eighteen inches wide, but almost as long as the bed. (The Serbian had emptied half the water and tried to carry this away too, but had abandoned it in the corridor because of the weight.) In it she nurtured a collection of tiny, violently colored tropical fish which she bought in the so-called pet market at outrageous prices. She read widely in the literature of this subject, limited as it is in Russia, and had started a correspondence—in German, with the help of a language teacher—with Konrad Lorenz, whose books she herself paid to be translated. They began by writing about cichlids and blue triggers, but soon drifted to Lorenz's observations of human behavior, Gelda being curious about her own psychological make-up. But she was summoned by the Party Secretary of the Retail Book Trust and 'advised', as the euphemism has it, that the correspondence was 'not in her own best interests'. She was forced to drop Lorenz. Then remembering that her own uncle was engaged in behavioral research, she began meeting him. The old man, her father's elder brother, had also suffered badly during the most virulent anti-Semitic years and developed near fatal cases of ulcers and diabetes simultaneously. But he survived, and now worked in the medical department of the Moscow City Soviet. According to Gelda, he had recently presided over a massive public health survey about a supposedly secret subject. Its purpose was to determine, by means of obligatory physical examination, the sexual habits of Moscow school-girls. The team found, among other things, that twenty-seven per cent from the ages of fourteen to seventeen were virgins. The younger doctors were said to be surprised that the percentage appeared so high. Variations of this story are so rife in Moscow that I was at first sceptical of Gelda's uncle. But she, of all people, had no reason to misrepresent such things, and since she mentioned the survey to me only once, I came to believe her.

To Oktyabrina, however, Gelda mentioned the survey not once but a dozen times in my hearing and presumably still more often in the seclusion of the bedroom. 'Brinchka', as Gelda called her, was exceedingly curious about the team's statistics and methods of obtaining them: did the school-girls actually uncover their all in the presence of male doctors? *Flare their lower limbs?* Can any doctor be absolutely certain about a woman's virginity, knowing that certain of them experience *mystical* erotic . . . er, episodes, even in youth?

'Yeah, it's terribly mysterious,' said Gelda through the teeth clenching her *papirosa*. 'A stiff prick finds its mark, even during a blackout. Is there radar in the tip, or an uncanny sense of smell?'

We were having a snack in the kitchen; Oktyabrina blanched and spilled her coffee. When she had recovered,

117

her expression was like a young boy's when given a taste of beer: while shuddering, he pretends to smack his lips.

'How absolutely to the point, Geldechka—if you'll pardon the pun. Anyway, what's so important about who's a virgin?'

Despite this, and her shock at Gelda's graphic bluntness, Oktyabrina's interest in the survey persisted. She steered the conversation frequently to the subjects of 'chastity', 'deprivation of chastity' and 'the inauguration of carnal gratification'. Gelda was impatient with this level of analysis. To her, sex was interesting as an expression of human nature, about which she was caustic. 'Let's face it,' she'd say. 'Human beings use others and discard them when they're through, like squeezed lemons. We're animals—why expect anything else?'

'Darling Geldechka, at a certain point, cynicism about human nature becomes utterly *tragic*. Your faith can be restored by using a bit of foresight. For example, *I've* always found that the hairiest lovers are also the most . . . well, ruthless. So you must be exceedingly *cautious* about future moustaches.

But Gelda had tired of this theme. She returned the conversation to her passion of that hour, a bizarrre pre-revolutionary writer named Vasily Rozanov. Rozanov was unknown to all but a handful of Russians: a mystical, anti-Semitic Jew, obsessed by sex, death and the Orthodox Church. Gelda's extemporaneous discourse, intertwined biographical detail, literary appreciation and historical perspective—a dazzlingly instructive performance.

Without a break, she turned to an examination of Vsevolod Meyerhold, the brilliant avant-garde director who was shot in 1939. Afterwards she tossed her *papirosa* stubs into an untouched cup of coffee and went to the bathroom, leaving the door open while she coughed and urinated. Before she'd come out, she was declaiming again, but Oktyabrina led her to the bedroom and closed the door.

On Sunday evening, I took leave of the girls through the bedroom door, eager for the respite of a walk alone. My head was buzzing with information and emotion. A weekend of Gelda was like a non-stop wade through both *Crime and Punishment* and *War and Peace*. I hoped to see more of her—but in hourly doses.

When I returned to the apartment around midnight, she was gone, together with Oktyabrina. The bedroom was a mess: ripped pillowcases and a shattered glass, which had apparently been hurled against a wall. On my desk was a note from Oktyabrina, obviously written in great haste: 'Dearest Zhoe will explain absolutely everything later love me.'

Monday was the anniversary of Lenin's birthday. The campaign to 'befittingly greet the sacred day'—by over-fulfilling production norms—lacerated the country like the fanfare of a million film-set trumpets. Oktyabrina did not visit the apartment that morning, but telephoned with a scrap of stale news. Her voice was overly off-hand.

'Where are you?' I asked. 'At the bookshop?'

'*Where?* Oh, you mean *that* noisome bookshop. No, I'm not there—why should I be?'

'Gelda's not working again? Why don't you bring her around for coffee—tomorrow, I mean, or the day after.'

'Zhoe dearest, what's this sudden fascination for shop-girls? Gelda's not exactly my sister, you know.'

'What was the brawl in the bedroom yesterday?'

'As a matter of fact, she's not only not my sister, but that's probably her underlying trouble: naturally her family's madness makes her frantically envious of my own parental bliss. . . . Anyway, Zhoe darling, I've some

119

important people to meet now. I'll probably see you to-morrow.'

This confirmed my supposition that the bedroom mess had been caused by tension between the girls. Other clues followed quickly: Oktyabrina declined to talk about Gelda, and took pains to avoid not only the book-store for several days, but Petrovka itself.

'I'll tell you what caused the ordeal,' she said when we first returned to Petrovka. 'Only you must pledge two things on your honor. Do you promise?'

'Will it hurt?'

'Do you promise? Believe me, Zhoe dearest, it's for your own peace and sanity.'

'I promise, my love.'

'Then you must never condemn Gelda for what I'm about to tell you—it's not her *personal* fault. That's one vow. The other is that you must never try to see her again. You see, Zhoseph, Gelda is *eine katatonische Schizophrene*. You can look up the rest in Konrad Lorenz.'

'She's a what?'

'Neither you nor I can help in the slightest,' Oktyabrina declared. 'Or anyone—Gelda suffers from incurable *fits.*'

'I suppose she has every reason.'

'It's not my duty to rock other people's children.'

Oktyabrina adjusted her bonnet in the reflection of a window and changed to her strolling-on-the-town expression. As far as she was concerned, she said firmly, the subject of Gelda was now—and for evermore—closed. But a few days later, she found a fishstore with a supply of cod liver and arranged for twenty-five tins to be delivered to the bookshop.

'Gelda is society's debt,' she explained. 'I'm sorry that I can risk no more than this gesture. It's simply too perilous: that glass just missed my face, you know.'

'I was afraid of something like that. Still, there's something splendid in that girl. The best hope is her awareness of her own affliction.'

'Zhoe darling, maybe you and I need less outside . . . er, *divertissement*. I used to think we were both a little daft, but compared to other people, we're pure, old-fashioned *euphony* together.'

'Oktyabrina darling, let's make another pact. We'll try to steer clear of strays and passers-by. Now slip your arm in mine. . . .'

Two days after this, we received separate notes from Gelda. Oktyabrina thought it best not to show me hers. Mine was inside a crumbling old book by Rozanov. It was full of explanation and apology about the inevitable bad end to her, Gelda's, friendships—which she very much wanted to prevent with both of us. She felt rotten about losing us, but at least we had each other. Marriage, she wrote, was a piteous hoax, but she was sure we'd try it one day—more she would not reveal of Oktyabrina's confidences—and bon voyage to us both.

## 11

☐ On May Day, I was up early to cover the parade in Red Square. The entire center of the city had been sealed off—a much wider area and with far stricter security than for funerals—and reporters had to be in their places by eight o'clock. The vigilance smacked of an occupying army preparing a major roundup: platoons of soldiers patrolled the otherwise empty streets, ensuring that only people with passes entered the restricted area. Starting at the metro exit, there were six checkpoints within the few hundred yards to the stands, and I had trouble at all of them because one letter of my name had been misspelled on my pass and 'contravened' my passport. Finally, I convinced a colonel who I was, and he escorted me to my place in the foreigners' section opposite the Lenin Mausoleum, and beneath a gigantic 'FORWARD TO THE VICTORY OF COMMUNISM!' banner. Bedecked with painting and signs in this vulgar evangelical style, the great, austere square seemed scaly, like a medieval dragon.

The ceremony started at the chimes of ten o'clock. Marshal Malinovsky, the Minister of Defense, reviewed the troops from a bulbous limousine, while thousands of soldiers shouted battle cries in unison. A violent harangue from him followed, warning the enemies of socialism. Then the parade itself in the traditional sequence: thundering tanks and missiles the length of football fields, accompanied by divisions of soldiers, sailors and cadets. Finally the massive civilian procession was set in motion. The thought that some of the tens of thousands of floats, banners, and portraits of Marx and Lenin had no doubt come from Evgeny Ignatievich's warehouse provided the long morning's only moment of relief.

For nothing in the world less conveyed the impression of spontaneous joy it sought than the elaborately rehearsed pageantry streaming through the square. Everyone knew that all of the hundred thousand odd 'demonstrators' had been drafted and painstakingly drilled—and that no one would dare refuse to 'volunteer'. Hundreds of signs read simply 'HAPPINESS!'—one of the blessings that Communism has officially conferred on the Russian people. This was the moment when the full sorrow of the paradox descended: deeply unhappy Russia with its cruel climate and history, its crushing political backwardness, proclaiming to the world that it has established Happiness on Earth. The land of Ivan the Terrible, Stalin, and mendicant mystics is somehow fated to go on this way, limping from tragedy to tragedy, sacrificing generation after generation—and always searching frenziedly for the path to paradise and redemption. The deeply religious roots of all this were demonstrated again that morning by the thousands of portraits of radiant Lenin, just as icons had been borne aloft by the Orthodox Church's ragged, unquestioning faithful.

Yet most Russians themselves would dismiss these 'insights' as patronising foreign humbug. The procession's hundreds of thousands of participants were thinking not about historical or philosophical abstractions, but about the big bowl of borscht waiting for them at home. It was a holiday, after all, and people *were* in a holdiay mood. They might have preferred to stay in bed rather than spend the morning on a forced walk; but the sun was shining and May the First had fallen on Friday, meaning

123

that absenteeism on Saturday was going to be prodigious, and a self-declared three-day weekend had begun.

When I had filed my copy and arrived home, Oktyabrina was also in a holiday mood. She dashed to the door in a lacy white dress, a kind of peasant bridal gown—her 'homage to spring'.

'Do you really approve?' she said, twirling happily. 'May Day, you know, is the opening of the "love season" —it's an old Russian tradition. I've a marvelous inspiration for how to celebrate.'

Her inspiration was to see *La Dolce Vita*. Somewhere, she'd heard the news that it was to have a private screening that evening at the Cinema Workers' Club. Oktyabrina had an idea of the movie's motif from a story in one of my old magazines, which convinced her it was *precisely* her kind of thing.

Foreign correspondents get passes fairly easily for these closed screenings, and I telephoned the office which makes the arrangements. But I had no luck there, or with any other of the calls I made during the afternoon. The reason was obvious: foreign films like this one are screened under the fiction of inspection for possible purchase, but in fact to allow a handful of chosen people to sample the forbidden fruit. *La Dolce Vita*'s reputation was known, and the news of its one and only showing had raced through the city's intellectual elite.

Besides, most of the tickets had already been requisitioned. A thousand Party first secretaries, heads of censorship departments and ideological specialists on The New Soviet Man and other moral themes were dying to treat their wives or sweethearts to a really choice evening of bourgeois decadence. Tickets were simply unobtainable; not even Kostya's excellent contacts produced results.

Oktyabrina removed her white dress and sulked on the davenport. 'What a way to start the love season,' she said,

124

fixing an eye on me. 'This year things aren't exactly *aus-picious.*'

Suddenly, she jumped up and lifted the telephone herself. She searched through my notes on the pad and picked out the number of the Party bureau in the Cinema Workers' Club. While she dialed, her face turned hard; for a second I saw a resemblance between the faintly Mongoloid cut of her jaw and Marshal Malinovsky's much fatter one at the microphone that morning.

'Whom am I speaking to?' she said in a vicious, splitting voice. '*Oh yes?* Well, *you* are talking to Comrade Vinogradova.' She paused. 'I'm with five Comrades from the Ukrainian Central Committee. We're here on the May Day project and require recreation. Reserve us six tickets for your film tonight, is that absolutely clear?' She paused again. 'Of course not, no. We are far too busy for any picking-up. Have them waiting at the door directly before the start—and *no slip-ups*, do you understand?'

She slammed down the receiver with all her might. Then she turned to me with her triumphant grin. 'I'm hungry, Comrade correspondent. You may serve tea.'

It was a chance in a hundred, but when we arrived at the large stone building that houses the Club, the burly doorman, while holding back the crowd with one hand, produced an envelope with the other. It was marked '*For Comrade Vinogradova, Ukrainian Central Committee Delegation*'. Inside were six tenth row tickets.

Oktyabrina was exultant. Nobody would have believed a story about *two* tickets, she explained in a vainglorious whisper—and with a corresponding gesture distributed the four extra ones among the swarm of beseeching hands outside the door. Then she collected five rubles from me, the winnings of our bet, and strolled into the auditorium with more self-importance than the celebrities who belonged.

The movie itself, however, disappointed her hugely—

125

so much so that she was fidgety and full of sonorous yawns after the first twenty minutes and dozed intermittently until the dunking-in-the-fountain scene near the end. Afterwards, when we stepped into the fresh air, Oktyabrina was irritated by the buzz of ecstatic praise from other members of the audience. The whole exercise was much too *talky*—nor could she understand why Marcello Mastroianni was so *spiritless* or what was so wonderful about that decadent life.

'I mean, those people didn't believe in *anything*. Didn't love anything, even *feel* anything. All those furs and cars and things gave you the creeps, like in some *mausoleum*. Please take my arm, Zhoe darling.'

'Fellini's a master at making you feel cold-bloodedness, you should see it as a modern morality play.'

'But why does he believe that beauty and luxury must be stone dead like that? Kostya's right—I wouldn't trade a hundred Romes like that for dear Moscow.'

'We're in our happy period now, aren't we, Zhoe? It's so unfair, how people squander the joy of plain domestic peace.'

Oktyabrina handed me an apple and settled in the armchair to attack hers. It was a Friday morning; she had recently arrived and I was finishing an article on arms limitation. The radio was introducing a drama based on Lenin's skill in reading and taking notes. The minor domestic traumas of the past weeks were forgotten; our understanding of each other was steadily waxing, like the spring sun. It was indeed our happy period—and also the calm before the storm. It broke twenty-four hours later.

Oktyabrina had never taken the slightest interest in my work until that Saturday—when it spoiled our plans. We'd meant to spend a happy afternoon at a French industrial exhibition in Sokolniki Park, one or two or three major Western exhibits a year, all of which are inevitably packed. Rows of giant machinery would seem to interest only engineers, but there are usually enough photographs of the magical sponsoring country to fascinate the general Moscow public. Displays of fashions and consumer goods are also bewitching, not to speak of in-the-flesh trouser-suited guides. Even Embassy wives, having forgotten these visual delights, spend days at the fairs.

Oktyabrina and I planned to consummate our tour with supper at a restaurant just outside the fair grounds. The ordinarily dismal establishment had been temporarily taken over by Maxim's as the exhibition's most alluring 'side show'. Oktyabrina prepared for it during most of the morning; her outfit was going to be a surprise.

Just before we planned to leave, the Press Department telephoned. I was informed that an interview I'd requested exactly seventeen weeks before had been granted, and could be conducted that afternoon—and that afternoon only. The man I was to see was the Vice-Minister of Public Health, the author of a long article in *Komsomolskaya Pravda*, the newspaper of the Young Communist League. It was an indignant attack on Siberia's spoilage by ruthlessly expanding Soviet industry. If the man was anything like his prose, an interview with him would be quite a prize.

Oktyabrina's disappointment over the interview's scheduling was mild compared to mine over its substance. I drove to the Ministry of Public Health with real hope; this was a non-political story, after all, and once in a blue moon a Soviet official says something meaningful. My illusions dissolved the moment we sat down to talk.

It was in the ubiquitous reception room of every public institution, with the bottles of mineral water arrayed on the green felt 'conference' table. The mere sight of this setting, Soviet officialdom's obligatory 'parlor', tends to stifle any free flow of ideas. But the more direct cause of rigidity and futility was the two at-

127

tendant supernumeraries. The Vice-Minister met me with an 'interpreter'—whose real function was instantly clear to all three of us, since not a word of English was used during the entire hour. The man sat silently at the Vice-Minister's right, wiping his glasses fastidiously, and unconcerned by the transparency of his disguise.

On *my* right was stationed a small jovial reporter from the Novosti Press Agency who, throughout the proceedings, beamed at me as if to indicate pleasure that the international fraternity of journalists had been reconvened, and occasionally jotted a note onto the margin of his newspaper. His presence was explained—by the interpreter—in terms of a 'remarkable but highly gratifying' coincidence: Novosti too happened to be investigating 'control of industrial waste'.

This might have been true, for Novosti does like to steal stories suggested by Western reporters—and then, having denied permission to these Western reporters, to hawk the articles (for hard currency) in Western capitals. However, Novosti's function that afternoon was not to poach my idea, but to send a back-up man for the 'interpreter'. This was clear from what I overheard when hurrying back into the building to retrieve the Vice-Minister's card, which he'd presented me ceremoniously when he at last appeared, and I'd inadvertently left on the table. The Novosti man was in the foyer, complaining to the interpreter: '*Tell* me next time, will you, for God's sake? At least the subject! *Pollution*, of all things. I could've prepared some statistics or something, instead of playing the friendly dummy the whole time.'

As it happened, statistics were the sole offering of the Vice-Minister himself. In crushing abundance: the percentage of *improvement* in air cleanliness, water cleanliness and pollution *controls*. . . . In his droning assemblage of figures, he not only said nothing in elaboration of his article, but produced a mass of mumbo-jumbo to refute it.

Obviously, someone higher had ordered him to correct the 'subversive' impression his crusade had produced in the Western press. There was no serious pollution problem in Soviet society, he was saying; and under socialism, there could be none. He slipped into a chronicle of the Russian people's miseries under Tsarism and the striking superiority of Soviet public health to that of American imperialists. 'Pollution is wholly insignificant in comparison to our people's immense strides under our Leninist Party's unshakable leadership. . . .'

Not one paragraph of this 'interview' was usable, except perhaps in a backgrounder about the mechanics of interviewing in Russia—which would have infuriated the Press Department. However, there was nothing unusual about the Vice-Minister's performance. The episode assumed importance only because of my ensuing discussion with Oktyabrina.

I'd dropped her at the exhibition grounds on my way to the Ministry. When I returned, only ten minutes late, she was waiting at the gate as we'd planned. Her fingers drummed against her handbag, to indicate that she was heroically controlling her exasperation.

'Don't bother to hurry, Mister Busy,' she called. 'It's too late for the restaurant. They said there was still an evening table if you'd reserved even an hour ago.'

'It's just as well really. I'm not in the mood for a grand meal just now.'

'*Just as well?* Thanks awfully. What about snails? What about crêpes suzettes? Your seductive descriptions.'

'We'll come back during the week, I promise.'

'How do *you* know I'll be free during the week? You *already* promised. For today, Saturday, the eighteenth of May, Old Style. Which is the fifth and my mother's

129

Saint's Day on the Gregorian Calendar, in case that fancy journalist's date-watch of yours has corroded.'

The disappointment of the interview was still in my throat, spoiling the taste for banter. And for fighting the crowds to enjoy the exhibition. Since Oktyabrina had already seen much of what interested her, we set out towards the northern, unpeopled corner of the huge park. It had turned cold again, like a raw day in early March.

'What's the matter with you, Zhoe darling?' Oktyabrina said at last.

'Nothing.'

'Something.'

'Nothing serious.'

'Something *rather* serious. One must doesn't ask a lady to supper and ruin everything that way for no reason at all.'

'*Well?*' she said again in her half-teasing, half-daunting contralto.

'Dearest Oktyabrina, believe me. There *is* a reason. It's the reason for everything miserable here. This hypocritical government of yours. The medieval *system*.'

'Zhoe darling, once upon a time you attempted to spank me for being "mysterious". Now stop brooding and tell your confidante what's gone wrong.'

In the end, I did tell—and everything. I traced the history of my campaign to see the Vice-Minister, and the worthless result. Once the dam had broken, a catalogue of frustrations gushed out, including several I'd forgotten. I described the straight-jacket I was in, the refined or clumsy obstacles erected around every story, the impossibility of doing even a half-honest job. Finally, I returned to the Vice-Minister, and the stupidity, the cynical *crudeness* of his muzzling and my being handed the old propaganda line. . . .

In releasing the steam, I momentarily forgot Oktyabrina. When I glanced down for her reaction, I saw that

130

she'd stopped a few paces back, where an elderly couple were walking their dog. She was fingering the little mongrel's leash—an old bathrobe belt.

'For heaven's sake, Oktyabrina. Let's go home.'

'What's the matter now?'

'I was telling you something. You didn't hear a word.'

'I heard absolutely everything darling, and I think it's positively hideous. You must be awfully worn out.'

'I'm exhausted and I'm sick of this place.'

'Only you do like to dramatize things a bit, don't you?'

'Wait a minute. I said that man didn't utter a single honest word. That's a statement of fact, not a dramatization.'

'Of course it is, darling. But why torment yourself about it? Put down what you like—that man won't mind.'

I assumed this was badinage—an offshoot of Kostya's standard quips about *Pravda* journalism. But Oktyabrina was in dead earnest. She was offering me what she thought I wanted: advice to write up the interview with that 'delicious diplomat man' in the way that would best suit me. 'After all, he'll never read a provincial American newspaper, will he? He probably doesn't even know English.'

'Good thinking; that takes care of him. But unfortunately there's still me. I'm a journalist you see, not a liar.'

She snickered. 'If you ask me, it's an *actor* your inner self is really seeking. You *might* do character parts. But I suggest a firm director: there's a tendency to over-play the "oppressed-and-aggrieved" emotion.'

'Most countries, you know, have the government they deserve. Lies are told because people want to believe them. The Vice-Minister didn't say an honest word—you haven't understood a single word.'

'I've understood every silly syllable. Despite your sour innuendoes—what it does to your accent, Zhoseph. What

131

I don't understand is you: whom you're trying to impress and why? Write your Very Important Article. Dash to your desk *this instant* if necessary; you've already ruined the evening. Only stop gnashing your teeth, the wounded-hero pose pushes you over the thin line into comedy.'

'I'm trying to tell you that I *cannot* write the article. Because I have no *facts*.'

She lowered her voice and organised her shame-shame expression. 'Really, Zhoseph, why shout? Posturing's so *unnecessary* with someone who likes you.'

'When I try to write. . . .'

'People particular about "facts" aren't in the habit of reading newspapers. Not to mention writing for them.'

'Why is this leaking out now? What are you getting at?'

'First you spoil our day, then you invent a castle of self-imposed "professional" hardships. Really Zhoseph, it's so simple. Your newspaper wants a tsk-tsk story about dreadful Soviet pollution. The Vice-Minister won't ever see the stuff you write. . . .'

Suddenly, I realised what she was driving at. What she'd been thinking—not just then, but ever since Kostya introduced us and she assumed the role of my coquette—'guide'. And throughout the months when she'd cooed about journalists being marvelously paternal. A stab of anger pinched my eyes.

'Do you really think I'm a journalist like Soviet journalists? Do you believe newspapers are a pack of lies in civilized countries? That's the worst of it: your newspapers lie and it infects you all. You all assume everyone else tells them.'

'Must you shout? Is that how people behave in civilized countries?'

'I do not publish lies. I write articles about what I know, not what might make me look good. Or my newspaper or my government. You can't understand that because in your country you've never learned the difference between fact, invention and pure lie.'

There was a momentary pause. I relaxed because she seemed to understand at last. But she answered in a harder tone.

'I suppose *your* country is better. Yes. Very much better—at burning villages in Vietnam. Lynching innocent Negroes right in your own homeland. Sucking blood from the poor and the defenseless everywhere—and then being very superior, of course, because you have sparkling kitchens and fancy cars.'

'We are talking about journalism. The pursuit of truth in newsapapers.'

'The pursuit of *wretchedness*, you mean.'

'The possibility of approaching the truth. And you are proving my point: a country's shortcomings must be searched out and *reported*. By journalists—that's our job. Otherwise, you'd know nothing about the treatment of Negroes or anything else that disturbs us both.'

'What a narrow view of truth you have. A collection of what you call facts, the uglier the better. Digging out other people's mistakes and misfortunes, then shouting your head off about them with all that glee. . . .'

'That is nonsense.'

'Yes, you're secretly happy when you find something painful. Then you can parade your righteousness—although you've done *zero* to improve anything or help anybody.'

'The first step towards alleviating misfortune is knowing the facts. Progress is impossible without them.'

'Your sermons insult my intelligence.'

'*Use* your intelligence. Face the issue.'

'Face your own issue—I happen not to be fascinated by newspapers. I'm interested in something called life, the mystery of existence. Journalists think "newspaper" is a password that excuses every rudeness and selfishness. That they can invite people to dine one minute and abandon them the next. Be so very superior about. . . .'

'I see. What really bothers you is Maxim's and nothing but Maxim's. Your blather about people's misfortunes is as synthetic as the line about my being your father. . . .'

'Find fault and be so very superior about a country that bled itself white to defeat fascism and keep carpers like you alive. Yet you preach about "the truth" as if you speak for humanity. It's the people who suffered and died who have that right—and above all, that means the people of *this country* you hate so much.'

'Let's end this farce. You're up to your ears in sophism —in propaganda. According to you Hitler attacked Stalin and people suffered terribly—which justifies continued suffering today. You confuse. . . .'

'We don't need foreigners telling us what we confuse. Or how to run things. I'm sick and tired of all you Great-God Westerners coming in here like missionaries to tell us what we do wrong.'

'That's a parody of my attitude and you know it.'

'*Preaching* to people to do everything your wonderful Western way. The way you dropped the atomic bomb on yellow people. The way you yourself shake your head oh-so-mournfully if you must stand in some line for a minute—oh yes, we're *backward*, you feel so infinitely superior. The way you dole out your hallowed Camels and expect people to kneel in holy gratitude. . . .'

'*Camels?* You must be ill, you know. Or simply can't tell right from wrong—you steal my cigarettes and then think you have a right to. . . .'

'*Your cigarettes?* You're so wrapped up in capitalist morality that you don't know how to *live*. Your precious cigarettes—and let a million people in Hiroshima burn. I never stole cigarettes. I distributed a few to people who needed them. Who just happen not to be rich enough to

134

afford them because they weren't born in seventh-heaven America and raised on imperialist silver spoons.'

'Why didn't you ask me? I'd have given you a carton a day. Or ten cartons, if that's patronizing—a hundred cartons. But try to be sensible. Taking someone's things without asking is wrong—under Communism as well as capitalism.'

'And by the way, if you were so certain you only write the truth in that fabulous newspaper of yours, you wouldn't be beating your breast about it. Why all the Hollywood speeches about *facts?* I'll tell you: because you know somewhere that you don't write the truth of truths.'

'Please let's stop. You can't follow the line of your own thought.'

'It's *you* who won't follow. I said that without Russia, you'd be in some concentration camp. That it was the people of *my* country who died to stop the Nazis—and my father happened to be among them. Yes, our suffering was sometimes caused by our own political mistakes too. But only because we were trying to practice the "brotherhood" Westerners preached for a thousand years. We took the sermons seriously—because that's what Russia really means: a kind of purity and striving for genuine goodness. We've always taken the *important* things seriously—like higher ideals, not newspaper "truth". So we suffer. And you gloat over our tragedies because it makes exciting journalism.'

'Just answer one thing. How does this justify lies—the Vice-Minister's or anyone's?'

'I don't wish to explain anything further to you. Until you learn to listen.'

By this time we were no longer at the top of our voices, but snapping spitefully at each other. We had come to a bench bordering the path in a secluded part of the park. I shall never forget the pain of the young girl

135

sitting on the edge of it. She was deeply humiliated, perhaps even frightened by her parents. The father, a large unshaven man, tried to force her to eat a large dill pickle while he swigged at his bottle; the mother was a disheveled hag with a mass of filthy hair. Both were very drank.

Lost in their vodka and wretchedness, the parents were oblivious to us. The girl looked up, almost pleading that bitter sounds from us too would be more than she could bear. Oktyabrina and I were silenced. Tired and unhappy, we turned back towards the exit of the park. When I resumed the discussion, it was to make peace—to offer a truce on issues she and I were powerless to resolve. What hurt me was not so much her disdain for my work itself, but for my intentions.

'So you do understand that I don't invent things,' I said. 'I didn't want to blacken Russia. Pollution is a critical problem in America. I genuinely wanted to hear the Vice-Minister's ideas.'

'Do you really want to continue this?'

'I don't. I want you to understand just that one thing—about me, if not about journalism in general.'

She said nothing for several minutes. Then she hissed a declaration she'd apparently been preparing.

'Journalism in general is prostitution. No matter who you work for and in what country—it's using words for something cheap instead of literature. Instead of art.'

'Please don't.'

'Newspapers are for wrapping fish.'

'Nicely put,' I said—now calmly, because I suspected this would be the last time I'd see her. 'Now, please explain what a person of *art* is doing with a prostitute. And half living off his immoral earnings.'

'I've got nothing against prostitutes. They can be as noble as . . . *doctors*. It's self-righteousness I can't stand.

That line about bleeding for the truth, it makes me sick.'

'I think I'd better take you home.'

'I think we *may* meet again one day. If and when you've learned you can't shunt people around at your convenience. Like serfs.'

It had started to rain. Oktyabrina pivoted on the wet path and strode again towards the depths of the park. I watched her, but watched myself watching instead of trying to stop her. The scene expressed something inevitable, as if I'd lived through it before; as if it were fated. It was not the first time a rage of misunderstanding had dissolved one of my friendships. Then I was invaded by an irrelevant reflection which prevented me from thinking about what I should have: the injury to our relationship. I was sure she would take the metro home because it was quickest and she didn't know the bus routes. I also knew she would be dying to get back because she'd been without a bathroom for several hours. But just to be stubborn, she sallied forth in the opposite direction. It was typical. And the rain now plastered her stringy hair to her skull and to the rayon remnant meant to be a cape.

## 12

☐ On Sunday, an envelope lay under the front door of
the apartment. It was postmarked Saratov and addressed
to Oktyabrina, care of the old pensioner at Domolinart.
Inside was a letter to us both from the Minister.

The Minister's handwriting was cursive and surprisingly elegant. Most of the letter was a profuse apology for
not having written to his 'dear friends' sooner. Nothing
in the world could excuse his negligence, he explained,
but there had been a few extenuating circumstances. The
most weighty was the search for a place to live amidst
Saratov's housing shortage. At last he'd found a room in
a communal apartment. This was surely temporary; soon
new housing for the teaching staff would be completed.
Construction had been interrupted because the Chairman
of the Construction Trust had been convicted of embezzlement after a long trial also involving senior city
officials. The new Chairman, wary that he too might be
charged with something, would not complete the change
of command without an inventory of every nail.

Otherwise, life in Saratov was satisfactory—even pleasant in many ways. Only the food was . . . well, frankly,
rather woeful. You had to queue all Saturday morning
for stewing meat, and who would have thought there was
no salami in a city this size? Luckily however, forty-five
carloads of canned crabmeat had arrived in Saratov instead of Moscow by mistake. This meant a whacking trial

of railroad engineers and certain Food Trust officials, but meanwhile, stores were stacked to the ceiling with the wonderful cans. . . .

In general, however, he wouldn't want to give the impression that he was unhappy. Far from it; in many ways, life was more honest and rewarding in Saratov than in Moscow. You had a feeling you could trust your colleagues more—except, of course, the young bureaucrats who would sell their mothers to the devil for a chance of promotion to Moscow. You could walk the length of Lenin Boulevard, the central thoroughfare, from its far end to Lenin Square in twenty minutes, and a strand of neon never looked so good. You could fish for almost anything your heart desired in the Volga—who could tire of Dear Mother Volga?—and there was a rumor that the sport store had been allocated a case of reels for the coming financial year. . . .

But enough about boring old him; how were *we* getting on? Were we keeping alive the traditional Sunday outings? We mustn't forget: the rent on the cottage was paid up until next autumn and . . . Yes, he missed us. Why try and hide it?—Especially now, when the spring verdure begged for a camera and *friends*. As soon as he could get time off he'd be coming to Moscow for as long as a week. Unfortunately new teachers were saddled with supplementary sessions of the Dialectical Materialism courses. . . .

The letter was signed 'M-m-minister', and followed by a PS: 'I just wanted you to feel as close to me as I to you. Oh yes, please answer poste restante. Unfortunately, the minute we moved into our room, my wife started issuing orders to everyone in the apartment. She'd forgotten how touchy provincial people—her own kind, actually—can be. Then somebody took revenge by informing the local security police we were secret Khrushchev sympathizers, plotting his restoration. So our post is opened.

Frankly, I can't blame the informer. On the other hand it's been hell for the wife: no chocolates, no canasta. She tries to tell everybody whom she used to have tea with in Moscow, but not even the old watchman believes her. . . .'

I reread the letter before folding it back into the envelope. After yesterday's disaster and the apartment's bleakness without Oktyabrina, it deepened the Sunday gloom. The refrigerator clicked on and whirred at intervals. There was no taste in my mouth.

I set out on a walk, but because it was still raining, turned back for my car. With the heater on, I went for a drive where the wheels took me—which turned out to be a purposeless tour of some dull, wet countryside. The radio offered a drama about a Finnish schoolgirl who'd learned Russian in order to read Lenin's letters to his mother; it was so bad that I stopped to take notes. The rain continued to pelt the windshield and I remembered the old peasant saying: 'A downpour is no real help.' The one comforting thought was that it had been Oktyabrina who'd slipped the Minister's letter under my door. This meant she too didn't want an irrevocable break. Or was she trying to shame me into feeling worse?

When I returned home, there was a note tacked to my door, scrawled in crayon and in Oktyabrina's unmistakable, childish script. 'Mind your own business about my country. YANKEE GO HOME!'

I waited until Wednesday to pass Domolinart. Two black Volgas with 'MOS' plates were parked near the entrance, and I decided not to drop off the note I'd written. On Thursday morning, she telephoned.

'Good morning, it's Tanya.'

'Good girl. Would you care to meet me today? At one o'clock—*please?*'

'No. Now.'

'Now it is. How late will you be?'

'That's not amusing. This is no time for banter. Now or not at all.'

When I arrived at Sverdlov Square, she was pacing around the fountain, clearly agitated. Having seen me, she turned away and made for Petrovka, indicating I should follow. Before I'd quite caught up with her, I suggested lunch at Maxim's with a bottle of their best champagne. I felt it would be quite Russian to seal our reconciliation in extravagance. Oktyabrina said nothing, but maintained her rigid march until we were beyond everyone's earshot.

'I didn't meet you,' she sputtered nervously, 'to discuss your personal debts to me. This is serious. *You must help.*'

'What's wrong now?'

'Something awful. Leonid is about to be destroyed.'

This sounded like her usual hyperbole, but I was glad of any excuse to patch things up. Then she began a shaky narration, and it was soon clear that Leonid was in fact in desperate trouble.

Last year, she explained, he had signed 'a pronouncement'. It was a letter of protest against the persecution of Alexander Ginsburg, the young intellectual who had compiled a record of the trial of Andrei Sinyavsky and Yuli Daniel. This was what had brought about his dismissal from the physics institute. Last month, he signed a second petition condemning the persecution of Alexander Solzhenitsyn. Against everyone's advice, he had included his address. This second offense, regarded as insolence, incensed the KGB.

Four angry officers had raided Domolinart the evening before. They tore through Leonid's things and removed all the written material, together with Leonid himself. Oktyabrina saw them manhandling him into a car as she was returning home from an errand. He just had time to

141

call a goodbye to her before he was slapped and the two cars drove away. Oktyabrina ran off and, too terrified to go home, spent the entire night walking.

That day came to be called 'Black Thursday'. We both knew that something had to be done—and also, at bottom, that we would do nothing. Because nothing *could* be done except to implicate ourselves. When Kostya patiently expounded this to us, we reproached him for his cynicism, but knew he was right—and he knew we had to hear it from someone else.

'Believe me, I know the score. If the KGB has him, he's finished and you haven't got a chance. A bit of sausage and cheese will help him a hell of a lot more than getting yourselves arrested.'

Nevertheless, Kostya did go to KGB headquarters on Dzerzhinsky Square—the dreaded Lubyanka—to inquire what would happen to Leonid. It was an act of considerable bravery. Oktyabrina and I waited a block away. Kostya was told—rather politely, to his surprise—that Leonid would be exiled from Moscow for five years. He would probably be sent to a construction settlement in central Siberia and assigned to hard labor—mixing cement and handling blocks—for a new dam on the Angara river. 'It's the largest in the world,' said the neatly-groomed KGB officer blandly to Kostya. 'Now, are there any other questions? Or do you want me to ask *you* one —I mean your name?'

When Kostya returned he took me aside and gripped my arm. 'Leonid's finished, Zhoechik. As we say, they've slipped the sickle around his balls. The solution for us lies in some Egyptian rum.'

In the evening, Oktyabrina and I sat on the bench in Gogol Boulevard and tried to think. 'But it's not fair,' she said. 'Leonid's a beautiful boy, a living *martyr*. He's suffering for his purity and his *ideals*.' She dropped the little-girl whine. 'Can lives really be crushed like this? I always thought it was dramatic accentuation.'

Later she was troubled by her own role. 'I always suspected he was involved in those things. Was it my deep moral obligation to stop him?'

'I don't know,' I said. 'When a friend wants to make a sacrifice for public good—I honestly don't know.'

'At least you can do something about it.'

'I wish I could.'

'What's written with a pen . . . can't be expunged by evil men. You can write an absolutely sizzling article about it. Stir up the Western world.'

'I've been thinking about it. It's probably better to write nothing.'

'Why?'

'Anything I write about Leonid, can only stir the wrong people in the wrong way. They'll investigate how I got the information, and eventually narrow it down to you. Then you'll be in trouble—and probably Kostya. With no hope of changing anything. Is it worth it?'

When she answered, her tone was more weary than challenging. 'This is a crucial article. What about your dedication to the truth?'

'I sometimes make compromises. Which makes me scream all the louder about honesty now and then, and sound self-righteous.'

She waved away my offer of a cigarette and I lit one for myself. 'What about your scorn for journalism? Exploiting people's misery?'

'I sometimes make generalizations. About journalism, for example. The silver lining is what I've learned about you.' She reached for my hand and pressed her palm to mine, as she'd never done before. Her hand was tired and unaffected—as womanly as her voice at that moment.

'It's been a terrible day. I didn't sleep last night. I'd

rather not go back to Domolinart just yet . . . Zhoe, let's go to the apartment—I can snooze a bit on the davenport.'

Again I felt the kind of stirring that had disappeared since the final acid months with my wife. I knew that Oktyabrina was less frightened now. Had it been another evening, were I not so wary myself, I would have taken her to sleep with me. 'You'd better have the bedroom Oktyabrina—after what you've been through. I'm used to the davenport.'

'I'd love clean sheets. And a *bath*.'

Inertia kept us on the bench for another half-hour, soothed by the mild May evening and the neighborhood's sights and sounds. A mother called to her daughter from an open window of an apartment house: 'Natasha, Natashinka, come home *this minute*. It's terribly late, you should be in bed.' 'Please mamachka, just five minutes more, *please*.' On the next bench, a girl pleaded to her cloth-capped swain from under his embrace. 'Oi, Andrusha, Andrushka mine, not here, I beg you. What are you doing to me?' A peasant woman passed, flopping in the remains of her slippers. She was carrying a heavy bundle on her back, and stank of herring and onions. A young man helped his sleepy son to urinate on a tree stump.

'But you don't *want* life to continue,' Oktyabrina said, 'when something like this happens to your friend. How can we treasure spring with Leonid in a dungeon? Or is that being synthetically dramatic?'

'Have you ever really been in love?'

'I might have been. I *can* be.'

'Because life goes on afterwards. Even though you feel like a traitor for taking part in it again.'

'That's it exactly, Zhoe dearest. Life's so *indefinite*. All these lack-luster compromises instead of something shining and solid so you know what to build.' But before we

144

got home, she was experimenting with a story about how her love for Leonid would have made his exile bearable, if only the tragic arrest hadn't cut the bud before it bloomed.

The next day Oktyabrina slept as if drugged until noon. Then she left to sound out the possibilities of a new room among her 'underground people'. She returned in mid-evening with an excellent find. The new room was in a dreary district called Ismailovsky, a good forty-five minutes from the center of town by metro. But she was happy to exchange the crabby old pensioner for a kindly widow. Her new landlady had lost her four sons as well as her husband in the war, and she took in paying boarders as a kind of charity and comfort to herself, giving them more in food from her tiny pension than she charged in rent.

Oktyabrina never collected her things from Domolinart. We thought it too dangerous; the room might still be watched, or the old pensioner under orders to turn her in. Luckily, at least half her wardrobe was in my apartment. All she really missed was a new leotard and a box of Czech face powder. But even this loss wasn't painful—or rather, the pain was sweet, because she was planning to wear no make-up at all for at least two weeks. It was to be an outward sign of her inner remorse over Leonid's fate—for her own part in it, as well as the state's.

For she would never forgive herself for not having given body and soul to him. Love was *there*, literally under her nose—love with a tragic, heroic figure—and she hadn't fully realised it until too late. Was she *congenitally* unresponsive to love? Would she die an old maid No, she'd learned her lesson; the very next time love appeared she would seize it like a water gourd in the desert. The trouble was there wouldn't *be* a next time. Anyway,

145

she *couldn't* seize it, out of respect for Leonid. Or, with his penchant for martyrdom, would he *want* her to be happy with another man?. . . .

She arrived at the apartment later in the mornings now because of her long metro ride. Some days, she did not appear at all, although she rarely went to Evgeny Ignatievich's class. When she did come, we resumed the old routine. We knew each other much better now, and Leonid's tragedy had cemented our friendship. Still, the old bantering ease we'd had was never quite reestablished. The argument gave us something, but also took something away.

# 13

☐ In late May, a cable arrived from my foreign editor with instructions to go up to Leningrad. I was to cover a conference between a delegation of American Senators and Deputies to the Supreme Soviet. I intended to go for the three days of the conference only, but ended by staying over a week. This was by personal rather than professional choice. Once away from Moscow, I realized how much I'd needed the break. Five months of steady routine made the overnight trip a happy adventure.

The conference was the usual kind: wholly uninformed and puffily ignorant politicians seeking 'mutual understanding' and 'the path to lasting amity between our two great nations', and exchanging toasts, banalities and disingenuous misinformation generously on both sides. The texts of the solemn official declarations contrasted predictably with the participants' behavior during off-hours. Souvenirs, dirty stories and free alcohol were the real preoccupations.

As usual, the most interesting stories were the unreportable ones. The American delegation was headed by a rabid anti-Communist and the Russians by a notorious Stalinist who once published a vicious magazine attack in *Kommunist* on the 'worst club in the world, the malodorous American Senate'. Yet these two patriots got on together better than anyone else at the conference—got on, in fact, as splendidly as old members of a small town

Rotary Club. It was only fitting that they also looked like brothers: both with roughly the same amount of surplus weight on short frames, distributed to match their gleaming pates and constricted by boxy suits. They exchanged tales of Kansas and Voronezh Province while measuring the relative merits of bourbon and vodka.

Each fed the other's self-admiration, fondness for 'plain country folks' and loathing of effete intellectuals. At the final banquet, they grasped each other around the waist, and through the smoke and my own slight alcoholic haze, I remembered Orwell—for it was impossible from my seat to make out which one was the dirty Commie and which the blood-sucking imperialist.

After the conference, I stayed on in the old Astoria Hotel. Many people exaggerate the differences between Moscow and Leningrad. You can be pushed around just as roughly by Leningrad crowds, and the waitresses can snarl just as nastily. But especially in spring, Leningrad can have a light and civilized—almost European—air, and you can avoid Moscow's peasant cloddishness. I wrote a story about an exhibition of paintings by young artists, and another about a department store on the Nevsky Prospekt where the salesgirls actually smiled and asked the customers if they needed help. Afternoons, I walked along the glorious quays and in the Summer Garden. No one knows what would have happened if *this* Russia had been allowed to grope its way towards the realities of the Twentieth Century. But when you compare the relics of the *ancien regime* to vast aesthetic wastelands of Soviet construction, you sometimes wish it could be revived, for all its grievous faults.

When I returned to Moscow, the trees were maturing into their full summer green. Oktyabrina greeted me nonchalantly, grumbling vaguely that the lilies of the valley she'd bought for my arrival had died days ago, and the place was again a mess. It was, but she'd placed

148

bunches of wild violets in cups and glasses, filling the living-room with a pungent smell.

'Aren't you happy to see me, Zhoe darling?'

'I'm delighted to see you. It's rotten to return to a dead apartment.'

'Yes, *do* look around,' she said slyly. 'Don't you perceive anything *new?*'

She broke into her triumphant-smile-that-cannot-quite-be-suppressed look, which announced she was enormously pleased with herself. And indeed: love had come her way again, miraculously. She could hardly *believe* she deserved this *bliss.* The new suitor was named Alexander. And Sasha, Sashka and Sashinka, in ascending order of endearment and delight.

My first view of Alexander was in the form of a photograph that had been clipped with bobby pins to a cardboard backing and was propped against the lamp on the table beside the davenport. I wondered whether the subject of such a gloriously propagandistic photograph could be real flesh and blood. But that very evening, Oktyabrina displayed him in person at a metro station called Kirovskaya.

They came together, Oktyabrina curled seemingly two or three times around his smartly-angled arm. She was in step with him and a half step behind; from my angle her legs were wholly hidden behind his boots, and she appeared to be floating. The impression was reinforced by her face, which was raised towards his with adoration and beatitude.

'How *wonderful* to see you, Zhoseph dear,' she said gaily when she saw me. 'You're terribly sweet to take time off from your work.' She slipped between me and Alexander to introduce us. 'Sasha, this is an old, dear friend. He's a leading correspondent from . . . fraternal Poland. Zhoseph writes about our Soviet achievements and simply *adores* everything here.'

149

The officer clicked his heels effortlessly and brought a graceful salute to his gleaming visor. His voice was a twangy tenor and his speech the Russian equivalent of a small-town GI's.

'Greetings, brother. The name's Zavodin, Alexander Sergeevich. But please don't call me anything formal like that—I'll think I'm in hot water.'

He shook my hand vigorously and flashed me a winsome smile—which, together with his beaming eye, flitted over my shoulder for an instant to several flustered, short-skirted girls hovering about in the hope he would look in their direction. His smile returned to me and broadened. I smiled too—as did everyone in the plaza. It was the kind of happy appreciation and involuntary uplift you receive from watching a well-drilled marching band. Alexander was obviously accustomed to this, for he paused to give everyone a full minute's gaze. Somehow this emerged as a gesture of indulgence to them rather than of vanity on his part.

Yet he had justification for limitless vanity: Alexander was as dazzlingly handsome as his photograph, and his uniform, in sharp contrast to most Army officers' crumpled sacks, was as neatly pressed. The body underneath was proudly carried and obviously solid—perhaps two or three inches short for Greek-statue perfection, but with a gymnast's proportions.

His face was even more impressive: the classic Nordic type, garnished with flaxen hair. From head to toe, Alexander was the picture of the glowing, resolute-yet-carefree young proletarian soldier of propaganda posters, standing guard over the map of the Soviet Union—or the grateful world, depending on the theme of the campaign —with a collection of serene children playing at his feet.

And in fact, Alexander had been a model for one of these very tours de force on the cover of a magazine called *Soviet Warrior*. It was a copy of this very photograph, smiling and invincible, that Oktyabrina cherished. Alexander had presented it to her on the afternoon of their first meeting, having penned an inscription in a loose hand over the lower corner: 'In War and Peace, in Our Metro and With Our Missiles—On Guard for You Always, Sasha'.

Alexander's splendor prevented me from getting a more comprehensive impression of him, especially as our first meeting was so brief. He had to report at his dormitory by seven o'clock sharp. 'Regulations are regulations,' he informed me with an ambiguous wink, adding that 'Chipmunk', bless her, understood nothing about military timing and discipline. He adjusted his cap so that—or was this accidental?—a lock of lemon hair fell effectively across his forehead.

Alexander offered me his hand again, pivoted and stepped briskly off. Oktyabrina shouted after him petulantly: he'd forgotten her goodbye kiss. He hurried back to peck at her loftily offered cheek. When he strode off again, the sight of him caused a succession of double-takes from passing pedestrians. A little Irish-looking imp in a school uniform tagged by his side.

When he had finally passed from sight, Oktyabrina confessed that the meeting had not gone as well as she had hoped. Alexander was terribly distracted by his work at the moment; it was something fiendishly important and dangerous, which naturally made him appear preoccupied. Besides, he was actually very shy—with strangers, that is. Which made his passion for her—when they were all alone, one and together—all the more precious and *unique*. 'And when you take all these difficulties into consideration, the romantic brilliance of our first

151

meeting was all the more . . . well, frankly *transcenden-tal.*'

For the next two weeks I was to hear about Sasha and nothing but Sasha. He was 'delicious', 'madly gallant', 'sensitive in a very special *natural* way' and, of course, 'the absolute quintessence of manliness'. Oktyabrina's day was a lingering preparation for the evening—not the entire evening, alas, but for the few minutes that Alexander squeezed from his exhausting training schedule. If he couldn't manage this, Oktyabrina planned and primped for the following evening, or the one after, keeping up a steady stream of talk to herself at the mirror.

Several facts were repeated often enough to seem reliable. Alexander was in training at a new, highly prestigious establishment called the Tactical Missile Academy. The curriculum was merciless. And although young officers merited liberal passes, this had to be understood in the context of Soviet Army traditions—which meant a precious few hours a week. Alexander's rusty mathematics and physics sometimes made him forgo even that. This is what kept him from seeing Oktyabrina 'as much as he was *burning* to'.

When they did meet, it was usually for a few moments at Kirovskaya metro station. Sometimes Alexander brought along a somewhat younger officer named Petya, in which case the conversation, understandably flowed largely between the two soldiers. Oktyabrina came to have mixed feelings about Petya's presence.

In fact, she had mixed feelings about certain aspects of the romance itself. 'I'm going to be excruciatingly honest with you, Zhoe darling,' she said one morning, 'because you know me best. This entanglement is not idyllic, and I'm not the kind to build castles in the air. Because one part of me has remained entirely clear-headed while the other part is hopelessly swept off its feet.'

I checked the wire services. When I returned, her monologue seemed grounded at exactly the same point.

'The sober part tells me he worships me and rejoices. He even has the grace to court me patiently, I mean for my carnal favors. Which is simply *inspired* for a warrior— they're usually so animal . . . are you listening' Zhoe darling? What's that dreadful cackle on the radio? . . . But I *do* recognise that our affair has imperfections. For one thing, it requires utterly fantastic patience from me. And positively superhuman love from him—because the trouble is, there's no time to kindle the ardor. I sometimes don't know what's greater, my happiness or suffering.'

However, she had one source of comfort. 'At least my Sashinka doesn't look at other women. That's probably his clean country upbringing. It's so terribly vulgar, the way city-bred men ogle every passing skirt. . . .'

At this point she was silenced by a blast of Tchaikovsky on the radio. It was the opening bars of the First Piano Concerto, which resound four or five times a day to diverse patriotic themes, this time was as background music to a story about Lenin's First Reading of Marx. But the crashing chords were oddly appropriate because Oktyabrina was preparing to narrate the story of her own discovery again: the First Meeting with Sasha.

Oktyabrina recounted the story—'the incredible *saga*' of that first meeting almost daily. But the account finally made sense only after my second meeting with Alexander, at a café on Kirov Street, of the same class as those on Petrovka and elsewhere. Because I'd come along, Alexander was able to free himself for a full half hour. His cap lay on an empty chair to avoid smudges on the plastic visor. While Oktyabrina performed the narration, he studied her; his open face expressed a slight amusement that made it more handsome and likable than ever.

It happened on Alexander's first day in Moscow—his

very first day in the capital, and one of his first in any metropolis. He'd arrived by train in the morning from a base in the western Ukraine, on orders to the Academy. He reported to the duty officer and was given an afternoon pass to see the city.

He was overcome by its fantastic size and sweep. He walked from one corner to another, drinking in the famous landmarks and fabulous sights. At last he understood the Red Army saying: 'Give your life for Mother-Moscow, the jewel of the whole wide world.' Thrilled, exhilarated, awed and (yes, he confessed it) slightly nervous, he sat down on a park bench to rest. For he was also exhausted—more so by the asphalt sidewalks and city noises than by a week of maneuvers. And when a sad peasant woman pleaded with him to buy her flowers, he succumbed, even though he'd never done anything remotely similar in his life. He bought her largest bouquet, simply because of his triumphant mood and eagerness to share his good fortune. The old woman blessed his kindness and promised the flowers would bring him love.

As the time to report approached, he found his way to a metro station. He'd never seen anything like it in civilian life; the expense and engineering, the incredible sweep of the concept! And the hydraulic mechanism of the escalator! It could only be compared to the artillery's best shell-handling equipment. But on his way down to the trains, a power failure occurred—the first one, Oktyabrina later established, in over a decade. (It was all *undeniably* fated.)

The escalators stopped dead; everything was plunged into total darkness. No panic threatened among the crowds, but on the up escalator just below Alexander, a girl began whimpering in fright. Gently but firmly, he directed her to take control of herself: Soviet citizens, after all, must be courageous and self-disciplined in any emergency. But the girl's sobs gew louder, and he felt her trembles from the opposite stairs.

He was confused and apprehensive. As senior officer present, he knew that he must take command of the situation, but he'd never been tested by a crisis like *this* before. Perhaps it happened regularly in Moscow. On the other hand, continued crying by the girl might lead to demoralization, even defeatism! Then he remembered the bouquet, whose stems had grown slightly sweaty in his hand. He reached across and placed it near the girl's face. The weeping subsided instantly—Sasha thought of a kitten being distracted by a string—and slowly diminished to an occasional sighing sob.

'Lilac?' the girl asked, barely audibly.

'I just bought them, just now.'

'And narcissus? Tulips?'

'I think so. Yes of course—you've got a fine sense of smell.'

'My name's Oktyabrina. I'm not frightened any longer.'

'I'm Alexander—they call me Sasha. Everything's going to be all right.'

In the darkness, they talked about themselves, recited capsule biographies, and reached for each other's hands. His were strong but gentle; hers were as delicate as the promise of her voice. The bouquet kept sliding down the railing. Someone had a sneezing fit and they began to laugh.

Then the power came on as suddenly as it had failed, propelling the escalators apart at their usual speed. 'We waved frantically to each other as his escalator hurled him downward and mine bore me on high—as if on a pedestal. At the bottom landing Sasha dashed onto the up stairs—but at the top, I dashed onto the down. We zoomed past each other again, laughing at our own predicament as if we were the oldest, fondest friends. . . .

155

By the time we actually met, dear Zhoseph—well, neither of us is religious, of course, but we both perceived that this was something anointed.'

'Aw shucks,' said Alexander softly. 'You're too much, little Chipmunk. You add something new every time.'

'Shame on you Sashka darling. You've forgotten half already. If *I* don't remember, who else will?'

Oktyabrina gazed at him aglow with a delirious-happiness-at-my-man's-side expression. But a moment later, a discrepant expression took command: the desperate-need-for-a-bathroom look, no doubt caused by the excitement of her long narrative.

'I'll be *right back*,' she warbled. 'Don't *dream* of saying anything juicy while I'm away.' She dashed towards the door, trailing her gauzy mantilla over the dirty floor. When she'd gone, Alexander gracefully withdrew a quarter-liter bottle of vodka from under his tunic and offered me a swig. Under-the-overall vodka boozers in that kind of café are usually the sort who literally drink away their pay and lurch home to punch their wives. But Alexander's gesture was so open, and he in general was so artless and good-natured that I would have been coarse to refuse.

He retrieved the bottle and wiped the lip with his palm. His boyish smile remained fixed during his own swig, allowing a trickle of vodka to escape down his chin. He wiped it with the back of the same hand and examined the bottle.

'I'm not really fond of this white stuff,' he admitted. 'But the pressures of modern life. . . . Frankly, I'm beginning to spot plain hogwash—higher up, where there should be solid sense.'

'What seems to be troubling you, Alexander?'

'Nothing really. Only I wish they'd stick to the missiles and battle games, without all that ideology we have. Ideology, political vigilance—all that stuff makes you stiff in the ass.'

The second swallow of vodka was more pleasant than the first. Alexander was in an uncommonly loquacious mood.

'I don't know how you teach it in Poland, of course. But what's troubling me, frankly, is the confusion in our Party line. On one front, we're battling the American imperialists—that I understand. But now the enemy's also inside the socialist bloc—Yugoslav revisionists, Chinese adventurists . . . What do *I* care? Let them all catch the plague. . . .'

He inspected my cigarette lighter at arm's length. One eye was closed, as if he were sighting a rifle.

'What do you do for your political exams?' I asked, sensing a story. 'I'd imagine "catching the plague" is a fairly weak answer.'

'That's the trouble: I keep forgetting the *new* answers.' He leaned closer and lowered his voice. 'But whenever I'm in real trouble, brother, I reach down in my memory for a juicy quote about the Party's relentless struggle against *all* enemies of the working class. And sprinkle Lenin's name everywhere—it gets them every time.'

He treated himself to another large swig. 'Yes sir, most people is just aching to be bamboozled.'

'Never mind, Alexander. In vodka veritas.'

'The girls, for instance. That yarn about never seeing a big city before—it *always* gets them, every darn time. Works even better in Leningrad—you should *see* the broads dying to drop their drawers in that old town. You should see the drawers up there—genuine nylon!'

It was no doubt my expression which caused the swift transformation of his. Suddenly, I felt a wave of repugnance for this fop of a soldier and his implications. To take advantage of Oktyabrina and boast about it required a special vulgarity. Just as suddenly, he became humbly repentant, like a Norman Rockwell kid caught at the wheel of a neighbor's car.

'Listen brother, you've got things wrong. I didn't mean to insult your gal. Anything *you* do with the Chipmunk is fine with *me*. The more loving you do, the less fighting and hating you'll get into, I always say. . . . So about the Chipmunk: relax, *I* don't mind. If you're poking her, good luck to the both of you!'

This was too much. First he seemed to be bragging about his conquests—now about mine.

'Now listen yourself, Zavodin. She's not my "gal" and I'm not making love to her. Nobody is. Can't a veteran Romeo like you see that?'

'Sure I see that about the Chipmunk, I ain't blind. Only I didn't see it then, on the escalator—you couldn't see nothing until the power came on. A city packed with classy nookie and I meet *her* the first day! Skin and bones —and her rags for camouflage. . . . Foul luck, brother— and now *you* won't drink with me.'

It was my turn for repentance. 'So you did meet in the metro,' I said. 'That's something, at least. Tell me exactly what happened, from the beginning.'

'That's where we met all right, but not the way she likes to invent. I never knew nothing until she was shoving some posies up my nose. Posies make me *sneeze*. Then, out on the street, she keeps tailing me—I can't hurt her feelings, can I? I never do, even when I don't want to poke them. So I say "hello Little One"—and that's my mistake: it gets harder to escape, day by day. *You* tell me how to slip the collar, I can't think. The wrong word from me—it'll break her little Chipmunk's heart.'

At this moment an outburst shattered the café's listless routine. A filthy man at the counter began cursing the girl who was dishing out the soup. While gazing at Alexander, she apparently scalded the man's hand with a misaimed ladle. He reached for her, slipped, and demanded a glass of vodka. The girl was joined in defense by several colleagues in dirty smocks.

Without a word, Alexander and I rose, and went to the door through which Oktyabrina had gone. When she reappeared a few minutes later, the mantilla was wrapped around the lower part of her face.

'*Guess who*, darling,' she sang to Alexander. 'For a man in love, no disguise conceals the eyes. . . . *Please* don't go back to those dreadful barracks now. Succumb to your instincts and let's do something glorious tonight.'

Alexander glanced at me with puzzlement and desperation. He took Oktyabrina's hands in his; she touched her head to his shoulder. He flushed, making an interesting contrast between the smooth skin of his neck and the starched olive drab of his collar.

After this, it was painful to see them together. I joined them just often enough to have a picture of their 'wooing' moments. They would meet at the metro station and set forth on a short walk. Two or three saucy working girls would be sure to follow them, swinging their handbags gaily and chattering to be overheard. This was a daring deed; however submissive Russian girls are, they almost never take such obvious initiative. But Alexander was strong bait, and gave them the necessary encouragement: when Oktyabrina's attention was momentarily deflected by a shop window, he would glance back, hardly moving his body, and transmit to them a devastating come-closer smile.

But of course Oktyabrina's attention was not really caught by any shop window; she was scrutinizing Alexander's every movement through his reflection in the dirty glass. She was also fighting back tears of despair, for

159

she'd pretended not to notice the girls. Finally, her control would give way. 'Those *pathetic* creatures' she would say, 'making a spectacle of themselves. Shall I chase them away, Sashka beloved? Are you exhausted this evening?'

'Chase who away?' Alexander would ask, frowning intently. 'Gosh, you mean them girls? Ain't they a silly sight!'

Eventually the girls would turn a corner, to Alexander's disappointment and Oktyabrina's greater relief. But before they'd parted, more pairs would have succeeded them. Alexander kept track of the last pair's movements, for after having kissed Oktyabrina goodbye, he would search for them. After the resolution of our misunderstanding, he confided to me that his secret was always letting girls give the first signal. When he tried to 'corral' one of his own liking, he invariably felt awkward; and in ten to twenty per cent of the cases, the girls wouldn't 'take the poke' the first time. But when they took the initiative, success was almost certain. The trouble was finding a place. He often did it by standing a girl against a tree in a park and 'coming in backwards'. But this sometimes bothered him because he remembered certain men's fondness for farm animals in his old village. 'Maybe we're animals too,' he said solemnly, 'but at least we can make it comfortable for our mates.'

There was an old Army saying that particularly disgusted him: 'A sheep's face will do—it's the cunt you screw.' He may be a bit of a rogue himself, he admitted, but there was something beautiful about girls, each and every one of them. They were more like butterflies than sheep. The trouble was there were so many of them to admire, and they all died so soon. . . .

# 14

☐ Meanwhile, we had settled into the steady warmth of early summer. Throughout Russia, it is a quietly joyous time—more fervently embraced and venerated than elsewhere because winter is so much longer and more cruel. A burden is lifted from the psyche as overcoats are lifted for the shoulders. Hope and levity, even frivolity, infuse the air—intensified by everyone's repressed knowledge that the escape is ephemeral: in a dozen weeks, winter's avant-garde will be waiting to numb you again. You receive warm days with reverence, therefore—not because you deserve them, but because the Russian psychology of siege and hardship has convinced you that the reprieve is *not* deserved.

I was working now at somewhat less than my usual pace, which was far too slow for someone running a bureau alone. But my conscience had melted soon after the last dirty snowbank, and I surrendered to belated spring fever. My office window was wide open, filling the room with diesel exhaust from trucks lumbering below the building. But there were also whiffs of moist earth and greenery, and I thought how strange it was to savor the smells of Michigan and Minnesota at a distance of ten thousand miles, in a disparate world.

I found myself spending more time than in winter with two American colleagues—somewhat younger men who wrote for influential East Coast newspapers. Perhaps

161

the nostalgia of summer smells prompted this; perhaps a shift in my feelings about America and Americans. Like most other aspects of life here, this one is subject to stages.

I'd now reached the stage where I could do without the American Embassy's mothering, and avoid almost all of its social calendar without wholly sacrificing the company of American themselves. I hadn't had a close American friend since the correspondent of the other Chicago paper had been reassigned over a year before. But I liked to pass an occasional evening with my two younger colleagues, perhaps because their freedom from wives also freed them from Embassy obligations and tensions. One man was a summer bachelor whose wife had departed for a long Florida vacation, the other was recently divorced and badly wanted the company of a Russian girl friend—almost badly enough to dismiss the Embassy's dire warnings about such arrangements. There was no need with these men to exhibit love of everything 'back home' and disapproval of everything Soviet, or vice-versa. It was simply a few hours of poker and beer—which began under natural light, since it was now bright well after supper. Bourbon and old locker-room stories often supplemented the beer.

Kostya and I were seeing more of each other too, almost in direct proportion to the rise in temperature. Our meetings took place not in his room or my apartment (in which he prudently never set foot) but in the great Russian outdoors. Every year Kostya waited impatiently for the first faint hint of warmth from the sun's rays through a closed window. When the signal came, he dashed to a nearby pond, reservoir or river to tear off his clothes and 'soak up Helios's potence'.

'As everybody knows,' he'd say in his pseudo-somber voice, 'Communist sunshine blindingly transcends capitalist. Because it's free for all the people. Unobstructed by the clouds of exploitation, etcetera. Thank you again, dear Party—and let us not forget the sky and stars, together with the Lamp of Heaven—oops, of Lenin.'

Alongside the river or pond, it could still be too chilly to take off your jacket, not to speak of shirts and underclothes. But Kostya would strip to his prized Japanese swimming trunks and spread-eagle without a towel on the damp clayey bank. It was often in Silver Pine forest, a river-bound island that serves as a municipal retreat. Trucks and barges shuttling to raw construction projects jarred the ancient countryside's beautiful harmony, but enough old houses and stretches of eroded river bank remained to evoke the spirit of old Russia and its serene sadness.

We would laze about on the rich-smelling bank—together with a grateful 'lassie' or two, if Kostya had brought them—and the afternoons slipped away before we'd fully settled in. Kostya talked about his Navy days and plans for his summer vacation, already well advanced. Almost every year, he contrived to spend two full months in the luxurious south, on or near the Black Sea. This meant wangling permission somehow for double the normal leave from his job, then finding accommodation in one of the resorts—usually by means of a healthy, well-placed bribe—and scraping together the comparative fortune needed for finance. Altogether it required a considerable effort in his metier of metiers; beating the system.

At the moment, he was maneuvering to secure a place on a hiking tour of the Caucasus for the girls of a Geology Institute. He'd sold his beloved Philips tape recorder, and was using the proceeds to 'encourage' the tour's organizer, an elderly assistant professor, to 'co-opt' him on to the expedition. His aim was to be classified as a patriotic volunteer to carry the sleeping bags and pitch the tents.

'Who needs Monte Carlo? What sane man would spend his vacation in the rat-race called Capri? Listen, Zhoe, buddy: all those spots are unhealthily overcrowded, and the profound humanity of our Public health services saves us from risking our vigor there. Write an article about me with twenty-two exploration-happy University females, two strong-limbed lassies to a tent, and every Riviera playboy will beg to swap places with me in my naked mountain pass.'

Kostya asked about 'the kid'. Oktyabrina, he complained, had stopped coming around since meeting 'the sniper boy'. She'd told him she had no time; Alexander took every minute and was madly jealous besides. Kostya was uncharacteristically annoyed by this, perhaps because he had a record of staying in touch with all his old girls. He disapproved of soldiers on principle, and for some reason, felt jealous on my behalf. 'If I were you I'd boot the boy in the jodhpurs and lay it on the line with the kid.'

'I knew a career officer in the army once,' he said. 'It was back in '37 when we were working twelve hours a day down coal mines in the Donbass. This lovely fellow was in charge of the People's Security—vigilantly averting sabotage by the likes of us, the happy working class. The Colonel used to get rather annoyed by losing his monthly salary in our poker game. So he arrested the steady winners and exposed them as enemies of the people. They finished life in labor camps, and he began taking a few pots. Yes sir, the regular Army's the place for Soviet humanism—all brains and heart.'

A man with a badly matched wig and blaring transistor radio settled himself above us on the bank. The program was about a cement factory that had volunteered for higher production norms. When Kostya could stand it no longer, he shouted a request to change programs. The man tuned in the other station, which was offering a medley of revolutionary marching songs.

'That's a bit better, don't you think, Zhoe buddy?' asked Kostya. 'I've heard that you Westerners actually love that patriotic stuff. Maybe I'll cut an album and ship it to Hollywood. I'll call it *Music to Vote By*. Make a fortune—but of course I'd never agree to touch the dirty dollars without gloves.'

It was inevitable that Oktyabrina would one day see Alexander outside their rendezvous time. Whenever we were out of doors together, her neck was craned and eyes peeled for him like a gazelle at a water hole. When it came, their encounter was the product of an extraordinary combination of circumstances. The first element was a sudden blistering heatwave, in late June. It had the usual Moscow characteristics: a searing sun generating tropical vapors and occasional prodigious clouds, with lightning seemingly changed by the whole of the continental land mass. The hardest element was the lack of air. Russian buildings were made for Russian winter; many windows have been permanently sealed, and without an edict, shop managers are reluctant even to open both panels of a door.

The noon news report announced the temperature was ninety-one degrees and climbing. I wrote a brief story about the heat, omitting any mention of the smells it generated—a sudden shortage of toilet soap a week before had emptied store shelves—and planned to stay in refuge in the flat. Oktyabrina was profoundly listless. Alexander was on duty that whole weekend, she reported. He couldn't manage a single meeting.

Our patience ran out in mid-afternoon. The humidity

was oppressive, yet exhilarating—even exotic. A steamy, sensual throbbing pulsed on the streets. It lured us towards some cheap distraction.

We followed the call to Gorky Park of Culture and Recreation, which houses the largest collection of what the day cried for: amusements and rides. Unfortunately, half the city's population had hearkened to the same call. Like a double-header crowd converging on Wrigley Field, a torrent of amusement-seekers surged toward the park from the metro exit. Once swept into the sea of damp flesh blocked up at the entrance, it was impossible to get free, even if we'd changed our minds. The smell was overwhelming. A ludicrously pretentious, totally super-fluous Greco-Roman portal straddled the gate—the final Coney Island touch. At last Oktyabrina and I reached the end of the sieve and were shot into the park, like particles by a cyclotron.

Inside, fractionally more air and room were available, but a convoy of farm trucks bearing down on a village could not have kicked up more dust from the paths. Crews of maintenance workers hosed them down—taking pleasure in dousing everyone in range—but it was so hot that the water evaporated instantly, and a hundred thousand pairs of shuffling feet continued to propel gritty clouds into the air and our faces.

'Shall I give you an old Russian saying about heat?' asked Oktyabrina gaily. 'Or about crowds, if you prefer. Close your eyes and you can picture Hades with a short-age of gas masks. . . . But there's something marvelously *abandoned* about all this holy mess, isn't there, Zhoe, darling?'

'I haven't had so much fun since KP in basic training.'

' "KP" meaning *Kommunisticheskaya Partiya?* You rascal, why didn't you *tell* me?'

'Careful, Oktyabrina darling. That ice cream is headed straight for your nose.

166

The threatening cone was held aloft by a hand whose owner was untraceable in the tangle of bodies. How he or she had managed to buy it was a mystery: the lines at the stalls beggared description. Even without lines, it took minutes to negotiate a few yards along the paths, and policemen were busy trying to drive everyone from what was left of the grass. Oktyabrina and I found ourselves entrapped in a monumental jam behind the open air auditorium, where a political agitator with a microphone was delivering a deafening harangue. The subject was 'The Victory of Leninist Proletarian Internationalism in the Yemen'. To this hymn, weary hundreds were gratefully dozing in their seats. At least they'd found *some* kind of entertainment, and a place to rest.

Elsewhere the noise was equally devastating: caterwauling babies racked with thirst, charwomen shouting in snack bars, a public address system blaring Sunday Leniniana. . . . Yet the extraordinary thing was that most people were enjoying the day not as something camp, but at face value. Just being in the park was a treat; it was enough to watch the lucky few who had secured places on the ferris wheel, and were now ooh-ing and ah-ing in appreciation and alarm as their gondolas swung upward towards cleaner air and a splendid panorama of the baking city.

Oktyabrina and I watched the ferris wheel too. A rare helicopter hovered over it for a moment, then flew off on its limping way up river, towards the Kremlin. Because of this, or because of her trouble seeing over the wall of shoulders, it is possible that she did not notice the olive-drab in a gondola starting its descent. The uniform belonged to Alexander—a model, despite the weather, for a Coke ad in Times Square. Across from him was a smaller officer with a crewcut—evidently Petya.

Petya's girl was attractive in a clean-cut way; Alexander's was a sizzling young tart. She had a gymnast's build

—the perfect complement to his—and was fully aware of it, even while making a show of fright on the wheel. She thrust her cheeky breasts towards Alexander's face and gripped him in the armpit. The sun's hard rays blazed on the chemical topaz of her hair; one poster-perfect leg, visible through the gondola's mesh, wound itself round Alexander's. Altogether, she was a sexy combination of vulgarity and health.

I called Oktyabrina's attention to a young father near us, carrying handsome twins on his shoulders. She was enchanted by the sight. Then we pushed our way towards the river bank in search of fresh air. Alexander was not mentioned. I now felt there was a good chance she hadn't seen him; otherwise, she'd surely have wanted to examine the girl. As it was, she soon wished to go home and lie down—to lose herself in *sacred solitude* for at least a *year*. But this could have been caused by the crowds and an entirely understandable exhaustion.

When we staggered home at last, Oktyabrina poured herself a glass of milk, the 'liquid of life', but her 'Pull the teats without heart, the milk will be tart!' emerged as wanly as her smile. She retired to the bedroom and closed the door. I made a mental note to forgo amusement parks for another ten years, and congratulated myself on preventing a too-brutal confrontation with the truth in the park. Why is self-congratulation so often premature?

## 15

☐ On Monday it was even hotter and the infatuation with the novelty of sweltering had turned to general fatigue. The newspapers had already begun their campaign for Metallurgists' Day on the coming Sunday, but half of Moscow's metal workers, together with anyone else who had the imagination, were playing truant from work.

On Tuesday, it was a shade cooler. Shortly after Oktyabrina arrived at the apartment, we went down for mineral water and beer, since the supplies were certain to be exhausted by noon. When we stepped out into the dazzling sun, a company of soldiers was trudging up a street leading from the Ring Road. They were presumably headed for the Central Club of the Soviet Army, a half mile away. The marching order was sloppier than usual, no doubt because of the heat. In their ponderous, year-round boots and coarse tunics they looked as happy as polar bears in an African zoo.

Oktyabrina's practiced eye explored the ranks rapidly, and for some reason she appeared relieved that Alexander wasn't there. Then we saw him simultaneously: he was *leading* the company. Sweat had soaked through his tunic in the back, and for the first time he looked older than twenty.

Before I missed her, Oktyabrina had ducked into the food shop where we'd been headed. She must have jumped the line at the dairy counter and slapped down a ruble without waiting for change. For in less than a minute, she emerged with a half-liter bottle of milk.

The scene that followed was not as remarkable as it might seem because there is an old tradition of Russian women pressing loaves of bread and jars of water into the hands of grateful soldiers and convicts trudging dusty steppe roads. Nevertheless, the glint in Oktyabrina's eye suggested not almsgiving, but revenge.

The bottle was pearly in the sun and dripped freely with condensation. She held it with outstretched arms like an offering, and marched steadfastly towards Alexander. He observed her from the corner of his eye while his head wheeled in a search for an escape route. In vain: the ambush was perfectly laid.

When Alexander turned directly to Oktyabrina, as a last resort, his blue eyes gushed pain and pleading: *please* disappear, I'll give you anything you want *later,* but not in front of my *soldiers.* Oktyabrina marched resolutely towards him with a serene face and Mona Lisa smile, through which she was humming 'Forward Comrades for Party and Motherland', a well-known Army song. By this time, several people on the sidewalk had noticed the spectacle and were spreading the word about it. Sensing a good laugh, the ranks of Alexander's company revived.

Alexander raised his arm and was about to say something, but Oktyabrina got in the first word. She was now directly across the street from him, but she shouted loud enough for the last rank to hear and savor.

'Aloha, Sashinka, darling—wait for me. I brought you something wonderfully refreshing. Take this and *sip.*'

Alexander looked despairingly at his men, hoping against hope that they would take Oktyabrina for an eccentric stranger.

'My beloved, you've lost at least a kilo since Friday.

170

On duty all *weekend* like that in the heat . . . you're dangerously *dehydrated*. Now stop this silly marching for a moment and refresh yourself. Drink drink *drink*.'

'I always knew it,' said Alexander miserably, humiliation disfiguring his splendid countenance. 'You're no Chipmunk, you're a polecat—you need a cage. Now *scram*, before I . . . before I . . .'

Oktyabrina strode on through the bunched soldiers. They had broken rank for the view, but now parted again to clear her path for presentation of the 'refreshment' to Alexander. Their guffaws concentrated on the implied slur of the bottle's contents and possible connection with Alexander's pretty face. It was 'baby's milkie' instead of the drink of real men, above all Army men—especially *Russian* Army men.

'Shame *shame* on you,' Oktyabrina chided them collectively. 'A cow in the yard means milk on the table—*that's* the kind of national heritage you big burly things are supposed to be defending. Only a dunce sees pleasure in vodka.'

This struck the soldiers as so charmingly zany that they seized Oktyabrina and flung her into the air in the traditional Russian toast to heroes and good fellows. A happy cheer and spray of sweat accompanied each airward trip. Oktyabrina clutched the bottle; her expression alternated between rapture over the attention she'd secured and terror of physical hurt. Alexander tried desperately to restore order, knowing that were a senior officer to drive past his career would be mangled.

Traffic stopped and a crowd of onlookers gathered. They began recounting their VE-Day experiences, the last time they'd seen such public spontaneity in an army unit. It was only after the troops were finally back in a semblance of rank that Alexander caught sight of me.

'How could she do it?' he moaned. 'Wasn't I trying to

be *nice* to her? That outfit she's wearing. And *milk*—do you realize I can never be in the saddle again?'

His men quickly supported this contention: although Soviet soldiers sing in response to specific commands, they broke into a full-throated chorus on their own initiative as they moved off. It was 'Forward Comrades for Party and Motherland'.

'How could I do *what?*' said Oktyabrina as the company disappeared. Her voice was like a wounded bride's. 'But it's still so dreadfully *hot*. Sashinka was sweating so —ought I to stand aside and watch him become *ill* for lack of liquid?'

Back in the apartment she made one of her statements of prepared ambiguity. 'My Sasha could have all the girls with licentious legs he wants—if he wanted them. I'm not blind to that. But I'm the one who loves him only for himself—enough to brave scorn and supervise his health.'

Alexander's note was delivered by Petya. Oktyabrina found this 'outrageous'. 'That pretty-boy lacks the courage even to say adieu to me in person.' But in fact, she was pleased by the triumph this acknowledged, as well as by Petya's behavior when he handed her the note. He scurried away, evidently in fear that Oktyabrina might select him as her next victim.

The note was entirely straightforward. Alexander wasn't angry, didn't even blame her, but she was plain dangerous. Although he wasn't calling her a subversive element, it came to the same thing. 'Because a hundred like you exposed to the troops and morale will be busted. Believe me, the Chinks won't stop at Siberia. . . . I know you could track me down, but I am warning you. I always promised I would never hit a woman because of Mother, but I'm warning you. . . .'

Oktyabrina placed the note next to Alexander's photograph and studied the documentary evidence of Beginning and End. 'Yes, Lieutenant Zavodin and I must go our separate ways,' she sighed, pondering whether to rip up the photograph and/or the note, or preserve one or both. Diffuse post-mortems followed throughout the day. 'If the love lacked joy, the parting will be sans agony,' she said. 'That's Lermontov, of course. Only sufferers fully understand his genius.'

The next day, we strolled down Petrovka in the post-heat-wave breeze and Oktyabrina suggested a visit to a church still functioning inside the ancient Petrovsky Monastery. It was attended by wretchedly poor women wrapped in almost a winter lamination of dingy shawls. They kissed smoky icons, sank painfully to their knees and prostrated themselves on the cold floor—all of which Oktyabrina saw in a new light.

'It's rather *exalted* in a way. . . . Do you think the Lieutenant was a sign for me to become a nun? I've long suspected that my life was consecrated for the pursuit of physical purity. . . .'

Religion, she thought, might be the answer for someone capable of giving a whole heart and all fibers of the soul. Love was such a boorish substitute. The trouble was that all women's monasteries were probably closed now, because of the opium of the people they used to dispense. 'Still,' she said, 'I could use some opium myself right now, or morphine.'

When we emerged onto Petrovka again, she considered a visit to the building directly across the street, a bizarre eighteenth-century mansion now identified by a red sign as 'The Institute of Physiotherapy'. 'I spared you most of the details, dear Zhoseph, and shall continue to spare you. The Lieutenant's coarseness should not be inflicted on any innocent third party. Still, you should know the general fact of my suffering.'

Her last comment was spoken quite happily. 'On the other hand, it was rather fascinating. A valuable life *experience*, you might say. The thing is, I can't quite make up my mind whether it was ennobling or degrading to have been desperately in love with a bastard.'

# 16

☐ I no longer try to analyze my attitude towards this country. There are too many layers and too many moods. The more 'Russianness' I see, the less I'm able to separate its virtues and deep flaws.

A tourist has a better chance of making up his mind. He may, for example, belong to the category that has a deep-rooted craving to be thrilled by the Soviet people and prove to himself that socialism works. In this case, he'll recognize an expression of universal humanity in a waiter shoving a menu at him after an hour's wait. When taken on tour of dreary housing developments, he will marvel at Soviet achievements. When his Intourist guide (bored silly and long past embarrassment over the half-truths she recites) preaches about the productivity of socialist labor and purity of socialist-realist art, he'll be moved by her shining wisdom. Above all, he'll confirm what he's always known: that Americans and Russians have a profound natural affinity. He may meet a Russian —the kind allowed to consort with tourists—and make the discovery that both peoples share the habit of brushing teeth. With toothpaste! From a tube!

On the other hand, he may belong to the category that despises the country at first sight. Even in his Intourist accomodation—beyond ordinary Russians' dreams of luxury—he will be irritated by the hopeless inefficiency: daily breakdowns of elevators, plumbing and nerves. He may not know he's paying thirty-five times what a Russian does for the same room, but he'll sense Intourist's ruthless fleecing. When he ventures from his hotel, he'll be depressed by universal shoddiness and shabbiness: the absence of smiles; unholy contrast between the paradise of propaganda and dreariness of everything else. By the third day, he'll yearn to board a plane—any line but Aeroflot—and resume a real vacation in Rome.

If this categorization sounds snide, the trouble is that my own reactions bounce as fitfully from pole to pole. Neither Intourist's transparent fictions nor the gloominess of the streets are a guide to anything important, but aren't the country's inner qualities equally contradictory? An extraordinary warmth and sensitivity survives under the surface Soviet rule. A heightening of perceptions and flooding of senses—the same qualities that have made Russian literature the most moving and universal in the world. Yet the country is obscurantist, backward and exhausting. It is a cruel dictatorship in the grip of evil men: Southern-sheriff types who trample on civilized standards without even understanding their crimes. And their marks are everywhere, in slovenliness, darkness and weight. Libraries are written explaining Russian in terms of one or another theory: Marxism-Leninism; the artistic temperament; the mysteries of the Russian soul. But these abstractions manage to ignore the starkest fact: the country is dismally *poor*.

Why, then, am I drawn to it? Because I feel richer by comparison? Because I'm lionized for a pack of Camels or an old Beatles' record? Because it's easier to live where the problems are external—society's fault rather than your own?

But these obviously aren't the sole explanations, for it was also in a poor and backward country that I began to miss Moscow in gentle swells. The first weeks of my va-

176

cation had been blissful. As my plane crossed the Soviet border, an inexorable weight disappeared; back on the ground, I took pleasure in the luxury of shop windows and ordered drinks for the sake of holding a graceful glass and watching civilized service. The sun and sea were glorious, the food spectacular by Russian standards. But something was missing.

I lay on the beach at Taormina, on Sicily's eastern coast, and relived my last day in Moscow. It was frantic because, as on every trip 'outside', I didn't know whether I'd be allowed back in. I'd been issued a double visa, for re-entry as well as exit; but the former is sometimes annulled when an 'unfriendly' correspondent is abroad and the authorities want to be rid of him. Leaving Moscow, therefore, is as different from leaving other places as living there is: you risk never seeing your friends again.

This thought makes you feel dramatic, but also frightened. The goodbyes have an altogether special meaning because they may be the last ones. You and your friends look into each other's eyes and promise to remember, even if work, politics or someone's revenge happen to separate you. You thank each other for being friends and bringing some meaning into each other's lives. Wars, famines, purges and midnight disappearances have familiarized Russians with this kind of parting; they perform it honestly and well. I haven't yet learned to have grace, as Hemingway put it, under the pressure of this searing nostalgia and pathos.

Kostya gave a luxurious farewell supper the evening before my flight. It was attended by his new girl friend, an enchantingly pretty medical resident called Tamara. She'd been living with him for over a week, which indicated he was extremely fond of her and she would become a member of his permanent 'brood' after the cooling of the romance. Having teased him about public

177

health violations, she'd done the impossible in cleaning his Augean room, and Kostya gave her an ounce of Chanel, a magnificent gift, in appreciation. She used it that evening, even though perfume made her shy; and sprinkled a liberal volume on Oktyabrina's lavender frock.

The summer plans were fixed. Kostya and Oktyabrina would be leaving for the Black Sea three days later. Kostya's trip with the geology girls had fallen through, but a former lassie of his was the mistress of a secretary in the Union of Composers, and had arranged for him to have a cabin in one of the so-called 'Creative Retreats' directly on the sea. The retreats exist under the fiction of providing creative artists a sequestered place to work, but in fact are a supplementary reward for the 'working intelligentsia' who produce politically acceptable art, and are usually used for inexpensive and rather uninhibited vacations in luxury unavailable to the general public.

'People can't spell any more,' said Kostya. 'All these new ComPart abbreviations are turning the great Russian language into a science-fiction code. It's *pro*creative retreat—not "creative". And nobody in the whole Union gets it right.'

He made sure to explain how composers use the colony to duck their wives. 'There hasn't been a chord written there since Stalin ordered a requiem to himself in 1953 and shot a few "saboteurs" for composing below Mozart's standards. At noon, every composer gets up and suns away his hangover. At sundown, they open their bottles and examine the girls they've selected on the public beach. Last year there was a proposal to chop up the piano for campfires, but the keyboards come in handy for hanging panties where they'll be found in the morning. . . .'

Oktyabrina was going to travel with Kostya as far as

Sochi—the largest resort on the coast, a kind of 1930s Miami Beach—from which she would survey the scene. It was her first trip to the Black Sea and she was full of the inevitable chatter about palm trees, luxury and romance. Nevertheless, she occasionally remembered to be blasé about the trip. 'I simply *can't* remain in Moscow,' she would say with heavy exasperation. 'Everybody who's anybody is leaving for the season. I've stopped fighting these boring conventions . . . and besides, *someone* must look after poor Kostya. . . .'

As a going-away present she gave me a small sixteenth-century icon. She'd had it cleaned by a restorer who removed several layers of overpainting to the original richly colored image. The subject was the Birth of Christ, an unusual one for the Orthodox Church, painted in the northern style. It was one of the most beautiful icons I'd seen outside a museum, and Oktyabrina declined to say where or how she got it, except that it had *not* been snatched from the Tretyakov Gallery. Even Kostya was impressed. He identified the three Magi in the painting as Brezhnev, Kosygin and Suslov, but studied it respectfully during breaks in the preparation of the supper.

Tamara helped him expertly in this, for she'd already mastered some of the secrets of his cuisine. She was very happy to be with him, even though she knew the romance would not last. Kostya gave his 'steady' girls, defined as those who were with him eight or more consecutive days, an intangible but unmistakable deepening, which never left them and for which they were forever grateful. Many came to see him years, even decades, after their brief affairs, and he took great pride in recognizing them all, no matter how many husbands and children they'd had, and however drastically their shapes had changed.

Tamara's farewell gift to Oktyabrina was an almost new Italian silk scarf that one of her medical colleagues had bought from a Western tourist. Kostya gave me a slim volume with yellowed pages and a tattered cover. It was a collection of poems by Osip Mandelshtam, who died in a labor camp in 1938 and has never been republished, although most of the 'underground' literary intelligentsia consider him Russia's best twentieth-century poet. Kostya had kept the book throughout the darkest Stalin years, when mere possession of literature by a liquidated writer terrified most people and could lead to denunciations. Inside the grease-stained cover, he'd written an inscription: 'To Zhoe, whom we'll miss whether he's gone two days, two months or . . . well, longer. If it's the latter, try to understand these poems and think of us. We'll never forget *you*. From your buddy Kostya.'

It was when Oktyabrina read this aloud that the realization we might never see each other again suddenly became real and immediate. We all stared at the floor for a long moment, feeling everything, but with nothing to say and no need to say it.

Oktyabrina broke the tension by presenting me with a 'memorandum' which she'd been preparing for a week. It was a list of 'import commodities' I was requested to bring in with me when I returned for the 'Moscow season'. There were thirty-five items, all numbered in pencils of different colors. Most were Woolworth articles such as ribbon and zippers, and of course cosmetics, among them nail polish remover and lotions for pimples, all carefully described with trade names she'd taken from advertisements in my magazines. Kostya snatched the list and added item thirty-six: 'One small collection of jade, to be delivered in the glove compartment of a sky-blue Buick sedan, with a musical horn and snow tires'.

After the huge supper, Oktyabrina lay back on the

bed, her arm still clasping Tamara's waist, as it had for an hour. Suddenly she jumped up and kissed Kostya on the lips and was back on the bed, sitting with mock primness, in a second. She examined me directly for my reaction, instead of from the corner of her eye. Our gazes became transfixed; for a moment we seemed lifted out of the flyblown room and on to a luxurious balcony in Monaco. 'So this is what it's like,' Oktyabrina whispered. 'Parting from a faithful friend. . . .'

She snapped to herself. 'Want to hear a new Russian saying? Please turn down the tap recorder, Kostya . . . "Whether far or near/Zhoe's our special dear/And when he returns to us . . ." ' She hesitated. 'Help me, you rats! Something better than "fear" or "tear".'

The 'celebration' came to life again, spiced by Kostya's latest jokes. Tamara swallowed a large glass of vodka and for the fun of it, unraveled an entire sleeve of a sweater she'd been knitting. Then she plunged into deep pensiveness and said something about the incomprehensibility of separation that would sound sentimental in the retelling, but on her lips had a perfect purity. Oktyabrina kissed her forehead.

Near midnight, the sky still held a faint trace of light, the remnants of early summer's White Nights. I got up to leave because my flight was very early in the morning. Kostya reminded us of the old Russian custom and we all sat down again for several silent minutes to gather our thoughts and put our lives in perspective before a long trip. I said my goodbyes in the room and Kostya hurried me down the corridor to the front door and fragrant night.

Later Kostya told me that Oktyabrina cried after I'd left. She had a premonition, she said, that something terrible was going to happen to me in over-rich, overstrung Europe. I might be run over by a sports car or arrested as a Russian spy. No, the real danger was worse: I would fall into the clutches of an overdressed, oversexed American heiress.

Sicily's beauty was rendered irrelevant by the invasion of Czechoslovakia. My first news of the Soviet tanks came at breakfast on the twenty-first, through the medium of a florid Austrian at a neighboring table. He was outraged at the 'barbaric Russians' and feared their troops would march straight through to his beloved Vienna. But he was also sneakingly pleased. The Czechs deserved something like this, didn't they? For being Communists themselves, of course. Besides, they were only *Slavs* in the first place: backward peasants who could never hope to govern themselves.

The morning passed in alternation between packing in my room and monitoring the grim radio reports in the lobby. My expected cable from Chicago arrived before lunch: 'Proceed soonest to Prague' to assist our East European man, who was already on his way. I got as far as Rome that evening.

The next week was exhausting. I couldn't get a flight to Prague; every journalist in Europe was competing for seats. By the time I did secure a reservation, the Soviet army had established enough control to ensure Western journalists were refused visas at the border. This meant I now had no means of entry. When this became clear, Chicago sent me to Vienna to backstop our East Europe man, who had rushed from there to Prague on the twenty-first.

Vienna was a hard slog: relaying cables, culling secondary sources, interviewing refugees who'd already begun to stream from Czechoslovakia. I'd forgotten what it was like to do a real story, and keep at it round the clock. My Russian gave me the drift of Prague Radio's underground reports: the heart-breaking encounters

182

with Soviet tanks. My mind reeled with the tragedy and I think my stories conveyed its depths. But after five days of this, Chicago asked me to return to Moscow. The bureau was unmanned except for a stringer and they wanted the Soviet side of the story covered more fully. I got a seat on the Aeroflot flight to Moscow the following afternoon.

# 17

☐ When the plane landed at Sheremetyevo Airport, I
felt a wave of vertigo. I was *here* again in this stifling,
hermetic, bafflingly remote world. How can Russia be
three hours from Europe—yet belong to a wholly different time and place? Everything seemed totally alien,
yet achingly familiar, as if I'd come to see grandparents
who died before I was born. The sharp smells of Russia
seeped into the plane even before its doors were opened;
a new neon sign proclaiming MOCKBA was sputtering
in three places. Fifteen long minutes passed before we
began disembarking: the crew assigned to the ramp—
four ramps for a hundred odd planes—was lost somewhere on a smoke break. Nothing had changed; nothing
*would* change. On the drive into Moscow, the woods
were deep in yellows and browns: autumn in August. In
the new, prefabricated outskirts, the inevitable lines for
food attended bare housing developments: solemn people
in plastic raincoats putting in the necessary hours for
something dreary to eat. I'd forgotten how poor everything was.

A stack of cables awaited me in the office. They were
full of queries that only members of the Politburo and
General Staff could answer about details of the invasion's
preparation, of where Dubcek and the others had been
held hostage, of their reactions during the sessions with
their kidnappers. In the heat of an important story, state-

side editors forget—because they've never fully understood—that the hard news they want simply doesn't exist. The Pentagon reveals more about the battle plans of Polaris submarines than the Kremlin about its workings. My stories were lumps of dough after Vienna's ringing cries. The most I could hope was that a straight report of the screaming lies of the Russian press would demonstrate how far the Soviet government, in manufacturing its own logic and standards, departed from Western notions of truth and justice.

In the absence of hard news, Chicago asked for local color and man-in-the-street reactions. But the strangest aspect of the invasion—the aspect my editors could least understand, suspecting laziness on my part—was that the Moscow man on the street had no reaction at all to what their tanks were doing, except a mild 'serves the Czech wise-guys right'. When it became clear that the invasion would not involve Russia in a new war, few Russians gave it another thought. It was something taking place in the mythical, inaccessible 'outside', about which Russians have no reliable knowledge and in which no real say— and therefore little interest. The whole world was holding its breath or trembling with indignation over Czechoslovakia and its consequences, but in Russia the problems were to find a dry-cleaner for your overcoat and elbow your way into department stores and busses. A few stunted apples and pears had appeared on the counters of selected grocery shops. Now was the time to grab them, five or six kilos at a time, or forget the taste of fresh fruit for another year.

Kostya obtained his fruit, including whole armfuls of fine Bulgarian grapes, without waiting in line: the supervisor of a nearby peasant market had been his girlfriend twenty years ago, when he was a young steel rigger in Magnitogorsk.

'Czechoslovakia?' he said with sham fervor when I

tuned to a news report. 'I'm delighted you're taking an interest in the way we free citizens run our affairs. The entire Soviet people, all progressive mankind, is profoundly grateful to the Party for offering fraternal help to the happy comrades in Prague.'

He poured two tumblers of white Crimean wine, which he was serving with fresh zander bought in another market, and fitted a new tape onto the recorder, a decrepit replacement for his Philips.

'But what the hell's all the fuss about, I wonder?' he continued. 'I myself remember the Czechs inviting our comradely army into the country, pleading with us to help save them from fascism.'

At this signal, I took out my notebook and pretended to jot down his *Pravda*-like quotes for publication throughout the world.

'Let's see. . . . The Czechs extended the invitation in the summer of '38—just before Munich, I think. Naturally we thought it over carefully before sending our tanks in—thirty years and two months later. Our Leninist Party spilleth over with humanitarianism; it never likes to rush for its guns.'

Kostya was tanned to a deep terra umbra, which lifted ten years from his appearance. He was now in splendid physical shape, having swum miles every day along the coast just outside Sochi. One day he struck out directly to sea to test how far he'd get before being stopped—frontier guards in the guise of life-savers patrol the whole of Russia's Black Sea coast to prevent defections by water. A motor boat intercepted him about two miles from shore, and that very afternoon his papers were examined by a Sochi KGB agent posing as an ordinary policeman. For the fun of it, Kostya produced several bottles and drank the agent, who'd boasted of his capacity, under the table.

Otherwise, his vacation had been only a moderate

success. Much as he loved the sun, Sochi was losing some of its luster after sixteen consecutive summers. He could hardly make a new conquest there; most of the beauties he spied on the beach turned out to be part of last year's catch, or the year before's. So many familiar physiques. . . .

As for Oktyabrina, he'd quickly lost contact with her. She went to sleep the first night with the intention of spending several weeks in exploration alone. But she soon found she wasn't 'transported' by Sochi and gave notice that she was moving on. The beach displeased her most: she hadn't expected crowds of people 'practically rubbing stomachs with each other—obese *hairy* stomachs'. And she disapproved on principle of deep tanning, or 'the charring of flesh'. Although it's true that Sochi's beaches are packed to bursting with some of the largest and least attractive bodies on earth, Kostya sensed that Oktyabrina's aesthetic disappointment masked her own embarrassment to appear in a bathing suit. She wore long skirts and high-necked blouses in the sun, then fashioned a parasol out of an old umbrella frame and some emerald fabric, and pinked a pair of white work gloves into 'lace'.

'I caught her sniffing the sea like a baby seagull,' said Kostya. 'This was a few kilometers up the coast, on an empty beach.'

'I wonder where she is now.'

'I wonder where I'm going to get a new bathing suit. This one's shot. Plus about a thousand rubles I borrowed down there.' The Japanese suit was indeed very worn; and Kostya refused to wash it because of the magic smell of salt. He slipped a pack of Camels into the limp elastic.

'The theater season's already started,' I said. 'Why don't we go just once this year?'

Kostya wrapped his arm around my shoulder. 'Relax: she'll turn up any day now. It rains down there in the fall. Pre-ci-pi-ta-tion. Why the hell do you think any-body comes back?'

'She didn't say where she was going?'

'Of course she did—she announced it. Departure for the Yalta because it was "certain to be more refined". The Tsar's summer palace, etcetera. Actually, I once knew a man who had quite an adventure with the daughter of the Tsar's former cook. No—the daughter of the former Tsar's cook. Anyway this happened back in '32 when. . . .'

'Did she have any money? She doesn't know anyone in Yalta.'

'Zhoe buddy, you don't understand how it works down south. It's *warm*. So-lar energy. Puts everybody in a generous mood. Stop worrying: even skinny girls do fine.'

'I suppose so. . . .'

'You need another vodka—helps when you're short on emotional self-discipline.'

'Or on bullshit.'

'A few weeks away from Mother Russia in those Si-cilies and Viennas and you come back oozing pessimism again. It's hellish, what imperialism does to a good man.'

We filled our glasses again and listened gloomily to an extremely worn Ray Charles tape. Kostya balanced the empty bottle on his pyramid of empties. Every few months he hired a taxi, returned the heap to a neighbor-hood store and had a big 'rejuvenation' celebration on the sum of the deposits. But now the prospect of a party seemed hollow.

'Let's head down to Kalinin Prospekt!' he exclaimed with attempted enthusiasm. 'They say a juke box's been installed in a new café. A juke box is the latest Russian in-vention—know what it is?'

We did drive to Kalinin Prospekt, a recently recon-structed boulevard flanked by East German-type skyscrapers, and there was indeed an Italian juke box in one of the cafés—but also a tight knot of disappointed teenagers studying the tantalizing object through the window. The café, a crude imitation of a pre-war Howard Johnson's, had opened during the summer with considerable ballyhoo, and was already closed for general repairs.

We spent the rest of the evening strolling up and back along the wide new boulevard, which Kostya kept comparing unfavorably to Sochi, where you strolled in soft moonlight and balmy air instead of cold drizzle. 'You Russian Question people never get to primary causes,' he said. 'Everything wrong with this country starts with a single simple reality: the shock of slipping from a cosy womb into an angry climate. The plumpest foetus can get paranoic.'

He told a tale about the latest promise of Soviet science. The country's roots, he said, would be cut by fantastically powerful laser beams and the entire Russian land mass drifted fifteen degrees south, where 'weather suitable for homo sapiens' begins. The operation was highly secret because it was going to be implemented in honor of Lenin's hundredth birthday the spring after next. 'Oh yes, a few hundred million Indians, Chinese and the rest will have to be squashed down a bit towards the equator. What the hell, they'll be jubilant to make way for Lenin's homeland. . . .'

Before the lights were extinguished on the boulevard, Kostya told me about his first evening with Oktyabrina in Sochi's tender moonlight and gentle air. She kept reminding him that he mustn't seduce a girl on the first night out of respect to Tamara, and volunteered as his chaperon. Near midnight, they walked down to the port, where a horde of tourists and local peasants were struggling to pack themselves onto a cruise liner about to cast off for Yalta. Gentle wavelets rippled against the quay and the moon made a wide 'road', as Russian poets call it too, across the water. Oktyabrina breathed deeply of the tropical air. Nevertheless, the Black Sea, with its Moscow-style cafeterias and lines for newspapers, fell far short of its promised *exotika*.

Oktyabrina began to question Kostya about his youth. Were his parents alive? Did they introduce him to *vodka?* Cautiously, she steered the conversation to sex. In Omsk, she informed Kostya confidentially, some people still believed that the size of a woman's mammary glands affected her capacity to experience sexual pleasure. That was one reason she just had to rip herself from her *roots*.

Her own enlightenment, thankfully, was early, complete and joyous. Being a sensitive, modern woman as well as a doctor, her mother had told her everything with great simplicity and beauty before she died. But the ignorance in the orphanage was so massive that the staff feared Oktyabrina's knowledge would upset the other girls. Some thought that babies were conceived by the wife sitting in an armchair immediately after the husband, while the cushions were still warm. . . .

Her own problem was not sex but children. Society made hideous demands on young women: how could anyone be both a mother *and* an artist? That's why her policy was to abandon men, even *cruelly*, rather than to bear their children at this stage. But even if certain nineteenth-century prudes rejected the logic of this modern solution and called her promiscuous. . . .

'That's enough theory, kid,' Kostya interrupted. 'I'm convinced—let's go to bed.'

Oktyabrina dropped her scarf—Tamara's present—on to the sidewalk and watched the breeze play at its corners. To gain time, she protracted the retrieving of the handsome silk.

'Let's go to bed, kid,' Kostya repeated. 'I've been mortifying my flesh for far too long—it's a terrible toll on my health. I want to let my passion burst right into you.'

'What about Tamara?' asked Oktyabrina shakily.

'Tamara will understand. If it's *you*. Better than a stranger, after all—she's very fond of you.'

'Well . . . yes,' said Oktyabrina, obviously trying to think of an escape. 'You're absolutely right, Kostya darling. When would you suggest—back in Moscow perhaps?'

'I'd suggest in about ten minutes. I need an experienced woman like you.'

'What an absolutely brilliant inspiration,' she said uncertainly. 'Sex is always best when garnished with a good laugh. With us, it's bound to be a huge giggle. And dynamite too. . . .'

Walking home, Kostya put his arm low on Oktyabrina's waist and felt her hip socket gyrating like locomotive connecting rods. Her mind seemed to be churning with equal energy to hatch a deliverance.

Not far from the composers' colony, they heard the familiar strains of a famous pre-revolutionary ballad, that had recently become popular among students searching Old Russia for their roots. The singers, a group of young men and women on a walking tour, mouthed the refrain listlessly, probably because it was the day's tenth repetition. But aided by the sea noises, the old melody had enough heart-melting melancholy to generate a mood.

> I was on my way *home*,
> Riding home and thinking of *you*.
> The moon shone sadly,
> Through the coach's dingy windows . . .

Oktyabrina held her breath. After the second verse, she sat down on the curb, clutched her face in her hands and mumbled through her fingers.

191

'Kostya dearest, tell me what to think. *Those* words. *That* melody. I can't begin to explain their meaning.'

'Give it a try,' said Kostya huskily. 'Don't worry about me, kid. I can take it.'

'It was *our* song. Intrepid Vyacheslav and I. I never dreamed I'd hear it again like this. . . .'

'And Vyacheslav,' prompted Kostya, 'was one of your most treasured lovers.'

'Not *one* of the most. That son of heaven, my one and only idol—it was *his* children I so longed to bear.'

Kostya helped her gently to her feet. 'I'm heartbroken,' she whispered. 'But of course you understand. I can't possibly give myself to you just now. This wound will take time. . . .'

'Of course it will,' said Kostya. 'Tomorrow's another day. C'mon, you'll need help to struggle to your room.'

The following day, Oktyabrina appeared in black on the promenade bordering the beach. She shouted to Kostya that she was going to a sanatorium called 'Lenin's Path' for treatment of her 'ballad-shattered' nerves. The day after that, she boarded a boat for Yalta.

# 18

☐ Winter's first spearhead arrived in late September. A grim, gunmetal cloud descended on central Russia and hung there, immobile, smothering all hopes for a break. The trees were already naked black and the streets swept clean of their soggy leaves, removing the city's last trace of color. Cotton wadding was stuffed again into the cracks of window frames, symbolizing the general mood.

By October the first wet snows had fallen and the awful burden arrived that makes Everyman an unwilling martyr: the unrelenting, unfair battle against the climate. A month of this clammy rawness passed that seemed like three; by the time the press was building up to its usual exultation over the anniversary of the Bolshevik Revolution, a state of mental siege had returned.

This was stoutly reinforced by the Party's new line. Even before Czechoslovakia, an ominous hardening could be felt in all domestic affairs. Leonid was a victim of this, together with hundreds of fellow intellectuals who dared object to the return of a full police-state atmosphere. The invasion accelerated the repression. It became known as 'neo-Stalinism', which described the retreat towards Stalin's orthodoxy and restoration to power of many of his henchmen and admirers.

The general consequences of neo-Stalinism made subjects for carefully worded stories: 'liberals' dismissed from their jobs and exiled from Moscow; intensified censorship and corresponding deterioration in all branches of the arts; a furious campaign to root out 'bourgeois' influences—meaning anything not rabidly anti-Western—in every publication, television broadcast and film. But it was harder to describe the great depressive effect of this on the sliver of Muscovites who had aspirations for Russia's progress towards Western standards. Once again, their hopes for healing Russia had been crushed. They reacted as the Russian intelligentsia has for centuries: by withdrawing to an inner world of favorite books and close friends.

The weather was equally gloomy. Snow had already fallen often, but the temperature pushed up again to a few degrees above freezing, leaving only mud and slush as if to remind everyone that autumn is the worst season of the Russian year. Besides the rawness, waiting for winter causes a palpable strain. A librarian once compared it to two and a half months of pre-menstrual tension.

During her breaks, I used to take this elderly woman, a member of an old intellectual family, to tea in the Lenin Library's basement cafeteria. Now she declined my invitations with a rueful smile. It was again a time to avoid social contact with foreigners. Together with the general tightening up everywhere, there was a major campaign to warn about the growing danger of 'alien' thoughts and influence. This was classified by the newspapers—in at least one article daily—as 'ideological subversion', and it was said to be practised by a significant percentage of the Soviet Union's foreign guests. The press 'reported' case after case of innocent people having been duped by Western correspondents and tourists who *seemed* friendly to Russia, only to worm their way into citizens' trust and sow the rotten seeds of doubt. Doubt of the Party's infallible guidance—an odious vice.

The most maddening refinement was the hypocrisy. At the very moment the ideological xenophobia was

194

being whipped up, Intourist offices in every Western capital were straining to attract foreign tourists—meaning foreign currency. 'Visit the USSR! Land of Caviar, Ballet and Friendship!' A translation of a single *Pravda* article about heinous imperialist spies, double-faced rats trying to gnaw at Marxism-Leninism, and verminous enemies of all socialist peoples would have kept all but a handful of masochists out of Russia forever.

I wondered about a connection between the xenophobia and Oktyabrina's continued absence. Then I dismissed the thought and cursed myself for having entertained it. A certain kind of Russian ignores these campaigns, even when the peril to himself is very real. Whatever she wasn't, Oktyabrina surely belonged to this category. In loyalty to friends—the primary test of character in Russia—I knew she was above reproach. But why had she disappeared for almost four months? Wherever she was, why didn't she telephone? At least write?

Soon I began to doubt whether I'd see her again at all. This can happen in Russia, even with your best friends—and the fact that other old friends like Kostya are left alone only heightens the anxiety. Two years before, I'd been friendly with a young doctor whose passions were Tennessee Williams and Norman Mailer. We used to meet for walks and talks in Sokolniki Park, until one day he didn't turn up as we'd arranged only an hour before. I never heard from him again.

The disappearances are not necessarily sinister. Many Russians have a powerful, inbred wanderlust which seizes them periodically. Depite all the rules and required documents—the identity papers, labor books, *propiskas* and hundred other devices designed to combat Russian chaos and establish order—despite all this, these restless people move about the country like Dos Passos characters in *USA*.

When you're on a train in a relatively remote part of
195

the country and you keep your identity quiet long enough, vodka will appear and stories will be swapped. The jumble of autobiographies in your compartment will amaze you. One man will have spent his life logging in the far North, and a woman will have wandered through the South after being a truck driver during the war. A crippled man will have worked on the Volga or the Don, and his wife will have been Mikoyan's personal nurse. Not one person in six will live in the city where he was born. The vagueness of living patterns corresponds to the vagueness of the land: the greatest of all wide open spaces.

I pictured Oktyabrina on a train somewhere, talking nonsense and stuffing herself with someone's pickles and *pirozhki*. Did she still wince over a swallow of vodka? Was it really possible that I'd never see her again? I began to understand that I had been wrong to go abroad. If I'd taken her to the Black Sea, she wouldn't have disappeared. Hadn't she hinted that we should explore the Caucasus together, as we used to sightsee in Moscow?

I was no longer sightseeing now because the person I was keeping company with had only evenings free, and preferred to spend them at small dinner parties. Several weeks after my vacation, I'd met a woman who ended my paralysis at last: the Dutch Ambassador's personal secretary. She was tall and graceful, worldly and intelligent. She wanted no permanent attachments because of her career, and had half-a-dozen suitors among the foreign colony's bachelors. But she sometimes responded gaily to my calls and became a companion for a few of the long evenings and weekends. I told her nothing about Oktyabrina. She would have thought the whole affair absurd.

And what was there to tell? It couldn't even be called an affair, after all. Besides, I was more and more certain that Oktyabrina would never reappear; more and more

196

aware that with my usual insensitivity, I'd ignored a hundred opportunities to encourage her, to tell her why she was needed. As usual, I saw my mistake only after the friend was gone. Kostya heard a rumor that Oktyabrina had 'fallen in with' an important East German engineer who was taking a cure outside Yalta. He reported the news with unmasked sorrow. Selfishly, we were sorrier still when we heard a second rumor: she'd been picked up on the beach by an ageing film director, moved to Kiev with him, and was pregnant.

I'd not only stopped sightseeing, but for months hadn't had a proper walk along Petrovka. The street had lost its appeal; I now walked north, away from the center of town. Ordinarily tranquil children in the streets had become whiny and irritable because of the incomprehensibly protracted fall.

On 7 November, I covered the parade in Red Square. It was virtually an exact replica of the May Day affair and provoked the same reaction in me—only more intense because we were descending into winter instead of rising towards summer. 7 November marks the end of an era, when the last hopes for mild weather are laid to rest. I remembered Oktyabrina's new white dress and 'love season' chatter after the May Day parade. It was time to put these thoughts to rest too, together with the tenderness for her which I produced so abundantly in her absence.

We were approaching mid-November: Tankists' Day, Petroleum and Gas Workers' Day, Workers of the Fishing Industry Day . . . and then came an ordinary Monday, without a title—but which should have one in terms of Oktyabrina's adventures.

The day started in anything but a Monday mood: I had a new idea for a story. Since Czechoslovakia, they were harder than ever to find. The Press Department gave per-

197

mission for an interview only if your idea was not just merely neutral, but positively pro-Soviet. At the same time, Chicago wanted more and more hard news, which was as unobtainable as ever. A reporter could satisfy neither side—nor himself.

My idea promised to tread the narrow middle ground. A new movie about Isadora Duncan had just opened in New York and I thought of writing about her strange Russian adventure. The way to start, I thought, was through her husband, Sergei Esenin.

Esenin was a brilliant and debauched lyric poet, still revered by Russian youth. He killed himself in 1925, joining many of the country's best poets who could not work under Soviet rule. I made some telephone calls and discovered that he was buried in Moscow. An expressive lead to the story then suggested itself: a description of his grave.

I drove out to the cemetery after lunch. It lies behind the American Embassy, past the zoo and is bordered by a desolate old road called '1905 Street'. This is one of the city's forgotten corners of old houses, old logs, old unpainted doors—all having earned the compassion due old workhorses. It is fittingly expressed in the cadence and old Slavic resonance of the cemetery's name: Va-gán-kov-sko-ye. A plaque on the tumbledown fence announced that it had been founded in 1822.

Inside, I was immersed immediately in the eerie, almost occult atmosphere of all Russian cemeteries, which somehow evoke images of northern pagan rites rather than the Christian service. Although the grounds were extensive, gnarled trees and tottering shacks made everything seem as stuffed as a Russian sitting-room. The graves were also packed shoulder-to-shoulder, but each was defiantly segregated by a spiked, waist-high iron fence—as if a lifetime spent among the toiling masses made a claim to privacy vital in death.

198

The grounds were soundless except for the rush of the wind and cackling of immense crows. I found Esenin's grave and described it in my notebook. It was a large black slab of marble in the 'modernistic', 1930s style with a gold-painted bas-relief of the poet in profile. The effect was so heavily ceremonious—so unlike Esenin and his poetry—that it seemed vulgar. This was only partially redeemed by the flowers, mostly artificial, that had been deposited on the wet pedestal, apparently during the course of the morning.

Later, I made my way back to the crumbling church near the entrance and asked an old man, seemingly a warden, whether I might see a burial one day. His response was an outpouring of hatred. Apparently he mistook me for a Soviet official and thought I'd come to mock the church, an amusement of certain Russians. This triggered all his fear, disgust and rage against Communist outsiders who cannot destroy God but are systematically annihilating His Church.

When the old man's hostility abated, however, he said that there were now very few burials: almost all the ground was occupied, and the authorities would allot no more to the church. Burial in Vagánhovskoye was an honor, and even many Communists begged for a plot on their death beds—when it was too late. The last burial had been ten days ago: a poor one, without even a cross, although the deceased was so steadfast a believer that the Deacon had lent him hundreds of rubles from the Poor Box over the years. The new grave was 'down there'—he pointed vaguely—and I could go and see it for myself if I was so interested. . . .

I was interested. The grave was the last of a relatively new row in the farthest corner from the church. As I approached, I was aware that I knew the person standing over it, and also that I would not easily remember from where. Was she the child of someone in the Press Corps?

199

A girl from the courtyard of my building? She was about twelve or thirteen, with a fat, pouting face—not easily mistaken for someone else, but I did not in fact remember until I read the name on the new grave. It was printed in white paint on a homemade wooden cross:

'EVGENY IGNATIEVICH ZHADRIN.
Born January 5th, 1881; died November 4th, 1968.
Eighty-seven years: a trice in the history of humanity, a glorious hour for those who knew and adored him.'

A smaller stake had been driven into the wet, freshly-dug soil about a foot in front of the cross. To it was pinned a yellowed photograph of a dancer, perhaps Nijinsky, in a spectacular costume, probably from an old Diaghilev production. It was protected by a piece of cigarette cellophane. Beneath the photograph was a cardboard rectangle with two brief epitaphs, printed in green ink:

*Ars longa, vita brevis*—Hippocrates

Seek, and Ye may not Find;
Strive, and perhaps you won't Arrive.
But for a man with Courage and Imagination,
The World's wide open, and full of Fascination.
　　　　　　　　　　　　　　　　—Anonymous

The girl was absent-mindedly holding a hyacinth bulb. Her feet were planted in a wide stance and had settled several inches into the mud; she failed to register my approach. Perhaps she was lost in meditation or mourning for Evgeny Ignatievich, but her vacant eyes and unclosed mouth suggested not thought, but the absence of it.

'Hello,' I said. 'Don't be frightened. Where's Oktya-brina?'

Far from being frightened, she was in a kind of peaceful trance. Her lips spread into a smile like gravy creeping across a cold plate.

'I'm sorry about Evgeny Ignatievich,' I said more loudly. 'Can you tell me where Oktyabrina is?'

When finally achieved, the answer was in a delighted, sing-song soprano, as if the idea had titillated the girl.

'She's got an *old*-er friend. *I* know.'

'She's what?'

'A guardian angel to Auntie Oktyushka like Auntie Oktyushka is a guardian angel to me.'

'That's fine. Please tell me where she is.'

The girl backed a half step away and smiled triumphantly, as if having detected an attempt to engage her in a forbidden game.

'Oktyabrina's in Moscow, isn't she?' I said as soothingly as I could. 'I remember how nicely you danced with her.'

'She buys the flowers but I'm not to tell. She says I'm not to tell men if they ask any questions. So you see. . . .'

She did not finish her thought. Nor place the hyacinth on the grave—until I reminded her. This is what finally convinced her to 'tell', but she apparently knew nothing concrete about Oktyabrina's whereabouts. A tragedy had happened to 'Auntie Oktushka'—no! a transformation. She was very *busy* now and couldn't always come to 'Uncle Ignatich's new home. . . .'

'What kind of tragedy? *Where is she?*'

'I'm supposed to come every day. For thirty-three days, the crying period. If I don't bring a flower, Uncle Ignatich will be dug out of his bed and *burned*. And Auntie Oktushka. . . .'

She could not finish her thought again. 'Auntie Oktyu-shka what?' I asked.

She giggled. 'Auntie Oktyushka gives me a ruble every time I come. I'm going to buy my own um-*brel*-la soon. . . .'

I pressed for more information as firmly as I could. Suddenly she remembered that she had a telephone number for emergencies. It was inked onto a piece of cotton and sewn inside her mitten, to thwart loss.

# 19

☐ The telephone number was for a western district. The same man answered every time I called. He knew no one, he said politely, of that name or description living anywhere in the apartment. After the fourth call in four hours, he sounded irked.

The next day, the Dutch Ambassador gave a luncheon I couldn't miss. By the time I got to the cemetery at five o'clock it was dark and no one was within sight of Evgeny Ignatievich's grave. The day after that, I arrived much earlier. Oktyabrina was there, bent over the grave with a dust-pan. She was laboriously sweeping away the leaves and muttering to herself in encouragement and felicitation. 'Come on, just a bit more, see how nice that looks, look at all you've *done!*'

Her skinny fingers gripped the dust-pan as they'd so often gripped my arm while negotiating mud and ice. I was flooded by soap-opera sensations: a need to laugh and cry at once; many surges, canceling each other out.

If one mistake transcended all others in the history of my numbness towards her, it was not to follow my next instinct. I wanted to swoop down and hold her tightly. That was the critical moment—and having faced it, everything else would have fallen into place. I hesitated and was lost. Once the moment of spontaneity had passed, my heart beat as when I wanted to speak up at a professional dinner and knew I would not.

I swallowed my self-disappointment and inched forward, keeping half covered by a clump of hedges. Oktyabrina's appearance was puzzling. She was wearing a canvas raincoat streaked with soot and tattered at the cuffs. Underneath was a black high-necked sweater discolored by washing and face powder. Strings of hair—black, in the fierce tint of Soviet dyes—clung to her cheeks. The cheeks themselves were powdered white except for dark circles under the eyes. The combined effect was a stage simulation of a woman of substantial years and intellect who'd lived life to the full, suffered her share of tragedy, and was now and forever alone in the world.

She scooped up the leaves as if the job would test a laborer's strength. An elderly couple approached unsteadily from behind me. Oktyabrina heard their sobs, straightened up to look, and saw me.

A look of amazement and delight raced across her face, but was suppressed so quickly that I might have imagined it.

'Oh it's you, Zhoseph,' she said blandly. 'How are you keeping? You're looking somewhat peaked.'

'Hello, Oktyabrina. I'm just fine, how are *you?*'

'Frantically busy, actually. But otherwise extremely . . . *fulfilled.* I suppose you feel madly daring without a scarf on a day like this.'

'Not really, I just forgot. I wish I had someone to sew me a reminder somewhere—I mean the Auntie Oktyushka method.'

She strenuously rolled up her raincoat sleeves, betraying no reaction to the hint about how I'd found her.

'I suppose you might be feeling a twinge of guilt,' I said, hopefully sounding playful. 'You were going to call me the *instant* you got back from Sochi.'

'Busy busy busy,' she repeated, ignoring my chiding. 'Be a nice male and make *this* pile of leaves somehow go over *there.*'

204

Silence descended. A crow cawed furiously. The old couple disappearing down the lane looked like a nineteenth-century painting.

'How long have you been back in town?' I asked, trying a more direct approach.

She did not hear, or pretended not to. 'What an extraordinary noise this wind is making,' she said, squinting into the distance. 'It reminds me of . . . of when the splendid autumn zephyr whistles down the hills above my beloved Omsk.'

'So you've been home?' I asked, feeling relieved. Her having returned to Omsk after Sochi or Yalta might explain not only her apparel, but also the long absence.

'You might say home—yes, *spiritually* home.' She sighed. 'Have you read *The Kreutzer Sonata* recently?' she asked. 'A frightening, but in a way a profoundly revealing study. You must *read* more, Zhoseph.'

'Indeed I must. For goodness sake, Oktyabrina, let's stop clowning and talk.'

'*The Kreutzer Sonata* is a late work of Tolstoy, you know—I mean Lev Nikolaevich Tolstoy. There is also Alexei Nikolaevich, of course. And Alexei Konstantinovich Tolstoy—a rather more obscure writer, but quite important to students of that period.'

It was my turn not to answer; I wasn't sure how. I waited in vain for the punch line: Oktyabrina had nothing to add to her unaccountable interest in literature and the Tolstoys. Her new role was inscrutable.

'How did you like the Black Sea?' I asked, taking another tack.

'The *sea* is pleasant enough,' she replied thoughtfully. 'Actually, it's rather blue. Serene and welcoming like . . . well, water's the symbol of womanhood, you know. But the ghastly public! Males are at their most absolutely abominable on the beach. Half of you go just to stare at us. To *oogle* like animals, leer, make *remarks*. . . . Now

Zhoseph, *do* let me complete my work. Frankly, I never *seen* so many leaves in one place. Where there's a grove of oaks, there's also a clump of birches—it's an extremely old, extremely true Russian saying.'

The conversation died again. Oktyabrina bent to her sweeping, arms flailing and brow puckered in concentration. Everything was so disappointing—so unreal—that I hoped I was imagining it, and that we could somehow begin the reunion again as it should be. What had happened to her?

To gain time, I moved to the neighboring grave, which was adorned with the portrait of a general and an epitaph about the Motherland. Oktyabrina quickly straightened up. 'May I trouble you for the time? I'm always light years off without the sun.'

'It's almost one-thirty. Time for a National Café lunch.'

'Twenty more minutes and then I must *dash*,' she declared. 'I do wish that little man would hurry and repair my watch. It's difficult enough for a woman alone to keep herself. . . .'

A sharp gust of wind blew a cluster of new leaves from the adjoining grave against Evgeny Ignatievich's cross. Oktyabrina sighed wearily and turned to pick them up by hand. Then she stepped back to give the grave a final proprietorial examination, like a man who has just washed his car and can't understand how he tolerated the dirt before.

'How did he die?' I asked.

She sighed again, this time with *Weltschmerz.* 'How did he die? Old age. Just old age, weary old limbs. And a certain dislocation of the soul.'

'I brought him back a walking stick from Rome— which I never delivered, of course. I'm sorry about that now.'

'Please don't try to be sentimental, Zhoseph.'

'Plus some pretty things for his most promising pupil. . . .'

'Please throw them away. My destiny is to become a real woman, not a doll. Males crave jewellery, costumes, flesh—anything at all to distract from the love and nobility of the real person inside.'

'What's all this about? I can't help noticing a slight shift in your . . . credo.'

The wind blew up again; Oktyabrina turned into it with a defiant expression. 'Yes, it's wet and raw,' she said. 'And may continue to be for many more weeks. But people who are at ease with themselves hardly notice the weather. People who know what they are and aren't seeking heroes or magical changes.'

She rolled down her sleeves and prepared to leave. 'Zhoseph, I'm not trying to be mysterious and don't want to offend you. The sensible solution for us is for each to hold to the satisfaction of one's own depths and one's *work*.'

'You've found a new teacher already?' I asked, having waited in vain for an elaboration of *work*.

'I've dropped ballet once and for all, if that's what you're trying to ascertain. It's a joy to be *liberated* from that humiliating pretence. Anyway, classical ballet happens to be dying. Not least because it's every woman is a shallow caricature.'

'Then what about Evgeny Ignatievich? You seem to be. . . .'

'Yes, Evgeny Ignatievich had certain virtues,' she interrupted, wiping his cross clean with a handful of soggy newspaper. 'But an old oak is as young as its newest root. His roots were deep in the acid soil of sexual injustice. It wasn't his fault, of course. He was a *casualty* of his time and upbringing. But the truth is, he practiced his deceptions on women. Because women are exploitable, women have *hearts*. And he had the endemic masculine cruelty to bleed them. In this sense, his passing was . . . well, *inevitable.*'

This allocution was punctuated with short pauses, as if Oktyabrina had long pondered the key phrases but was surprised to hear them spoken. Together with the world-weary costume, they were undoubtedly part of her new identity. The natural thing would have been to take her by the shoulders and shake the makebelieve out of her. But a straight line was often the longest distance to her secrets. Besides, there was now a hint in her expression that she was really very happy to see an old friend, and that if I remained patient, she'd explain everything at the proper time.

'For someone who feels like that about Evgeny Ignatievich,' I said gently, 'you seem to be paying considerable attention to his grave.'

She thought for a moment. 'That's unquestionably true,' she answered. 'I'd almost forgotten your perceptiveness about certain things.'

'I'd almost forgotten your eyes.'

'Oh God, *don't!* . . . The hard fact is that I'm not fully liberated from the male myth. Indeed, if you didn't know the odds I'm fighting against, you might assume I've hardly *begun.* On the other hand, allowance must be made for my exposure to romantic pressures at an impressionable age. . . .'

Something of the old Oktyabrina returned as she began analyzing herself in solemn detail. The tending of the grave, she confided, was indeed a sentimental indulgence to her past. On the other hand, it was a kind of symbolic *last contact* with her old way of life and its mushy illusions. That was why Gelda approved of it— well, not exactly approved, but made allowances for it. Women's natural altruism must be patiently *cultivated,* like an orchid in. . . .

At last I caught the signal. 'Gelda?' I said. 'You mean you've been with Gelda all this time?'

'And when you compare me to my former state—no, I don't like even to *think* about it. The past is a receding nightmare.'

'When did you pick up with Gelda again, Oktyabrina? Do you still answer to Oktyabrina?'

This pleased her visibly, but she controlled her old triumphant-smile-that-can't-quite-be-contained   expression and gazed over my shoulder, into the distance.

'You never understood her inner nobility; I shan't attempt to describe it. I simply can't convey what Gelda stands for—certainly not to someone lacking our feminine instincts.'

I waited the required moments for the dramatic pause. Oktyabrina's voice was like a radio announcer's describing a steel plant. 'Gelda is a beautiful person. A woman who's learned that all women are *used*—and, in the end, remain alone. And she's taken me under her loving wing again.'

We had nearly reached the car when Oktyabrina stopped short. '*Spooks!* I've forgotten it!' she exclaimed, and dashed back into the cemetery. When she returned, my old Maxwell House can was clanging against her dustpan. She used to use it for storing hair-pins and rubber bands. Now it seemed to contain small worms—for Gelda's fish?—but Oktyabrina concealed it behind her hip.

We drove past the zoo towards the center of town, stopping only to buy ice-cream. Oktyabrina gazed at the wet, somber streets as if in wonder.

'It's no longer simply Moscow that enthralls me,' she sighed. 'Life itself is so wholly intoxicating. My waking hours are literally an orgy of happiness.'

209

'What's the secret?' I asked. 'I'd like to write a story about it.'

'The secret is simply to be *yourself*, with people who *truly* love you exactly as you are. Which stops life from being a mass of meaningless trivia.'

'I suppose you've found the elusive inner peace that puts everything in its proper place.'

'Exactly. For example, this very minute. The insides of my boots happen to be soaked with freezing mud, but I'm absorbing autumn's beauty and hardly even notice it.'

The illogicality of this was so blatant that we both chuckled. 'It happens to be true, Zhoseph, and I only wish it could be for you too. There are lots of ways a person can change, but self-understanding's the only real one.'

'I'm very happy for you. And that happens to be true too, even if you want to make fun of it.'

'Life's so odd, isn't it? Like when you return to a familiar place years later and stand there all dizzy because so much has changed—yet you're still somehow you. I know perfectly well you sometimes worried about me. And here I am now, worrying about *you*. . . .'

Oktyabrina sucked the last of her ice-cream, the noises demonstrating that at least one part of her hadn't changed at all.

'And what *about* you, Zhoseph?' she asked in an artfully casual voice. 'Working hard?'

'Not very. The usual.'

'And still living all alone?'

'Still living all alone.'

'I suppose you still see Kostya,' she said in a harder tone. 'How is our old exponent of the ethos of the bull?'

'Same as ever. No—something seems to be leaving him. Somewhere he's very sad, you know.'

'I'm afraid there's no hope for Kostya. To attain self-understanding and a sexual reality, I mean. But give him my . . . *compliments*.'

'They'll make him very happy. I'm sure he'll want to throw a big reunion celebration.'

'No,' she said sharply. 'I can't meet Kostya yet.' She lowered her voice, hinting renewed trust. 'I won't be coy with you about the reason why, Zhoseph. I'll speak with utter forthrightness out of consideration for our old . . . well, association. Whatever it lacked in genuine understanding, I'm certain you never *intentionally* misled me. But I simply can't consort with you two again. Say I'm not yet strong enough for social intercourse with notorious ladykillers, if you like. You know the rules for a reformed alcoholic.'

'Only at second hand. I know the rules are very rigid. But I'm very happy for you, Oktyabrina. You're obviously deep in something invaluable. I wouldn't dream of interfering.'

This clearly disappointed her. She gazed serenely out of the window again—which meant, of course, that she was trying to think fast.

'And yes,' she said at last, 'there's a more crucial reason—I'm not ashamed of it. If you must know, I'd go to *any* lengths to conceal our renewed association from Gelda. It would shatter my last chance irretrievably. To become a *real person*, I mean.'

'Quite right you are too. I admire people tremendously who sacrifice everything for their last chance.'

Then I resorted to one of her own favorite ploys—the purposefully ambiguous statement. 'You've sacrificed even more than you know for this chance,' I said, and squinted as if following a distant thought. 'You're one of the rare women who've defeated the tyranny of petit-bourgeois drives.'

She scrutinized me, but suppressed the question on her lips.

211

'It's funny how things work out for the best,' I continued. 'For months I've been trying to track you down just to give you the very thing you've resolved to renounce for ever. Now I see it would be sheer hell for you to have it.'

She sniffed my bait from every angle, like an old bass in a farmer's pond. When she finally signaled she was ready to hear what her sacrifice had been, and I revealed it was a flight bag of cosmetics and trinkets that I'd brought her from Rome, she affected annoyance over the 'teenage trivia'.

'Exactly,' I agreed. 'I'd hate myself if I'd actually tried to foist the stuff on you.'

'Zhoe darling, stop clowning. Precisely what do you propose to do with that flight bag?'

'What *can* I do? Empty it in the trash can, I suppose. Bit by bit, to avoid charges of hoarding deficit goods for black market speculation.'

Suddenly she slipped her foot past mine and jabbed the brake. 'Zhoe, this means "Stop" to your buffoonery!'

The car careered dangerously. Oktyabrina yanked back her foot in a fright, whacking her knee on the steering wheel. Pain and embarrassment somewhat tempered her subsequent speech.

Of course she didn't want that vulgar rubbish for herself. But it would be an absurd gesture, the very kind of theatrical posturing she'd been striving to shed under Gelda's patient guidance, actually to *waste* the materials. 'You see, I could very easily distribute the contents of that bag in an orphanage somewhere. Orphan girls absolutely adore that kind of thing—I can tell you myself. . . .'

In return for this, it was decided that Oktyabrina would not withdraw from my life again, but that we would resume a relationship of old friends who had lived through a certain disappointment, and therefore had a better understanding of each other's inner needs. To seal the new pact, I made two promises: never to allude to any erotic adventure of her past in Gelda's presence, and to shield them both from men on the make.

# 20

☐ The next day, Oktyabrina escorted Gelda to my apartment. It was Artillery and Missile Warriors' Day, which was a comic touch because of Alexander, whose graduation from the Academy probably took place that very morning to coincide with the holiday. A grimmer touch was the arrest of a husband and wife in Red Square.

The young couple had tried to mark the 'holiday' by protesting against the occupation of Czechoslovakia. From start to quick finish, their venture was a pathetic failure: plain-clothed KGB officers seized them before they could fully unfold their 'Hands off Czechoslovakia' banner. They had won no understanding, not to mention sympathy, from 'the people' they'd hoped to enlighten. Pedestrians uttered curses and angry threats, and several good citizens left their places in the Lenin Mausoleum line to march to the site of the commotion and express their patriotism by spitting in the 'sniveling traitors' ' faces.

This is the account I put together after covering the story that morning. By afternoon, predictions were circulating that the young couple would be sentenced to five years in Siberia for 'disturbing public order'. When Oktyabrina and Gelda arrived, I was in the mood that often paralyzes Russian intellectuals: black despair for themselves and their country, combined with searing anguish over the dictatorship's remorseless injustices and people's unconcern. On days like these, Russia is no more than a huge dungeon.

Gelda greeted me as if I'd last seen her six days ago rather than six months. Her features were unchanged, but it struck me for the first time that she had a considerable black moustache of her own. Her raincoat was an exact copy of Oktyabrina's—or vice-versa; when she took it off to reveal a black high-necked sweater, the inspiration for Oktyabrina's new costume became clear. Although I rarely talk of politics to Russians, the incident in Red Square had so depressed me that I turned up the radio to jam the apartment's 'ears' and whispered the news to Gelda. She was unimpressed.

'What did you expect from our Politburo pricks? A demonstration on Red Square yet; the kids can be happy they weren't beaten on the spot. At least they'll be crucified for something they *did.*'

Gelda then spoke of a friend who'd just been punished for something she hadn't done. Last summer, the girl who'd translated Konrad Lorenz's letters for her met a German tourist in a restaurant. Back in Hamburg, the German published an unflattering article about Brezhnev, about whom he'd never spoken to Gelda's friend. She was summoned to an office, called a 'stinking traitor and filthy whore' and informed she would never work again as a teacher or translator. She now washed dishes in a cafeteria.

'If I had a machine-gun,' said Gelda, remembering to whisper again, 'I'd go to the Kremlin and shoot every one of them. In the balls, where they deserve.' She swallowed a pill. 'On the other hand, what the hell for? Can anybody believe better bastards would replace them from the Russian masses?'

Oktyabrina hung tightly on her words; Gelda's ripe language no longer made her flinch. The translator's misfortune pained her, but she also seemed relieved: the rare

215

talk of politics had smoothed our reunion, leaving questions about the past months unasked.

After a glass of tea, we all felt better. As always, politics were pushed to the back of our consciousness—to make life possible. Oktyabrina studied our tea leaves, and for good measure fetched a crystal ball—in the form of an empty *prostokvasha* jar from her carryall.

'The spirits whisper to me,' she intoned. 'No—stop deflecting my concentration. . . . The spirits want it known that dish-washers will become princesses—female of course. And that winter will end in February this year. . . . And they instruct dear Gelda and Zhoseph not to be dispirited. Because they are together again, and will grow to trust and love each other.'

Oktyabrina then inspected the apartment with proprietorial thoroughness, commenting on the women seduced on the davenport—by a notorious American heartbreaker —in her absence. Gelda talked of her new intellectual preoccupation. She'd moved on from Lorenz to Freud. But even with her unexcelled contacts among bibliophiles, she'd had great trouble securing a single volume of Freud's papers published in Russian before the revolution.

When Oktyabrina took the tea glasses into the kitchen, Gelda spoke of her in the rudimentary Freudian terms with which she'd recently been acquainting herself. Oktyabrina's inhibitions about men, she reasoned, surely lay deeper than in the trauma of that summer: somewhere in the pattern of her early childhood. . . .

The trauma of that summer, she explained at my prompting, took place in a small seaside town called Alushta, just east of Yalta. Having exhausted her rubles, Oktyabrina was sleeping near the beach. As she lay there uneasily, a small boat approached from the sea and a large man in oilskins waded ashore. As luck had it, his torch quickly detected her. He was upon her in an instant, and since he'd been at sea for weeks, remained upon her for an hour. Oktyabrina's screams died in the night; no one was near enough to hear. Since she was unwell at that time, it was a particularly brutal rape. . . .

'Do you believe that story?' I asked.

'Not literally. But something happened; she returned to Moscow in bad shape. Someone bruised her.'

'You actually saw the wounds?'

'I didn't have to. She almost had a breakdown.'

Since then, Gelda—in the absence of Kostya and me from Moscow—had assumed the role of Oktyabrina's guardian. During the first few days, Oktyabrina was in mild shock. Having recovered, she resolved to write a story about her 'tragic adventure'. Weeks later, she burned the pages, all ten first drafts, because 'it would be wrong to capitalize on misery'. In September, Gelda's suggestion that Oktyabrina visit me was declined; Oktyabrina was already deep in her rejection of men. But Gelda felt that Oktyabrina's real reason was fear of appearing disloyal to her.

The relationship between Gelda and Oktyabrina was not as one-sided as it had seemed at first. When Gelda was suffering a 'fit', she released the whole of her brutal resentment on Oktyabrina. Her insults and curses were restrained only by instincts developed during long years in communal apartments. She was merciless to Oktyabrina. Her curses were bad enough, but she also attacked Oktyabrina's weakest spot. She called her a leech, a toady, a sponger, a sycophant, a parasite and a slut.

'You're as much use in this world as shit in an ice-hole. You're not whore enough to earn your bread from men. Not *woman* enough to have a man. So you lick my ass— the dirtier the better. I'm sick of it, do you understand? Disappear from my life, you cheap phoney—you corkscrew cunt.'

Oktyabrina bore everything, knowing Gelda's need for catharsis. And indeed, this therapy worked better than Gelda's usual assortment of pills and compresses. Her fits lasted only a day or two, and when she emerged from them, she hugged Oktyabrina's hips and stroked her hair. The hair was as close in shape and color to Gelda's as Oktyabrina could make it, although the texture remained much finer despite the dye's effects. The sight of the dwarfish, pitted woman with the *papirosa* in her teeth embracing the radiant girl with the imitative costume was as moving—and disturbing—as the recognition scene in *Anastasia*.

'It's better now?' Oktyabrina would whisper.

'It's gone, Brinchka. You little idiot, why didn't you run away?'

'I'm *starved*, let's go somewhere glorious.'

'You must fly away somewhere: in this domain, angels come to no good.'

To celebrate, Gelda broke her usual diet in favor of a long heavy meal. They usually went to a restaurant called 'Slavonic Bazaar', which lies behind GUM in a region of important government offices. The Slavonic Bazaar used to be a 'cafeteria' for high-level Party officials, admitted only with passes. The food then was immeasurably better and cost much less than that of ordinary restaurants; caviar and steaks were always available, together with delicacies like fresh fruits and vegetables, even melon in January! Underground passages linked the restaurant with nearby office buildings—according to rumor, even with the Kremlin—so that the Party oligarchs could avoid the twin inconveniences of mixing with The People and suffering a short walk in the cold.

After the government cafeteria had moved to more elaborate quarters, and the Slavonic Bazaar was opened to the general public, its menu became as limited and expensive as any in the city—meaning very. But Gelda, both relieved and penitent after her fit, would merely short-change a few dozen customers on the afternoon of their fling, providing rubles to spare.

Since women are not permitted into restaurants alone, Gelda and Oktyabrina would approach the most likely-looking men in the line outside the door. For the consideration of a carafe of vodka to be ordered to their table inside, they induced the men to play the role of their escorts. Once at the table, however, the girls spoke a kind of pig Latin which Gelda had learned in order to keep things from her mother and passed on to Oktyabrina.

This caused the men great puzzlement. It compounded the earlier riddle about who these two odd women were and why they seemed suddenly unapproachable after the promise of a sure thing. Sensing that the strange language was meant to mock them, the men often progressed to anger. This, of course, added to Oktyabrina's delight—a delight which was produced by literally every element of the evening. She adored the restaurant, with its name and former reputation. She adored an evening out in general, and in particular one with Gelda. Most of all, she adored the thought of clear sailing ahead with Gelda, until the next fit. From time to time, Oktyabrina would glance disdainfully at the men sharing their table, sharpening her I'm-a-million-times-better-off-without-men look until even provincial types took the point. Speaking straight Russian again, in a sexy tenor, she'd advise the men to beg the cook for more dill, since 'dill works wonders for masculine aggressions'.

Yet Oktyabrina's campaign against *men* was in no way inspired or encouraged by Gelda. Gelda was occasionally amused, but usually tolerated or ignored it, certain that it was a passing phase. Moreover, she continued to keep her own eye peeled for men—with moustaches, of course. She was no more lesbian than the burly Russian men who

219

kiss on the lips at airports and railroad stations are homosexual, or the peasant soldier-boys who hold hands while strolling through the wonders of the big city. Oktyabrina did not live in Gelda's room; Gelda never asked her to, although a cot could have been squeezed beside the aquarium. Oktyabrina flitted from one rented cubicle to another, bargaining for a place to sleep when her 'contacts' informed her that someone had left Moscow on vacation or assignment.

Otherwise, Oktyabrina copied Gelda in every possible habit and gesture except for smoking, swearing and cracking her knuckles. And was almost totally dependent on her, financially as well as psychologically.

In return, Oktyabrina made the motions of cleaning Gelda's little room. This was not difficult after the 'Serbian smuggler' had removed most of the furnishings—and even before, since Gelda was as unfastidious in her domicile as her person. Oktyabrina washed Gelda's stockings and smalls together with her own. She kept the room in fresh flowers, bought at sacrificial greenhouse prices, and presented Gelda with occasional prizes, such as pairs of imported tights. And she took charge of procuring the fish food.

She took along a book for the lines at the pet shop, for she had embarked on a reading crusade, also in imitation of Gelda. It was usually one of Gelda's, for she wanted to read what 'her dear friend' did, and resented the idea of being spoon-fed 'easy' literature. But the crusade was not proving a success; she hardly read more than a chapter of any one book before starting the next. With all of this, she hadn't forgotten her fascination for back copies of my magazines. I gave her a large stack that had accumulated in her absence and she in return—because she always liked to give things in return—gave me an outsized *matrioshka*: a wooden doll with a series of successively smaller ones inside. This one had ten.

'Take this, Zhoseph,' she said, 'as a companion for your desk. And may the symbolism improve your writing through an appreciation—however subconscious—of the infinite humanity of *women*.' But this was accompanied by a wink instead of tartness.

On Sunday mornings Gelda and Oktyabrina went to the so-called 'pet market', one of the city's most colorful spectacles. 'Market' is somewhat misleading, for there is nothing organized about this one: pet-lovers simply gather in a large empty lot, and the Sunday crowd spills out into the adjoining streets, milling about the vendors. No permission, tax or even registration is required to sell pets, provided they are raised domestically and without an intention to 'profiteer'. It is a last outpost of capitalism and the old Russian tradition of street markets, where people come more than simply to buy and sell, but for the sake of something to do and for the satisfaction of bargaining. Most of the sellers are middle-aged men in ragged clothing. They cradle their wares—a pot-pourri of mongrel puppies, kittens, hamsters, tortoises, canaries, parrots, snakes, monkeys, rabbits and an occasional baby fox—tenderly in their hands or under their threadbare jackets, since cages and leashes, when available, are wildly expensive. And, of course, the market offers a wide assortment of tropical fish, usually displayed in pickle or yoghurt jars. Their popularity seems incongruous at first: tropical fish in such a northern country? But many Russians cherish them as they do tropical plants, no doubt for the same reason.

The market is located in a nondescript area of nineteenth-century houses and slapdash prefabricated blocks, which Gelda and Oktyabrina reached by metro and streetcar. Gelda was one of the best known and most respected of the market regulars, combining wide experience in handling tropical fish with extensive academic knowledge of pets in general. She was a kind of Queen-

of-the-Gypsies to the other regulars, mostly poor pensioners who peddled a fish or two from dawn to dusk in
quest both of company for their lonely lives and of a few
extra kopeks to buy jam for their bread. They treated
Gelda as if she were a young belle who could have her
pick of husbands, but was waiting for one of her own
standards.

Oktyabrina took to the market immediately. It was her
kind of place; she was enchanted by the buying, selling,
haggling and milling about. Gelda encouraged her to go
her own way, and she quickly learned the market's secrets. Soon she was swapping small items of clothing,
cautiously peddled by traders along with the pets. The
patrolling of the market by plain-clothesmen—who kept
watch for this, as well as for pickpockets and 'speculators'
buying and reselling other people's pets—predictably en-
hanced Oktyabrina's enjoyment of the atmosphere. She
told Gelda she sometimes wished that they could open
their own little business together on the lot. Perhaps an
antique booth or the tiniest tavern. Gelda could manage
the business and do the accounts, while Oktyabrina swept
up and waited on customers. . . .

After the market, Gelda and Oktyabrina sometimes
went to a nearby cathedral, entering towards the end of
the long Sunday afternoon service. The massive structure
had been scheduled for demolition in the anti-religious
fervor of the late 1930s, but war intervened, saving it
through the general confusion and shortage of dynamite.
Now it offered one of the most elaborate and moving
services of the handful of Moscow churches still functioning as such. Neither Gelda nor Oktyabrina was in
any way religious; their interest was in the choir's brooding, pagan-sounding melodies, the shadowy candlelight,
the incense and faintly ethereal, faintly sinister atmosphere transmitted by bearded priests and the ragged,
gnarled old faithful. Gelda lectured Oktyabrina in Rus-

sian history, including the role of the church as oppressors who were subsequently oppressed—the inevitability of darkness producing darkness.

The pet market hardly existed except for Saturdays and Sundays; no more than a dozen hard-core enthusiasts were there during the week. But when one of Gelda's fish died, Oktyabrina traveled there alone, and secretly, to replace it. This was an act of compassion on her part; she wanted to spare Gelda the sorrow of a loved one's death. And Gelda responded in kind by pretending not to notice the replacement.

## 21

□ The first day of genuine winter was like a national holiday. One morning the city was silent and white. It had a strangely incorporeal, almost sanctified quality, like the garments of a nun. In the long run, this signaled the beginning of five or six months of grinding cold—but no one thought of the long run that morning. The greyness, mud and slush were gone at last, and replaced by something shining and exalted, something even joyous. Russian winter had returned like your father after a fishing trip—someone you knew intimately, and from whom you expected much, even if he was stern. It was almost as exciting as the first day of spring. Even the old pensioners in black overcoats who'd seen it fifty or sixty times were moved.

It was the kind of day on which you telephone old friends. I called Kostya early in the morning; sure enough, he'd invented an excuse to skip work and was planning a day in the countryside with his 'roommate', a girl he'd met the evening before in a dry-cleaning outlet. He was brewing a large pot of potato-and-barley soup for the outing and promised me my own thermos if I came along.

'You heard about the new furniture GUM just put on sale?' he exclaimed. 'It's a long-awaited breakthrough in our consumer goods production: an all-pine triple bed. They call it "Lenin Is Always With You"—and it's selling like crazy.' He chuckled happily and I could almost hear his grin. 'I've got a hundred of them, Zhoe buddy— but not for the telephone. Leave your place now and you can join us in twenty minutes.'

I couldn't leave until mid-afternoon at the earliest: there were morning newspapers to look through and another disarmament story to write. I went back to work, tackling a series of *Pravda* articles inspired by the intensifying campaign against 'hooligans', then a long, tragi-comic 'exposé' of new muddles in the distribution of soap powder. One investigation had revealed that over forty per cent of the soap production destined for Kiev was lost or stolen en route to the store shelves. I felt a wave of *déjà-vu:* hadn't this very article been run somewhere last year?

An hour later, a thunderous knock resounded from the front door. When I opened it, a liter-sized thermos plopped inside. A note from Kostya was tied around the neck: a man of my age, he'd written, should make certain to have soup every day throughout the winter. Instructions followed for meeting him in the countryside outside a certain village, if I managed to free myself before dark: '. . . after that last cottage, take the second trail on the left to a small clearing with a clump of birches. . . . Go five paces further and look under the large fir on your right. You may see a rubber mattress. If it's mine, you'll recognize it. If we happen to be embracing on it, wait a few minutes discreetly in the clearing—my roommate's strangely shy. . . .'

The soup was a meal in itself. I was on my second cupful when Oktyabrina called to tell me about the 'sublimeness' of the weather and invite me to share it with her, just the two of us, in some beautiful place. Gelda was unavailable because a team of government inspectors had descended on the bookshop to audit the books—'probably on *purpose* to spoil the day'. However, the snow had returned the old buoyancy to her voice and she cooed the 'Zhoe darling' with silvery affection.

'Do let's go somewhere,' she said. 'If you're not working too hard, of course.'

'I can't accept invitations from you—unless I set the conditions. I'm a dominating male, after all.' I said she'd have to discard her canvas rag and let me buy her an overcoat.

'You'll probably make me get something outrageously *ladylike*. Zhoe darling, I know your clever little stratagems. . . .'

Eventually, she allowed me to buy her a three-quarter length sheepskin at the hard-currency shop. It was surely the best and warmest coat she'd had: severe enough to let her pretend she cared nothing for style, yet stylish enough by Moscow standards to be stared at. After this we agreed on an afternoon walk in the Botanical Gardens, a favorite of our exploring-Moscow days. Driving there, Oktyabrina chattered happily about the novel she'd just started. She always knew, she confided, within the *first five pages* whether a writer was on her wavelength.

'For example, *you*, Zhoseph. I genuinely think you'd move me deeply if only you'd take up fiction. Because you're straightforward—kind of modern. Not full of melodramatic plot.'

The scenery silenced us. All the city's peeling paint and blemishes were concealed by white fluff, and the cupolas of a dozen churches cast an enchanting spell. Not only the churches, but also the iron fences of the grand old mansions—even, somehow, the sagging wooden cottages and old trolley wires.

The gardens were almost too pretty. Snow fell so fast that flakes stuck together before hitting the ground, like typewriter keys punched too quickly. Each tree was a picture postcard. The air smelled of fresh snow and of something organic, as if the autumn apples hadn't been harvested. Oktyabrina was so moved by the wintry glory that an hour passed without a call of nature. When the need did assert itself she walked ahead with no fuss at all and relieved herself in the fresh snow behind a clump of trees. Despite everything—I thought—she'd matured considerably in the year or so I'd known her.

When our faces were tingling we started back. Oktyabrina took my arm and snuggled up to me.

'Zhoe darling, doesn't this beauty make you feel terribly insignificant?'

'I'm not sure. Small and great at the same time.'

'That's it *exactly*—a writer understands. It makes you feel at peace with yourself because it puts things in *proportion*. How I hope my period of being silly has passed.'

She shook the snow out of my hat with her mitten.

'How's your embassy lady working out?' she asked.

'Not as well as I'd hoped. It's a kind of dead end at the moment.'

'I'm sorry, Zhoe darling. Really I am. . . . Funny—you never took me to meet her. Are you aware of that?'

'Would you like to now?'

'I'm not sure. I was simply *dying* to when your romance was at its most torrid. On the other hand, I was also secretly glad. . . . Because all this time, I never told *you* something rather important.'

'What's that?'

'It's why I didn't come to see you all that time in the autumn. You see, it had nothing to do with Gelda, really. The real reason is I'd heard about your sweetheart and didn't want to interfere.'

'You'd heard about what?' For a second, I imagined she was genuinely jealous, and my thoughts raced. But Oktyabrina reacted to my question as if to a challenge.

'You're right to doubt me,' she asserted. 'Why camouflage life's dilemmas? Your love affair was a pretext.

227

The *real real* reason concerned you and me—*only* you and me.'

She waited for my prodding. 'You're hinting that I somehow let you down before the summer vacation,' I said.

'Don't be a sentimental goose,' she said tenderly. 'I simply felt it would be . . . well, somehow *wrong* to go on seeing you after our farewell ceremony. Perhaps my decision was influenced by autumn itself. Because there's a time for everything in life: "Every season brings its own friends, like its own fruits"—do you understand?'

'Not exactly. I think we might have braved the fall together. It was fairly cold when we met, if I remember.'

'Zhoe darling, don't be so dense, this isn't easy for me. What I mean is, I thought our friendship had seen its summer. Certain emotions can't be relived. If you try to go back all you achieve is something dismally *artificial.*'

'But what about going forward? I was very fond of you, you know.'

'Going forward to *what?*—you were so distant, you gave me so little hope. . . . Besides, you've missed my main point. Which is that I'd changed *utterly* by the end of the summer. I simply wasn't the spoiled brat you once cared for.'

She gulped audibly. 'To come directly to the point. I feared you'd be bored with me after I'd shed all my . . . well, affectations. I couldn't bear the thought of you slowly drawing away from me. And not saying anything just to spare my feelings.'

'Silly little Brincka. I think you're serious.' I said this jocularly, but the lump in my throat reappeared. I felt it would not be long before we did go forward at last.

'I *was* silly, wasn't I, Zhoe? I mean, it turns out that we can still be friends. People don't have to thrill other people every minute of the day and night, as long as they're

228

fond of each other. We can be even firmer friends now—genuine friends.'

When we hugged each other, Oktyabrina's handbag fell deep into the fluffy snow and we both laughed. For some reason, it struck me that this was going to be a very long winter.

A few minutes later, we came to a greenhouse and this time I excused myself to go to the toilet. When I stepped outside again, it was to a scene that somehow reminded me of high-school days: Oktyabrina was engaged in a snowball fight with a young man. Her missiles fell apart in the air, his went wide—perhaps not purposely, from the look of his throwing arm. I felt like a father watching his daughter on a date. A fragment of her snowball nicked the tail of his overcoat, and she squealed in triumph.

I tossed my own snowball between them. 'Oh Zhoe darling,' called Oktyabrina. 'I want you to meet someone. Vladimir will be getting another degree very soon, *postgraduate.*'

The young man smiled nervously and hurried towards me, adjusting his hat. 'I'm extremely pleased to make your acquaintance,' he said shyly. 'All joking aside, I never meet girls this way—your friend fell, she needed help.'

He adjusted his hat again. 'Anyway, I was just leaving. Between you and I, I shouldn't be here now at all.'

When we had dropped Vladimir off at a nearby school, Oktyabrina sighed deeply. 'Do you think Gelda will be hurt?' she ventured. 'I'd hate to cause her anguish.'

'I'm sure Gelda will be delighted.'

'I'm not so sure. *And you?*'

'He seems a tolerable choice—now that you've shed your affectations.'

229

'Zhoe darling, you *are* a sweetheart. I do so want another chance. With someone suitable at last.'

Soon she began to hum: a Soviet ballad with a line about 'finding my beloved in twilight on a background of our Motherland's white'.

To my surprise, Gelda was upset. Vladimir's frequent presence—with Oktyabrina—in the bookshop made her feel cramped, she said; Vladimir was always *watching* her. And he was a teacher, whom she scorned 'as a class'. Besides, I think she was jealous of losing so much of Oktybrina's veneration, especially to 'a classroom creep'. The very sight of him got on her nerves.

This said more about Gelda than Vladimir, since nothing in his appearance could be offensive to anyone. He was a tallish young man with large feet and heavy rubber galoshes. His face was milky and slightly slack—distinctly intellectual except for a bulbous peasant 'potato nose'. His lapel sported a large 'Lenin-Is-More-Alive-Than-The-Living' badge; not necessarily a clue to personality, since many people wear them simply for decoration in the shortage of other costume jewellery.

He also wore an imitation karakul hat with the ear flaps down and string tied beneath the chin. The hat showed great signs of wear at the crown and was apparently a permanent fixture from September to May. This was because Vladimir was 'five minutes short', as the Russians say, of being completely bald, and his mother would not let him leave the house with an uncovered head. In short, he looked like a typical young member of the 'working intelligentsia': one of the tens of thousands who study all day in overcrowded reading rooms, wearing winter pallors and shiny trousers.

Vladimir sat all day not in a library, but at the teacher's desk of the geography room of School Number 628. On Sundays, he was a volunteer custodian in the Museum

230

of V. I. Lenin's Funeral Train at Paveletsky Station. In addition, he was working towards a graduate degree with a disertation provisionally entitled, 'The Exploration and Development of Natural Resources in Kamensk Province During the Period of the First Five-Year Plan, 1928-1933'. Kamensk Province borders the Ukraine. With funds from his mother—and, at first, her attendance—Vladimir had made several journeys there to interview local geographers. They were his life's adventure—until he met Oktyabrina.

Otherwise, his circumstances were typical of the Soviet professional class. He shared a flat with his mother, traveled to and from work by metro, and subscribed to *Soviet Geographer, Teacher of the Motherland's Schools,* and *Socialist Geography.* For sport, he concentrated on chess, in which he'd worked his way up in the hierarchy of these things to Chess Player Second Class. He instructed Oktyabrina for hours at a time. Since she hadn't known the game before—the name 'pawn' annoyed her at first, just as the knights intrigued her—it was probably their only activity in which the roles of teacher and pupil were clearly defined.

Oktyabrina and Vladimir saw each other almost every evening. At first, Gelda and I were dutifully informed of their plans, which usually featured the movies. On the evenings when Vladimir worked on his dissertation, Oktyabrina occasionally joined me. She was thoughtful and composed, in keeping with her position as the 'life companion' of an upstanding young man.

'He says I'm like a little fawn,' she said one evening over an ice cream. 'Always running, running, running—a frightened fawn in the faraway forest. But he's the gamekeeper. He's caught me once and for all, and now he's going to tame me.'

But if Oktyabrina's patter about Vladimir smacked of

231

the old hyperbole, other elements in her attitude towards him were new. For one thing, rather than resenting his research—lacking a pass, she could not join him in the library—she encouraged him wholeheartedly. She recognized the dissertation's importance not only as such, but for its enhancement of Vladimir's self-esteem.

'Every young man must prove himself in some desperate duel with his own will', she confided. 'It's rather like St George slaying his dragon—only harder in a way because modern challenges are in offices and less dramatic. . . . When Vladimir conquers the dissertation, he'll be a *man's* man. The least I can do is help.'

There was much to help with. Vladimir suffered the self-doubts of any shy, conscientious young man, plus several added burdens incurred by his position and his means of obtaining it. The headmistress of his school was an old chum of his mother from their days of volunteer social work in the 1930s. In fact, it was she who'd found Vladimir his job after graduation, as a favor to Mama: in her school, Vladimir would find support as a novice teacher. And indeed, the headmistress spent a few minutes in Vladimir's classroom most mornings, before the opening bell. She helped him wipe the woodwork with a wet rag. . . .

Oktyabrina recounted this with surprising candor. 'You're aghast at the lack of heroics, aren't you, Zhoe? Because I'm needed by Vladimir the *man*, not the symbol. His tiniest problems are mankind's greatest for me: that's the joy of being a *mature woman*.'

As a dedicated Young Communist, Vladimir took the organization's precepts seriously, especially those establishing the duty of teachers in instilling Communist moral principles. He sometimes wished he could ignore the responsibility, but everything in his background made him fight for right.

Thus, even if some teachers snickered at meetings of

232

the Pedagogical Council and Young Communist Committee, he knew his duty was to expose boys who smoked in the lavatory and sneaked wine into political instruction sessions. Punishing the boys wasn't the answer, but the problems had to be discussed. The headmistress deserved support. Vladimir's friends sometimes tried to catch his eye to suggest he sit down and relax. They knew that his vulnerability in class was as much the fault of his own zeal as the teenagers' cynicism. To some extent Vladimir himself recognized this, and promised himself before each meeting to be realistic. But rebellion in the classroom—spitballs and wisecracks—corrupted the children themselves, and the social fabric. . . .

'It's a genuine problem at last,' said Oktyabrina. 'How can I help?'

Vladimir's party waited for an evening when his mother was away at a conference, leaving their apartment free. It was the standard studio type in one of the new prefabricated developments. Vladimir slept in the kitchen; his mother on a convertible sofa in the living-room, which was crammed with mass-produced bric-a-brac and reproductions of cottage landscapes. A glazed bust of a pinkish Lenin on one of the sideboards told its own story amidst the collection of clay elephants. The furniture was protected by maroon slipcovers, a color that gives you a quick headache in remembrance of childhood Sundays visiting relatives.

Everything in the apartment spoke of a sizeable income, even by the intelligentsia's standards. Vladimir's mother, a senior inspector of schools, obviously poured most of her salary into furnishings. Her husband had left her when Vladimir was eight, and his name was not mentioned in the apartment.

Vladimir had invited a former classmate and his girl friend along with Gelda and me. He served a sweet wine and sliced bologna and cheese, both of which were sweating greasily when we arrived. The girl friend spilled her first glass of wine over her metallic party dress and suffered thereafter in tongue-tied embarrassment. Her boy friend, Vladimir's classmate, could not tear himself from the television set. The noise of the set and banality of the program hardly contributed to a party atmosphere.

Oktyabrina tried to play hostess, but it was her first time in the apartment too, and Vladimir was on tenterhooks lest she break something. She found herself sunk in one of the overstuffed armchairs, trying to interest Gelda in the small talk of evening entertaining. Gelda's irritation put an edge on the general pall. I yearned for a bourbon, or vodka. The wine was impossible.

At one point, I had a few words with Vladimir alone—what he called a 'man-to-man talk over a glass of good vintage'. 'All joking aside,' he said, 'I don't know wines very well but I prefer red to white. On graduation night from my Institute I got so sick on white that I had to sleep at a friend's. Mama wrote *his* mother a very strong letter about bad influences on me—I had to deliver it to her myself. Between you and me, I think white's got some kind of acid in it.'

Vladimir told me that despite his mother's severity on certain days, she was full of charity on others. He loved her for her honesty and devotion to him; they read plays together after supper. And oddly, their roles were reversing. Now a lonely lady, Mama needed the release of bossing him more than he was distressed by her strictures.

He refilled my glass, obviously eager to talk. Yes, life was proceeding according to plan, he said. But in spite of everything, he somehow felt *trapped*.

'I do all the right things. Volunteer work with the Pio-

234

neers, and I have a medal for helping at the Museum. But somehow everything seems so dull for me. Sometimes I daydream of throwing up everything and going north. To be an explorer or something . . . free and on my own.'

It was now clear that Vladimir was what he seemed, an exceedingly tedious young man—'as boring as an English Sunday', in the words of a beloved Russian poet. He reminded me of everything I like to forget about my own youth: anxiety, excessive intensity, sweaty concern about making a bad impression or going unnoticed. What could Oktyabrina see in him? I wondered. Where was the heroism—even the charm? As if he'd read my thoughts, the answer followed. 'I don't know why I'm telling you this, but you were her best friend. My Oktyabrina's made the whole difference in my life. It's a miracle, how I met her. But she's so free about everything—what if she leaves? . . .'

Vladimir noticed that his other guests needed attention. He suggested chess, but only his classmate responded. Then he played several records from his collection; current Soviet ballads as exciting as his mother's furniture. Oktyabrina had given him a recording of the song about finding one's beloved 'on a background of our Motherland's white'.

Vladimir asked Gelda to dance, but she merely picked up a book. Gelda left almost immediately after this. She had to have *air*, she said. Panic flickered in Oktyabrina's eyes as Gelda clumped down the stairs and she, Oktyabrina, remained at Vladimir's side.

Suddenly I too needed air. What really disturbed me in Vladimir was the crucial difference between us: watching him fumbling with Oktyabrina, I realized that he had the sense to embrace something good, instead of pushing it stagily away, as was my tender habit with every girl who showed interest in me. Vladimir was manifestly too young for Oktyabrina: wrapped up in his own anxieties, he failed even to notice her ravenous appetite. But it was humiliating to find myself making comparisons about who was more generous to a girl of Oktyabrina's age.

It was after midnight when I got home. I looked at the empty davenport and realized what a fool I'd been to send Oktyabrina home at night when she'd lived with me in the spring. Suddenly I knew that she was sleeping with Vladimir. I telephoned my embassy friend. Irritated by the hour, she refused my suggestion of a nightcap. Life was as empty as it had ever been. I went for a walk, wondering what force in life had delivered me to where I was, the ancient streets of comatose Moscow, empty except for rugged snow-clearing crews.

# 22

☐ Oktyabrina appeared at the apartment early the next morning. With a wry smile, she handed me a packet of aspirin. She took two herself with a large glass of tea.

Then she made her first casual mention of getting a job. By the end of the morning, she was talking about little else. It was not, she assured me, that Vladimir was pressing her. Still, she wouldn't deny that her enlightenment had come through his example. *He* worked and was a far better man for it. And although he treated her like a princess, she couldn't help feeling somehow . . . *lowly* next to him. While he toiled nobly all day, she queued for worms.

'In all honesty,' she declared in her all-honesty voice, 'I won't be comfortable at his side until I'm a person who earns his deep respect. I can't expect to live my life *through* him, sort of begging and borrowing from the dignity he's achieved for himself. I certainly can't expect to be presented to his mother. . . .'

By the next day, she was spouting what Russians call 'newspaper talk'. Where she'd learned it was a small mystery, for she never read a newspaper; her attitude towards journalism had been made clear. Still, her message was the State's message: she must become a *useful member of society*. And the key to this, as the Moral Code of the Builder of Communism ordained, as the Bolshevik ethic had posited for fifty odd years, was honest labor.

'In our socialist land, one must give his labor to society, then society will take care of the rest. It's the only way to be genuinely happy. I see that now. A person not only becomes depraved but frightfully alienated, actually *lost*, when he . . . oh for goodness sake, Zhoseph. Explaining something ethical to you is like asking a cow not to mess the stalls. Stop smirking.'

'Stop smirking yourself. I've always been dead serious about work—welcome to the sufferers' circle.'

'Shall I continue? This is important to more than me.'

'You don't know how right you are.'

'Where was I? . . . A person becomes not only depraved but frightfully alienated, actually *lost*, unless he's solidly rooted in honest toil. There's still time for me to cast off my old, corrupted ways and find a shining purpose in life. . . . I've discussed the whole problem with Vladik.'

Not merely discussed it, but explored his underlying convictions. That's why she *knew* her decision was right: it was grounded in Vladimir's own principles.

'He told me a person's past isn't crucial,' she declared. 'I come from the former exploiting classes, so my present personality may still harbor some frivolous strains. But social origin can always be mastered by application of *will*. Look at Dzershinsky. At Lenin himself. My vital task now is simply to fall in step with the working class. Then my lineage can't deflect me. . . .'

Whatever advice he actually gave, Vladimir himself was powerless to make Oktyabrina a working woman. She still lacked a labor book and all prerequisite documents. Anyone with reasonable contacts and roughly two hundred rubles could have fixed this easily enough—but Vladimir was hardly the man to negotiate a bribe.

As Oktyabrina's impatience swelled, Gelda realized

238

that she alone could provide the longed-for job. With considerable misgiving, she arranged for the bookshop to hire Oktyabrina. She was to work the regular salesgirls' week but be paid from the manager's fund, a small account achieved from profits, so that her name need not appear on the books. Gelda's sole *quid pro quo* was that Oktyabrina attempt no innovation in the shop's routine. Flushed with enthusiasm over her 'new position', Oktyabrina had considered leading the sales force in morning callisthenics, to the radio's daily ration of music for this purpose.

She began work on a Monday, having asked me not to visit her for the first week. 'Even the largest udders won't fill the pail in a new barn,' she explained. She made the motions of running her hand through her hair, but there was little to grasp. It had been cut short and bleached to look as close as possible to her natural dirty blonde. This was part of her new Proletarian Look, which also featured a secondhand overcoat and frayed 'salesgirl's' sweater. The effect of this costume, shared by literally millions of Moscow women, was ambiguous. It was conventional enough to let her pass unnoticed in a crowd. But the conventionality was so pointed—and her eyes so big and shining—that the first impression was of impersonation: the old Oktyabrina. The final touch was a kerchief with the Kremlin emblazoned in crimson and gold.

On the Saturday evening after Week One, Oktyabrina and Vladimir visited me in the apartment, on their way to a movie. Oktyabrina said she'd rather not talk about work, but about Vladimir, who was responsible for her first genuine contribution to the first socialist state in the world.

'Vladik has helped me shape my *personal* will to History's,' she said. 'By putting me in step with our society—

239

meaning in step with mankind's march to a far better world.' But her week behind the counter left her too exhausted to continue.

When she went to the bathroom, I persuaded Vladimir to remove his hat and try his first sip of bourbon. 'All joking aside,' he said, 'she's working too hard, and I don't understand why. I wish *I* could get exhausted for *her*.'

Vladimir told me that Oktyabrina insisted on paying him a kind of tithe of a quarter of her wages—to represent the taxes, union dues and Young Communist League contributions paid by official employees of the shop. Oktyabrina didn't want to give Vladimir the idea that she was working for mere material compensation. *Sacrifice* was necessary . . . 'and besides, she said a little more money in *my* pocket might help me with Mama.'

Vladimir shrugged his shoulders and manfully tried the bourbon again.

The following Monday, I went to see Oktyabrina at work. She had transmitted her final requests by telephone.

'Look to your heart's content, Zhoseph—but *please* do not talk. Don't even show me your dear face unless absolutely necessary. Distraction fills me with dread when I'm toiling.'

I walked to the bookshop after lunch. According to the exacting regulations for the protection of State property, the old door was festooned with iron padlocks and rusted bolts—although only a desperate burglar could have looked twice at these premises. Several bookshops in neighboring districts were closed again for inventory or repairs, making Number 44 more crowded than usual. Someone had dropped a jar of marinated mushrooms on the floor and the shopping herd obliviously wallowed through, spreading the slime with their boots. It was so slippery that two old ladies grasped each other for fear of falling and begged for help.

Gelda looked up from her abacus and nodded towards the rear of the store. Oktyabrina's black rayon smock—the uniform of Soviet salesgirls—blended with the darkness, obscuring her momentarily. She was in continual, fluttering motion, causing her glasses, which I hadn't seen since spring, to keep sliding down her nose.

The usual crowd was pressed up against her counter. Everyone in it seemed amused except a large man in the center. By contrast, he was choking with spleen.

'I said *Mussolini*,' he snorted. 'Mus-so-li-ni. Want to hear it *again?*'

'It's not necessary, Citizen,' replied Oktyabrina ingratiatingly. 'I'm not sure we have any volumes on *that* particular subject. Is it something those people eat?'

'It is a *man*,' he bellowed. 'The *leader* of Fascist Italy. I want a *biography* of him. Bi-o-gra-phy.'

'Of course, Citizen. I'll be delighted to fill your order instantly. We keep a list of every book. . . .'

'I *know* you keep a list,' the man broke in. 'For God's sake, look at it.'

Oktyabrina whirled as if she'd just misplaced something and was trying frantically to remember where. Then she made her hallelujah gesture and dashed to the master catalogue at an adjoining counter. The deep bite of her lip brought no help to her nervous fingers as she tried to flip through the cards. The thumb-worn cards seemed both unintelligible and impossibly sticky. Long minutes passed in the examination of a single tray, and after she'd advanced to a second one, Oktyabrina suddenly returned to the first.

At last she went radiant. 'We'll be delighted to satisfy your quite proper request,' she shouted, waving a card triumphantly. 'With patience and hard work. . . . I'm certain you remember the old saying, Comrade.'

241

His appeasement was brief. Oktyabrina now struggled to navigate the ladder through narrow, book-strewn aisles. This was a tiring operation, but amusing exercise compared with the ensuing ordeal of climbing. With a safe ladder, Oktyabrina might have been calmer; this one was as old as anything in the shop.

Each step higher required an act of will. Oktyabrina clutched the rungs like lifelines and tried not to look at the dusty floor below. Each time she did, an interval for recovery was needed. Her handbag dangled from her wrist, adding to her confusion about where to put what. The crowd at the counter grew tense.

Chance had placed the wanted book on the next-to-top shelf. Oktyabrina recognized the title and planned the move to net it, like someone confronted with a leap promising safety or death. Calculations of timing and balance registered on her face, together with deep sighs of do-it-*now* resolution. But they all came to nothing: she could not force her hand to leave the ladder and reach for the book. Her attempts were successively more feeble, sapping her courage not only to make the next one, but simply to remain on the ladder.

Real danger—of panic and played-out limbs—now faced her. But when she began to wobble, Gelda locked her drawer, climbed from her stool and drove ruthlessly through the crowd. She coaxed Oktyabrina down the ladder and into her arms.

Gelda herself then mounted the ladder and fetched the book, moving quickly despite her physique. 'Who requested this volume?' she asked joylessly. The fat man snatched it without answering—and roared again.

'I said Mussolini,' he thundered. 'Not Muscovy—*Mus-so-li-ni*. You people are idiots. I'm going to write a complaint.'

Gelda had returned to Oktyabrina's side; each had an

arm around the other's waist, and Oktyabrina was restraining tears. They were evidently waiting for the man's rage to spend itself, but he got a powerful second wind.

'The skinny one's a menace,' he shouted to the crowd. '*Non compos mentis*—or *corporis*. And the black dwarf encourages her—it's an outrage. I'll get them both.'

Suddenly Gelda exploded in Oktyabrina's defense. Since there was in fact no reasonable defense, she substituted a searing attack. I would have said she could not possibly have bested the man, had I not known about her fits. A voice in the crowd offered money on Gelda.

In short—for the struggle was brief and one-sided—Gelda's diatribe left the man stunned. He retreated awkwardly towards the door, where the two stranded ladies clutched at his overcoat. Gelda led Oktyabrina into a back room, ignoring the line at her booth, which had lengthened to some twenty people. One or two of them muttered mild curses, but the majority waited blankly until some higher force might intervene and provide them with service. This did not materialize during the ten minutes or so I remained in the shop.

A second week passed during which the job seemed a too-protracted joke. Oktyabrina confused Switzerland with Sweden, Romania with Bulgaria, Iran and Iraq. If these mistakes were explicable, others testified to massive gaps in her knowledge: what is the link between 'Moslem' and 'mongol'? Marshal Zhukov was mistaken for Andrei Zhdanov, Stalin's feared cultural overseer; and her failure to know Molotov caused another minor incident. Because Molotov has been an 'unperson' for ten years, a man whispered his name. Oktyabrina sang it out in her 'working soprano' to the hoots of half the crowd and growls of the other half.

She herself did not laugh—she seemed to have lost both the ability and desire. For her job was not a joke; it had become the crusade of her life.

She had more to overcome than the ordinary strains of a new job. They were aggravated by the pressure of the ubiquitous, clamorous throng, elbowing each other and screeching at her. Bred on the hard lessons of perpetual shortage, Russians break into an acquisitive fever as they cross the threshold of even a relatively peaceful store. Salesgirls at the front of the battle quickly become hardened or change their métier.

Finally there was the difficulty of mastering the 'stock'. Books are a serious matter in this country, and the secondhand shops are patronized by extremely serious people. Many make daily rounds of the dozen odd shops in central Moscow, hunting with heroic resolution for an old Proust that's been out of print for thirty years or a James Joyce in a Western language, one of possibly five copies in all Moscow because the novel isn't 'Soviet' enough to have merited publication here. In other words, Oktyabrina had to cope with the most dedicated and knowledgeable corps of customers among Moscow's hardened millions.

But she did cope; it *was* a triumph of will. And of brain—and, in a matter of speaking, brawn. For she prevailed only by enduring extreme drudgery and exhaustion. Mornings, she was in the shop with the cleaning women, an hour before opening time; evenings, she remained an hour after closing time, sorting, dusting and contemplating the titles of books. 'A feeble brain gives no rest to the feet,' she said, eager to reduce her flutterings behind the counter. She copied whole trays from the master catalogue on slips of paper—authors on one side, titles on the other—and studied them, like a student learning Chinese. She read literary encyclopaedias and pestered Gelda for lists of important authors, schools, periods and fields of learning. 'Memorize, memorize, memorize,' she chanted. 'A maiden's memory is like a cuckoo's—and it's time I stopped being both. . . .'

But most of all, she learned by sheer concentration during her long hours in the shop. All her inventiveness and tenacity surged into the fight to fend off exhaustion and to *remember*. Had it come five years earlier, this drive alone might have made her an acceptable ballerina.

To speak of a salesgirl being respected in Moscow is misleading. But by the end of the month, Oktyabrina had a following. She recognized more and more steady customers and more and more authors, and began putting aside the volumes they'd requested. People liked her; she worked quickly; sales increased. Even the manager was pleased—and since the shop's sales plan was being over-fulfilled, closed his eyes to Oktyabrina's occasional filching of a geography book for Vladimir's dissertation.

In time the long stints exhausted her less. Although she didn't quite believe it herself, she'd survived the test and become a working woman. She was making a 'real contribution' at last. But she'd grown thinner, paler and markedly more subdued.

In fact, she looked wasted. The Proletarian Look was no longer a costume: like so many of the working class, she was run down from too much work on too few vitamins, and had a nagging cold. It was now clear that by themselves, her features were entirely plain; it had been her dramatization of them, however outlandish, that had made her a personage—almost lifted her on to a higher plane. Unretouched, in the dull light of day, the peaked nose and thin mouth made her a provincial working girl, with the pinched look of English mill towns, despite the Slav accents of her cheeks. I never loved her more.

Oktyabrina had changed so much that when she came

to lunch one Sunday, the sentry in my courtyard didn't recognize her, and left his booth for a better look. I'd prepared a big meal of her favorite treats, but she ate without appetite. And praised Vladimir without enthusiasm, as if disgusted with her own talk of his 'shaping her destiny' with his 'tuitional wisdom'.

Suddenly she pushed away her plate. 'What's the point of this nonsense,' she whispered. 'Why am I lying to *you?*'

'What's actually happening with you two?'

'He keeps begging me to remember our beginning—to play chess with him like we used to. How can I tell him? What can I *do?*'

'What do you want to do?'

'First to tell you the facts of life. A salesgirl makes seventy-six rubles a month—a pair of shoes and two pairs of stockings. Vladimir makes two pairs of shoes. But it's not the miserable scrounging that's important.'

I waited for what was important. Of course, she said finally, she hadn't expected anything *uplifting* from a bookshop, anything heroic from Vladimir. But both had turned out to be so excruciatingly, hopelessly *dreary*.

'Last week I finally realized that I must make him suffer to become a man. To sacrifice something for his passion. Then I saw how silly that was. Because it's vice-versa, you see: only real *men* ever suffer over real things. Anyway, dear Zhoseph, I can't bear hurting him—so this is my last resort.'

She unfolded a sheet of paper from her handbag and handed it to me. It was so carefully printed that I hardly recognized her hand.

Dear Vladimir's Mother,

A million pardons for addressing you thus, but I don't even know your name. Vladimir always calls you 'Mama'. My ignorance of your name is natural enough. But your not knowing my name is—I must say it—unhealthy. Not knowing even that I exist, that Vladik has had a female companion. How can I persuade you that *I'm* not hurt by this; the damage is to *him.*

Having lost my own mother—also a noble woman who died for her profession—I understand and respect his devotion to you. And you must surely be proud of him, who has perhaps the highest human virtue: never wanting to hurt anyone. I know that no outsider can advise two people about their own relationship. But, respected Lady, Vladimir needs to breathe. You must cut the apron strings. Boys of his age have a need to run a bit wild, even involve themselves occasionally in—well, silly pleasures. And not-so-silly pleasures, although I am far from wanting to offend you. Vladimir is a sensitive person, and should spend more time with men to feel himself a man. And shouldn't he be allowed to lock the bathroom door without explanations?

I'd intended to write to you at respectable length, but these matters do not really befit a letter. If you accept the tone of my communication and my good will, please telephone me at my place of work. [Here followed the bookshop's telephone number.] I will tell you some things that I can't even mention to Vladik himself.

You might be relieved to know that I'll speak with total objectivity because I have no 'designs' on Vladimir. And that I'll deeply sympathize with your position: that of a woman who has sacrificed for her country and her son—for mankind in a very real way—and wants to embrace what she has achieved. Of all life's tragic trials, none demands more courage than watching one's child step forward on his separate rocky road. Perhaps I can help.

With great respect, with genuine feelings,

Oktyabrina Vladimirovna Matveyeva.

'What . . . do you . . . think?' she stammered. She was blowing her stuffed nose; I was letting my grin go at what was new in her, and what would never change.

'What is your professional *opinion*, vox populi Americanas? To save you embarrassment, my epistle wasn't penned as a joke.'

'I think it's very serious. Very beautiful.'

'And won't change anything. But I might know more about change than you think. . . . Give me an impressive envelope, please. I feel better already.'

She looked better too, and her appetite materialized. After the meal, she went to the mirror and laughed at her costume: the salesgirl's sweater was now positively ratty, but she'd rejected a subsidy from Gelda and couldn't afford even a good scarf on her salary.

'Don't think I'm in pain from this sacrifice,' she said. 'Vladimir's like you in a way—he never beats his women.'

'Or takes them to supper? Listen: if you come to supper with me, I'll buy you a fantastic new dress.'

'*Yes!*' She ran to the mirror again to stroke an imaginary gown. 'Let's be happy again, Zhoe.' Then her face fell. 'Don't be hurt, dearest: our revel must be postponed. I've come this far, you see—now I'm *obligated* to wait. For a reply to the epistle, I mean. Or maybe the young man himself will make some attempt. . . .'

Later, we walked down Petrovka to where she would mail her letter and catch a bus. It was snowing again and the wind burned our faces. The pole with the bus-stop sign also displayed a poster announcing the usual Saturday evening political lecture in a local club. 'SOVIET

248

FOREIGN POLICY IN THE LIGHT OF THE DE-
CISIONS OF THE SEPTEMBER PLENUM OF THE
CENTRAL COMMITTEE OF THE COMMUNIST
PARTY OF THE SOVIET UNION'.

I stepped round the corner to look for Oktyabrina's
bus. When I returned, she'd crayoned a simpler message
on the poster: 'Brinchka loved Vladik? *Guess!*' She
frowned at her handiwork and vigorously blacked it out,
leaving a crayoned rectangle in the shape of a coffin.

Oktyabrina flung the crayon across the street. 'Between you and I,' she said solemnly, 'my doodles were
in bad taste. Think of Vladimir's distaste for exposing our
intimate emotions on *that* kind of poster. . . . That's
what I admire most about him, actually. He's the most
superbly creative young man in keeping everything in its
proper place.'

Vladimir's mother did not respond. From Vladimir himself there was a telephone call during which he was so
upset that Oktyabrina had trouble understanding him.
He called from a telephone booth—not for the reasons
foreigners do, but in case his mother came home early.

What disoriented him most was not the loss of Oktyabrina but of a *girl*—any girl, the comfort of having one.
Finally Oktyabrina calmed him with a promise that
they'd be friends for ever and that he'd have a fine girl in
a year or two—he was only now entering the period of
his most powerful attractiveness to deserving women.
She splurged a week's wages to send him a lacy plant,
suitable for his mother. Then she called me to arrange
our 'revel'.

When Kostya heard our news, he insisted that he was
due at the opera that evening—'the premiere of something new called "Red Star over White Moon" '—and
that we use his room. He canceled all appointments with
his lassies, decorated the room with a handsome little

249

spruce tree festooned with birthday candles—he called it a 'Maypole manquè'—and left two bottles of champagne between his windows, together with a whole side of smoked salmon, procured from the director of a warehouse for export foods. We ate the tangy fish with fresh black bread.

'There are tons of fish in the sea, you can't catch them all,' said Oktyabrina. 'Who needs a saying to explain that? If you're happy, you love what you have.' She winked and handed me a fat sandwich.

It was one of the rare evenings devoted to gaiety that surpass their promise. Kostya's blowzy room was transformed by the candlelight. Oktyabrina wore a gypsy-like dress with a long skirt and puffed sleeves, and laughed happily when I asked when she'd found time to make it.

"But *I* didn't sew a stitch. A fairy godmother waved her wand—*your* godmother, Zhoe, because she wanted me *refined*, for you.'

We drank the champagne from Kostya's souvenir ram's horn because my godmother had forgotten to transform Oktyabrina's old shoes into slippers. Oktyabrina proposed an affectionate toast to Kostya, praising him for leaving champagne instead of vodka and for his 'occasional inspired insights into human nature'.

When the subject of Vladimir came up, Oktyabrina was ardent but unmannered. 'That role simply wasn't *me*. And why do I require roles? What are we afraid of, Zhoe? Why can't I just be *myself?*'

She was asking in earnest. 'I think we're afraid that our real selves look foolish or feeble,' I said. 'I happen to know something about that. The paradox is that the fear often sires creativity—your kind.'

'But I'm not frightened with you, you know—I never have been. Because—well, it simply feels right. . . . Did you know I'm tendering my resignation from the bookstore soon? I want to do something suitable just for the *change.*'

We danced to the tape recorder in the two square feet of floor space. I remembered a line from a Chekhov story called 'Champagne': a middle-aged man reminiscing about himself recalls that 'at that time, I was young, strong, lusty, extravagant and stupid'. That story, or perhaps our own champagne, made me think, and when we sat down again, something remarkable happened: I was telling childhood stories that I'd forgotten myself. The humiliation of an uncle's prison record and of a long illness of my mother. These memories had been stifled for decades, first by shame, later because they sounded like apologies. Then I began to talk about my marriage. Oktyabrina reached for my hand.

'Don't stop, Zhoe. Somewhere inside me, I have the capacity to understand. Somewhere, somehow, I have the ability to love. Really *love*—I know I have. . . . But these things may take years. It may be a very, very long time before I flower into the woman you deserve. *Will you wait?*'

My throat constricted again. Perhaps she was playing —but I saw her lead and knew I would bungle it again.

'Dearest Oktyabrina, I'm more than twice your age and I feel it. When we turn on the lights, you may notice that I can pass for an antique.'

She blew out a candle. 'A mature man's worth a *hundred* saplings—it's one of my most antique sayings. Now answer the question.'

But I did not. I was trying to picture us together in another country—to make the decison of my life.

'How old are you, Zhoe? The gospel truth, if you please.'

'Forty-four.'

'Goodness *me*—why do you pretend one foot's in the grave? What's this role you cherish?'

251

Long minutes passed—a silence that could not be broken by a joke.

'Of course I'll wait,' I said. 'I'm used to waiting. I can stick to it until you flower into the kind of woman *you* deserve.'

This was evidently more than she'd bargained for. 'Phoo, you don't expect *me* to believe that,' she said in her old all-men-are-rascals voice. 'I happen to be aware that Americans have no patience for *anything. . . .*' Then she began to cry. The sounds were softer than her sobbing of our kiss-after-bath fiasco.

'What's the matter now?' I whispered. 'Please don't say I've hurt you again.'

'Haven't you ever seen tears of joy, you big brute? Why do all the beautiful things happen to *me?*'

Her hair tickled my face. 'You have a remarkably serious "happy" cry,' I said. Her sobs grew louder. I held her, wondering whether they were genuine.

'I don't deserve this happiness yet,' she blubbered. 'Why don't others have it too? . . . I want to warn you right now: I'm absurdly demanding. Any man of mine will have to be stunningly rich: I want him to support an orphanage. We'll start with the poor little girl from Evgeny Ignatievich's class. She's not an orphan, but hasn't a chance.'

Wax sputtered onto the spruce, filling the room with an unforgettable spell. I poured more champagne. We sipped it silently.

'As long as I'm making demands,' added Oktyabrina, 'you had better be gallant to Mishka, my teddy bear. Because he's exceedingly jealous—I shall *not* sleep without him.'

## 23

☐ Then Vladimir was taken ill. It was the sniffles at first, but he was apprehensive. With good cause: a heavy cold materialized and culminated in a nasty case of Asian 'flu—probably the vanguard of an epidemic that had been spreading, perversely, eastward from England.

Perhaps sensing that this was the time to prove his manhood to Oktyabrina, Vladimir foolishly attempted to treat himself. This resulted in his being sprinted to a hospital for Ministry of Education personnel. His mother made the arrangements. With some reluctance, Oktyabrina recognized an obligation to visit him.

'What an *untimely* tragedy,' she said, mocking herself. 'I must go to him.'

'I must go with you,' I answered—superfluously, for we were together most of the time now.

We drove out after a concerted shopping effort. Oktyabrina bought apples, lemons, jam, honey, canned compôte and a bottle of a strong pepper-vodka called *pertsovka*, a peasant remedy for colds. 'I feel almost middle-aged,' she hummed. 'Being an angel of mercy for a *former* suitor.'

The hospital lay in one of those Russian tracts whose roads, such as they are, seemed designed to confuse outsiders. This might actually have been their purpose, since the adjoining woods contained government dachas, where the public is manifestly unwanted. When we finally arrived, it was to a locked gate. The absence of a flock of relatives bearing food parcels meant it was obviously not a visiting day. A sign on the gate confirmed this, adding that 'unauthorized persons' were 'categorically forbidden to enter except during specified hours. This was enforced by a brick guardhouse and watchman inside who refused so much as to approach the petitioners' window. He waved us away and returned to a tin of fish, morsels of which he consumed from the tip of a penknife.

Oktyabrina shouted about a 'supreme emergency', but it was obvious that nothing would move the guard. Having come this far, however, she couldn't abandon the 'mercy mission'. After we'd driven a few hundred meters back down the road, she asked me to stop the car. The fence of the hospital grounds was made of raw timbers, already sagging. Oktyabrina took the provisions from the car and I helped her climb over.

Her absence, she assured me, would be *spectacularly* brief—not a *tick* more than half an hour, for I was due for cocktails at the British Embassy. The newspaper in which the provisions were wrapped tore as I passed them over the fence. I retrieved a jar of Bulgarian jam and put it in Oktyabrina's little mitten, which peeked over the top board like a baby bird's beak.

'Thanks a million, Zhoe darling—for you and for absolutely everything,' she shouted. 'Half an hour, I hope to die. Please violate me if I'm late—even if I'm *not*. And darling, *don't worry*.'

I wasn't at all worried. Russian hospitals are notoriously lenient with strangers who've somehow sneaked inside. I heard Oktyabrina's rabbit steps crunching along the snow crust as she advanced through the woods towards the complex. Then she fell, squealed, giggled and picked herself up again.

I'd allowed an hour for Oktyabrina's visit. The woods softened the cold, and I spent most of the time outside the car. The newspaper from which the provisions had fallen had a wonderfully comic letter from an indignant grandmother, a Communist of forty years' standing, complaining of a fur workshop in her district that dispatched its workers to stores to buy up its own products at state prices, then resold them for double on the black market. I blocked out an article on the theme, softening the conclusion to avoid trouble.

A bowlegged man appeared on the road, mumbling to his large, sad mongrel. To me, the man rambled about 'ships from a foreign planet' that had landed in nearby woods. They had come to make a deal with Politburo bigwigs, he said, to sell them a thousand pensioners a week as slaves. He urged me to return that night 'for proof'.

Oktyabrina had been gone an hour when the man limped on. Waves of exasperation passed, and I returned to the gate in case she was waiting there. I scouted several hundred yards further along the fence in case she'd lost her bearings. When I returned to the car, she'd been gone almost two hours; I had to leave for the British Embassy. The epithet I drew in the snow crust for her was a favorite of Gelda's during her milder fits.

Gelda called the next morning: Oktyabrina had skipped work again. She was more irritated than worried—until the following day, when we faced the fact: Oktyabrina had disappeared again.

Gelda and I met after work to consider the possibilities. One theory of mine seemed worst: the emotions unleashed at our revel had somehow been transferred back to Vladimir. They had eloped.

Saturday was a visiting day at the hospital—but men-

255

tion of Vladimir's name stopped us at the guardhouse. A younger guard scanned the registry book and scowled. A policeman joined him to question us about our identity. Together, they announced that Vladimir had left the hospital—they could not say for where.

'We don't inform strangers about former patients. He's been discharged. You have no further business here.'

I drove Gelda to Oktyabrina's latest room. It was in the basement of a converted monastery not far from Vladimir's apartment. The windowless cubicle was empty; the family who let it hadn't seen Oktyabrina since the morning of the 'mercy mission'. They refused to tell us more: detectives had come to examine Oktyabrina's things—and to warn them that they faced prosecution for profiteering on their apartment.

The rest of the weekend was a see-saw of anxiety: we would dash somewhere on a fruitless lead, and return to pace Gelda's room. The secretary of the Museum of V. I. Lenin's Funeral Train at Paveletsky Station—a trite propaganda palace—felt certain that Vladimir was still in the hospital, since his mother had telephoned to this effect that very morning, explaining his absence.

We traced Vladimir's home telephone and Gelda called. No one answered until evening. Then it was a woman, obviously Vladimir's mother. When Gelda asked to speak to him, she replaced the receiver.

Sunday was election day for representatives to the Supreme Soviet. Gelda had to drop her ballot, pre-marked by machine, in the box at a school near her room; then we drove to the pet market. But Oktyabrina did not appear there during the whole of the long afternoon.

On Monday morning, the election results—99.4 per cent for the unopposed Communist-picked candidates—were reported as a 'magnificent demonstration of the superiority of Soviet democracy'. I was writing up the

256

story when Kostya telephoned. He had just heard from a typist in the Moscow City Council.

'The kid's been taken to Petrovka.'

Before we could uncover more, the article appeared which made Oktyabrina a celebrity at last. It occupied six full columns in *Komsomolskaya Pravda*. But her name leapt from the sea of compacted print.

### RIFF-RAFF
—A Feuilleton—

*The conversation was prolonged, painful and futile.*

*I went to the window. The street sparkled with festive lights, and happy smiles adorned the faces of thousands of strolling Muscovites. But I felt as if I'd swallowed a glass of castor oil.*

*Then she was led away by the warders. We all fervently hope that this will be the last time she is under guard. But she gives us no encouragement.*

*Even now she is smugly unrepentant. Despite all she's done and everything that awaits her, Oktyabrina Matveyeva clings to the intolerable squalor of her way of life. As our conversation ended, she told a last, pathetic story about her 'marvelous lovers' who would 'rescue her magnificently, like a tragic damsel in distress'.*

*Under the circumstances, after all that had happened, this fatuity was not affecting, but vulgar. Vulgar and gangrenous, like everything she stands for. Like the condition of her soul. . . .*

*But not like the first impression she makes. I met her accidentally: as I was leaving Petrovka 38 a slight commotion at the entrance interrupted the building's quietly disciplined, hard-working life. Eighteen-year-old Oktyabrina Matveyeva was being led in under guard.*

*My first thought was involuntary: had there been a*

*mistake in the arrest of this sapling of a girl? A girl who, by the wide-eyed 'innocent' look of her, belonged almost anywhere else? Everything I knew about the work of the People's police made this improbable. But in the end, I concluded that they had indeed erred—in not having arrested her much sooner.*

*She had been living in Moscow over a year. During this time, she was involved with nothing that was not illegal, immoral, degenerate or offensive to the Soviet way of life.*

*The contrast between her appearance and reputation intrigued me. I decided to follow the case—from Petrovka 38 to the place of detention to which she was subsequently delivered. It is a hard duty to report the filth I uncovered.*

*Oktyabrina Matveyeva was arrested in a hospital ward, where she had caused chaos and suffering to gravely ill patients—while remaining callously indifferent. This was entirely characteristic: screaming at doctors in a hospital ward—where she had no business whatsoever—was but the latest of a string of 'exploits'.*

*Nine months ago, she deliberately tried to help a known speculator escape arrest in a major railroad station. A month earlier, she created a disturbance in our capital's beloved Lenin Museum—an uproar which the words 'outrageous', 'scandalous' and 'revolting' cannot encompass. In short, she spat on everything most cherished by the Soviet people.*

*No one will be surprised that a person who endangers hospital patients and gleefully blasphemes our Leader does not value honest labor. By her own admission, Matveyeva has not worked a single day during her 'sojourn' in Moscow.*

He who does not work, neither shall he eat. *But how*

*does a non-worker exist? By being a parasite—a sucker of society's blood.*

*Each parasite steals in its own way. Matveyeva's was to leech on spineless men. Her list was long—and did not fail to include members of the so-called foreign press corps: mole-like creatures who rummage through our society's garbage, from which they concoct their 'reportage'. Matveyeva was not too fastidious to accept handouts from these pitiable outcasts. In other words, she was a prostitute.*

*And a speculator. For she also busied herself buying and selling rags. She never wasted an opportunity to turn a kopek in some back alley. Her compulsion to sell junk was as strong as to sell her body. . . .*

*One more 'detail': Oktyabrina Matveyeva had no business in Moscow in the first place. She came not to study or work, but specifically to live her putrid way of life— without a propiska, of course. She was a depraved individualist who not merely disregarded society, but sneered at it.*

*But more than this provoked my nausea on that brilliant February evening. I was alone with Matveyeva. The warden hoped that I might unravel what still puzzled everyone.*

*'What made you insult society at every opportunity, Oktyabrina? Was something troubling you?'*

*'Do let's discuss something more interesting. Who sold you that tie you're wearing? It's a fascinating piece—for a museum, I mean.'*

*'Look through the windows, Oktyabrina. All those people—they're happy because they've found their place in life. They work. Raise children. Contribute to the society that nurtures them. Does that mean nothing to you?'*

*'Who wants to have babies? Just to spend their lives at some desk hearing about obligations. . . . I might tell*

*you what one of my most marvelous lovers said about that. He was also a journalist, from Rome. . . .'*

*To many of my questions, Matveyeva produced an inane smirk and corresponding gobbledygook, insulting even the Russian language. But a fool is happy only in fairy-tales, as they say.*

*How is it possible that such a girl can 'flourish' in our socialist society? We once believed that the elimination of capitalism would insure the disappearance of her kind of decadence. But facts must be faced: 50 years have passed since the Great October Socialist Revolution—for which, with a final stinging irony, Oktyabrina Matveyeva was named. And although our achievements in those five decades have thrilled the world, we cannot be content while scum like she still poison our society.*

*Thus the answer is not in slogans but lies in a full and objective examination of the facts: what turned Oktyabrina Matveyeva rotten. We asked a reporter in Omsk to investigate her background. He visited her parents. They live in the quiet village of Nikolaiyevka, Omsk Province; and are long-standing members of the thriving 'Our Leninist Path' state farm. Vladimir Pavlovich, the father, operates a combine. Svetlana Petrovna, Oktyabrina's mother, works in a new brick dairy barn.*

*Oktyabrina herself was trained as a milkmaid. Her younger sister was a gold medalist in the local school. The family seemed to lack nothing.*

*But those who said this cared too little about Soviet responsibility for one's neighbors to look beneath the surface, where grave trouble lurked. Oktyabrina had hardly cut her pigtails when her 'career' as a parasite and cheat was launched.*

*She had left school. She treated her work with unconcealed contempt. She was often missing from the morning milking, her most crucial duty. A search would find her hidden with a fashion magazine, or trying to distract a young tractor driver. Her cows suffered visibly from her wilful neglect.*

*She was as cruel to her parents. Beneath the surface of innocent curiosity, a wholly selfish ego was running wild, like malignant cancer.*

*'Finally we had to send her to a colony,' said Svetlana Petrovna, wiping away tears. 'We were all so ashamed. But she was wild; we couldn't cope with her.'*

*Yet the family history is more complex. Sympathy for her parents cannot absolve them of their blame for Okty-abrina's deep moral flaws.*

*That they took no part in community life—avoiding meetings, even films, in the Palace of Culture—was in itself an ominous warning. The Matveyevs isolated themselves from the socialist collective—in order to booze. They were known on the farm as 'the moonshine pair'.*

*And when they drank, vodka's fever possessed them. Neighbors described repulsive, shrieking battles. More-over, vodka alone held them together. They were never heard to exchange an affectionate word. They never strolled together through the neat little village, went to the well together, or watched the sunset, hand in hand. . . .*

*But these details are not our concern here. Our con-cern is why intolerable cynicism and anti-social attitudes were permitted to fester. After six months in a juvenile colony, Oktyabrina blithely resumed her anti-social ways. Unobserved and unhindered. No one bothered with the festering sore. Because no one saw any immedi-ate advantage in intervening. No one cared.*

*This was the gravest fallacy. For when infections like those in the Matveyev family are allowed to fester, the whole of society eventually suffers. The people who must cauterize the infections suffer. You and I suffer.*

*And the greatest sufferers are our children, who are exposed to the infection before they are fully grown and morally strong. Everything we have built in our socialist society becomes tainted; everything we cherish.*

*This rottenness doesn't go completely unnoticed. Obnoxious youths are sometimes arrested and lectured. But too often without further action—because 'no specific crime has been committed'. Thus even the People's police too can forget their socialist obligations.*

*For what is hooliganism? Hooliganism is cynical actions committed as a barefaced challenge to society. Do the actions of Matveyeva express such cynicism? She behaved in full and conscious contradiction of our ethical principles. And her declaration as our 'conversation' was drawing to its wretched close summed up her brazen cynicism 'I don't understand what you're going on about,' she said, smirking. 'Nothing can stop me from living the way of life I like.'*

*By goodness, she was right! No court, no police officer, no prosecutor, not you or I—no one could prevent her from being a prostitute, disgracing Soviet womanhood and pouring filth on our Motherland.*

*But I suggest that these insects can be controlled. Energetic application of the legal sanctions against hooliganism will stop good-for-nothings taking advantage of our indecisiveness.*

*It must be made clear that insulting and abasing the national dignity of the Soviet people is no less a social danger than a punch in the face. Soviet citizens should not be required to live with this stain on the honor of our womanhood and citizenship.*

*We are all responsible for the moral cleanliness of our capital. So we can hardly find it onerous to take a broom and sweep this riff-raff out of the city. Cleanliness is the first step to health, as the old saying goes. Besides, our air will be noticeably purer.*

There was a time when I imagined something like this would be 'romantic'. It was intrigue in a foreign land; I was involved with someone in danger. Now the article brought only a dizzy weakness. I had to rest before reading it again.

There was too much to take in; peripheral points struck me first. The regular use of fabrication by the Soviet press: when Prague workers were needed to applaud the Kremlin's invasion in August, *Pravda* coolly invented them and 'quoted' their cheers for the Soviet tanks. Yet the report about Oktyabrina's parents rang terribly true. Her daily references to cows and barns—'pull the teats too hard, the milk will be sour' and all the others—flashed to mind, followed by waves of understanding for who she was and was trying to become. Yellow fever in Omsk? Vodka was the disease; now her repugnance for it made grisly sense.

Otherwise, I could only guess what proportion the author had been deceitful as opposed to merely misinformed. He was a regular contributor of feuilletons, a well-liked genre which permits important topics to be treated from a supposedly personal point of view: the indignant citizen-journalist appeals to the authorities to put an end to some moral abuse. Of course the opposite was true: without directions from above, no Soviet reporter would dare suggest the police were too lenient. Nor would a major newspaper print an article of this length without high-level editorial—meaning governmental—instructions. These were undoubtedly issued in pursuance of the anti-hooligan campaign.

Within an hour, we'd uncovered the first major distortion. The fact was that Oktyabrina had been taken to Petrovka on suspicion of stealing drugs! Finding her in one of the hospital's store rooms, the arresting policeman thought he'd uncovered something big. Oktyabrina was interrogated about narcotics for two days in Petrovka: once suspicion has been aroused, Moscow police—even more than most in the world—are loath to abandon it. The investigating officer did so only after the drug notion had completely disintegrated. He then transferred her—reluctantly—to an ordinary prison on less serious charges.

Kostya learned this though a former girl friend in the Moscow City Council. The author surely knew these facts, but failed to mention them lest they weaken his article. His feuilleton was typical in purpose as well as tone: it set the stage for a trial intended as a public example.

I read it again that afternoon, then drove to the hospital for my own investigation. Something told me that Vladimir, the unmentioned key to the puzzle, was still there.

The younger man occupied the guardhouse. He'd have recognized me, even if I pretended to visit another patient. If I were seen climbing the fence, I'd be expelled from the country with nothing achieved. I abandoned hope of slipping into the hospital.

But not of finding out. When a story is vital in this country, one method sometimes works: interview the janitor or cleaning woman. Many won't understand the story's significance, and therefore speak candidly. Others will know about the affair, but their attitude towards it may differ enough from the 'line' to provide an important clue. At last I could use my professional skills for a story that mattered.

Vladimir's ward number came back to me from the register the week before. I drove back to the point where

Oktyabrina's mitten last peeked above the fence. This was a good position for intercepting everyone who'd left the hospital and was making for the solitary bus stop. The task began of finding someone who worked in Ward 4.

I might have given up after several hours had not patience at this game been rewarded before. Dusk descended early, but the snow diffused a greyish light. I was relieved that my message to Oktyabrina had been erased by fresh falls, until I caught the fallacy behind the thought. When the moon appeared, the patter of animals enlivened the woods. I smoked a pack of Camels.

The information appeared in the form of three student nurses, chattering happily after a long shift. They were indeed from Ward 4, and solved the mystery of Oktyabrina's arrest as I drove them home.

The girls talked in unison: Vladimir receiving extra attention from the moment he was put to bed . . . his mother carping at everything in the ward, down to the Intourist calendar with a well-endowed girl . . . her position in the Ministry of Education allowing her to choose her own visiting hours . . . Oktyabrina appearing gaily in the ward and Vladimir flushing with conflicting emotions.

'It's you,' he cried from his bed. 'You've come!—but dearest, you must go away.'

'Calm yourself, Vladik,' said Oktyabrina. 'You'll be in marvelous shape soon. I know about hospitals—my mother practically ran one, after all.'

Far from calming himself, Vladimir raced into a series of exciting pleas: that Oktyabrina recognize the changes in him since her letter to Mama, that she return to him when he was well—but now leave, immediately. He had just overcome a sneezing fit when a woman with a muff entered the ward.

265

'Summon the duty doctor, Comrade Nurse. And I'd like to see my son's charts.'

When Vladimir's mother recognized Oktyabrina, her first reaction was a surprising nervousness. Moreover, she vented her feelings not on Oktyabrina herself, but on the hospital staff. How dare they allow outsiders into the ward during non-visiting hours. It was outrageous. . . . But she rather quickly drifted into her now familiar sermons about civic duty and reminders that when *she* was a Young Communist, people *respected* authority.

Someone recognized the moment to ease Oktyabrina from the ward, apparently ending the incident. But a moment later, Oktyabrina peeked into the doorway.

'Don't forget to wash the apples, Vladik.' She winked. 'And I want to wish you the best of everything in life— the most marvelous *good luck*.' She disappeared into the corridor again. Searching for the staircase, she opened a storeroom door.

Oktyabrina's afterthought was too much for Vladimir's mother. She strode into the corridor, demanding that 'measures' be taken. The open storeroom prompted her to add theft of state property to her accusations. Reluctantly, the staff summoned a security officer.

The nurses were certain that the bagatelle would end in a lecture. But Oktyabrina's lack of papers and a satisfactory explanation of her identity led to a call to the police—whom she had to avoid at any cost. When it was found that the storeroom contained narcotics and Oktyabrina had no *propiska*, the situation turned ominous.

When Oktyabrina was seated in the motorcycle sidecar for delivery to Petrovka, Vladimir's mother seemed somewhat contrite. 'Nevertheless,' she said, 'it was wrong to let my boy, with his advantages, carry on with her kind. She's a common shop-girl, just look at that old dress!'

Oktyabrina was puzzled. 'But I could have *escaped*,'

she kept repeating. 'I just stayed there and let her call the police. What a blunder for the sake of my new maturity!'

The following week I was in Belgrade to cover the trip there of a Soviet Party delegation. I then flew to Munich to meet an owner of my newspaper. When I returned to Moscow, Oktyabrina's case was still under investigation. She was in a prison called 'Old Sailors', whose charm is known not to extend beyond its name. We could not visit her: prisoners under investigation on criminal charges can be seen only by their immediate family.

Moreover, we were not permitted to visit even after completion of her investigation. This was accomplished with unusual dispatch, leading, according to Kostya's source, to indictment under paragraph II of article 206: malicious hooliganism. This article falls under Chapter Ten of the Criminal Code: Crimes Against Public Security, Public Order and Public Health:

> *Article 206. Hooliganism.* Hooliganism—that is, intentional actions violating public order in a coarse manner and expressing clear disrespect for society—shall be punished by deprivation of freedom for a term not exceeding one year. . . .
> *Paragraph II. Malicious hooliganism*—that is, the same actions committed by a person previously convicted of hooliganism . . . or distinguished in their content by exceptional cynicism or impudence—shall be punished by deprivation of freedom for a term not exceeding five years.

# 24

☐ The day of the trial passed, as these things do, in the semi-trance necessary for self-control. There is much to be said about the emotions of that day, but I'll keep to a reporter's account of the scene.

The courthouse was a few hundred yards from the American Embassy, a squat two-story structure in the old Russian style of logs and yellow plaster. The floorboards sagged and walls flaked from dehydration.

Kostya and I arrived at the same time. It was a clear morning, but so cold that fingers ached through sheepskin gloves. Nothing in nature moved except people, by sheer will. And things made by people: busses ghostly with frost.

A plaque beside the weatherbeaten door read, 'Ministry of Justice, RSFSR, PEOPLE'S COURT, Krasnopresnensky District'. Why the trial was held there was a small mystery—and also an apparent violation of the law, for Oktyabrina had neither worked nor lived in Krasnopresnensky District. In fact, she'd rarely visited this part of the city except to meet me occasionally near the Embassy and to visit the zoo. But this was the least disturbing violation of criminal procedure.

The most disturbing was the conduct of the entire trial in camera. There was no justification whatever for this; Soviet law requires all trials to be public except when state security may be jeopardized, or minors or intimate sexual matters involved. None of these exceptions applied to Oktyabrina. Yet not only was the door of her court-room shut and guarded, but a wiry police lieutenant cleared the corridor leading to it minutes before she was escorted through, from the prisoners' chambers in the basement.

Kostya inquired about the secrecy in the court office. No reason was given of course, but we guessed: hooli-ganism trials of women can be an embarrassment to the authorities. Especially when there was no guarantee that the defendant would exhibit proper contrition, efforts were often made to suppress the details, except as re-vealed through the unique prism of the Soviet press.

In any case, Kostya and I were permitted to return to a bench in the corridor only after the trial had begun. When we opened the door, it was slammed shut by a po-liceman inside. At the third try, he cursed and looked at his gun. During the split second the door was open we could see the prosecutor sitting beneath a steamy win-dow—a middle-aged woman in a blue uniform and her hair in a severe bun.

This was on the second floor of the old dwelling, a succession of former bedrooms converted to courtrooms. Clusters of workers waited outside adjoining courtrooms; the smell was of their clothes, acrid tobacco and the building's dilapidation. And of the toilet, a tiny cubicle whose door jammed against the slanted floor. Few people managed to drag it fully closed. From time to time, de-fendants were led to and from courtrooms. With their shaved skulls and ragged clothes, they might already have served years in dungeons.

Gelda arrived after ten o'clock, her face made fierce by Asian 'flu. The pits in her cheeks had turned purply in the cold, and she swallowed pills after every *papirosa*. Fifteen minutes had passed when I heard a distinctive swish-clump of galoshes along the corridor. I had just recognized these noises when the Minister appeared. Surprise flicked in his eyes at the sight of us, but the larger emotions were weariness, pain and disgust. He dropped his briefcase on to the floor and blew his nose into a dirty handkerchief.

'M-m-miserable b-bastard,' he said. 'M-miserable b-bastard.' It was the first I'd heard him swear. He removed a greasy notebook from his briefcase.

'N-notes,' he declared angrily. 'I'm g-going to c-catch the eight o'clock t-train.'

The Minister's appearance was wholly unexpected but more perplexing was how he'd learned about Oktyabrina's trouble—obviously before the *Komsomolskaya Pravda* article. For he kept alluding to his campaign to rescue Oktyabrina through intervention by his former chiefs at the Ministry. From Saratov, he had written, telegraphed and finally telephoned everyone he could think of in high places in Moscow. All this would have taken a minimum of weeks. The Minister himself called it tilting at windmills.

'I'll tell you one thing straight away,' he stammered, 'don't try to pull strings from the barn. Nobody wants to know you when you've been disgraced. You might as well have foot-and-mouth disease.'

The Minister's self-condemnation lacked his old, endearing whimsicality. He was now acutely sardonic, and berated himself cruelly.

He broke the nib of his pen writing in his notebook and rummaged his pockets for a stub of a pencil. He was irritated for having arrived so late, as if this would bear crucially on the outcome. Although he'd been in Moscow several days to continue his defense campaign, he confused the name of the district that morning and went to a courthouse in another part of town.

'M-miserable b-bastard. And w-who the hell t-told y-*you* people I c-can't go inside?'

His fur-collared overcoat was distinctly shabbier; Kostya's moroccan gloves might have been used for digging. Despite the gloves, the Minister ignored Kostya—and was also unaccountably chilly to me. Only towards Gelda, a total stranger, did he show any interest. This was more than reciprocated, despite Gelda's 'flu and gloom—despite everything. For the Minister's moustache was more prominent than ever on his newly haggard face.

I thought of soothing the Minister's self-disgust over his failure to save Oktyabrina, as I'd once tried to alleviate his failure to make films. In our cottage days, I talked of my own washout as a novelist; now, similarly, I could describe my own uselessness in Oktyabrina's defense. But this defeat was too new and too acid to mouth into consolation, even had the Minister wanted to listen.

In a real way, my failure to help Oktyabrina was more punishing than his: I hadn't lifted a finger. Kostya kept reminding me that the worst a foreigner could do, especially after the feuilleton's clear reference to me, was try to intervene, since this would joyfully be used against Oktyabrina. The Press Department too gave me to understand that they knew all about the affair, and were keeping an eye on me—that is, watching me squirm. They were somewhat cleverer than I thought, knowing that a person's feelings of impotence and guilt don't switch off on signals from Party headquarters.

So I said little to the Minister. Oktyabrina's plight had assembled us physically, but her absence dissolved our intimacy.

The save-Oktyabrina-campaign, such as it was, had been shouldered entirely by Kostya, with less ambitious and somewhat more promising strategy than the Minister's. Lacking contacts in that area and on that level, he had no hopes of influencing the prosecution.

The anti-hooligan crusade was so intense that only personal interest by some high official could have helped. However, Kostya did find and engage one of Moscow's best criminal lawyers. Alexander Kuperman was one of a handful of lawyers who tried to defend his clients on principle instead of advising them to exhibit profound penitence and throw themselves on the mercy of the court and the Motherland. 'He's far too expensive for the likes of us,' Kostya said. 'But he happened to take a fancy to a few lassies of my acquaintance.'

Kostya labored to imitate his usual jaunty self, and spoke of combining 'the kid's' acquittal celebration with a pre-Easter party. But this pretense soon evaporated. Most Soviet trials are dispatched in an hour or two; the longer they exceed this, the slimmer the defendant's chances. Oktyabrina's had run well over the average without so much as the door opening, except when a witness was summoned from a group gathered—hostilely —around a nearby bench.

Behind our own bench, a radiator hissed incessantly, intensifying the heat and smells. Our sweating little group was joined by a bohemian-looking couple, apparently from Oktyabrina's 'underground' contacts. The boy showed us an old triptych that Oktyabrina had given him.

A silver-haired *Komsomolskaya Pravda* reporter also joined us, explaining that he'd been assigned to follow up the case. He smoked expensive East German cigarettes procured from an attaché case, also obviously imported. Since the bench sat only three people, we took turns standing against the flaking wall. Policemen occasionally pushed past us like Cossacks dispersing petitioners to the Tsar.

The trial dragged on. By pressing our ears to the courtroom door, we could distinguish voices, but not words. When Gelda pulled open the door again, the guard furiously kicked it shut. Then he opened it himself to call the next witness. It was the wizened railway pensioner, proprietor of Domolinart. By this time, our little group had been reduced to sullen silence. I was glad of the chance to lose myself in old dreams of glory.

At last a witness—a prim girl supporting the prosecution on behalf of the Young Communist League—emerged from the courtroom and revealed that an adjournment was imminent. Extra policemen appeared to clear the corridor again. We sought a glimpse of Oktyabrina from the bottom of the stairs, but there was a separate route to the basement for prisoners.

On our way towards the main door, we met Vladimir, hunched in the squalid vestibule alongside a plaster Lenin bust. He hadn't come upstairs for fear of being seen by an informer or reporter. His plan was to wait for the verdict in the courtyard, and he had endured this torture until the cold actually numbed his limbs. He wore a new musquash hat, but his nose was still mauve and' his strength depleted.

'I honestly don't understand how they could get everything so wrong,' he quavered. 'Our own organs of socialist legality. . . . After everything she gave me, Oktyabrina being crushed like a butterfly on a wheel. Even Mama doesn't believe the article.'

The lunch break lasted an hour. Kostya used the confusion to smuggle himself into the courtroom. He was ordered out again in the security check before resumption of the trial, but convinced the police lieutenant he was an acoustics engineer assigned to run a test under actual trial conditions. Ten minutes later the judge ejected him permanently, but not before he'd had a good look at the proceedings.

Oktyabrina sat on the 'defendant's bench', guarded by a large policewoman. The judge was an elderly man with greasy glasses. The witness box enclosed the bookshop manager, who had carefully avoided Gelda's eyes in the corridor. Now he was nervously explaining his relationship to Oktyabrina. Both prosecutor and judge interrupted frequently to condemn his 'scandalous laxity' in the shop's management. The testimony ran on rather tediously for some minutes until the prosecutor turned her ire to Oktyabrina.

'You not only led a parasitic and dissolute way of life. You also disrupted an economic enterprise, causing direct harm to the state. Defendant, the court wants to know *exactly* why you spent so much time in Secondhand Bookstore Number 44.'

Oktyabrina sighed wearily. 'If you must know, Madame, the bookshop was a source of a certain enlightenment and self-understanding. I daren't tell you more. Anyway it's easy enough for *you* to be smug—you didn't get what I did for lunch.'

The court was jolted from its post-lunch drowsiness; the judge removed his glasses for a clearer view of Oktyabrina. Searching the room for the source of a snicker, he discovered Kostya and ordered him removed.

Kostya's report to our corridor outpost rallied us for several minutes. Oktyabrina was still concealing her job at the bookshop to avoid implicating Gelda and the manager—which showed that her spirit remained unbroken. Encouraged by Gelda's response to him, the Minister came to life and announced that his wife had divorced him. Gelda pressed her thigh against his on the bench. Vladimir had joined us and, overcoming his awe of the Minister's title, described his interrogations by the police, throughout which he staunchly rejected pressure to denounce Oktyabrina as a slut. This, he boasted, was why the prosecutor hadn't called him as a witness: he was too tough to crack. However no one asked the embarrassing question of why Kuperman hadn't called him in defense.

By this time, the finely-groomed *Komsomolskaya*

*Pravda* reporter was almost one of us. No one objected; the presence of this small pillar of the Establishment was reassuring. Besides, he was very friendly and optimistic about Oktyabrina's chances. He suggested I meet him some day after the trial to exchange professional notes.

But the afternoon quickly became worse than the morning. By four o'clock we sensed the dusk, even though the corridor was windowless. Fear of missing something kept us sweating in our overcoats on the bench, unwilling to make a move except for hurried trips to the toilet. The filthy cubicle was a reminder that Oktyabrina's plight was part of the larger, national one. Scraps of newspaper that had been used for toilet paper littered the floor. Gelda said what no one else would: after a newspaper 'exposé', no defendant was ever acquitted.

No waiting in the world is like a courtroom vigil. Our group smoked a hundred ritual cigarettes, adding heavy smoke to the powdering plaster of the walls. The resulting mixture produced rings around the light bulbs and an oddly subtle coloration to the Lenin-And-Law poster. Kostya found himself reciting poetry, something he hadn't done since his Navy days. He remembered only one poem in its entirety, and this he recited twice, in a voice I'd never heard before. It was from the Mandelshtam volume he'd given me:

> It needn't say a thing,
> Or even try to learn,
> It's sad this way—but also good
> A simple animal soul:
>
> It doesn't yearn to preach,
> It cannot even speak
> But swims, like a young dolphin,
> The aged oceans of the universe.

It was partly this wonder-struck curiosity—too 'nihilistic' for Soviet rule—which had delivered Mandelshtam to tragedy. And Oktyabrina? . . .

Finally the court retired to deliberate the verdict. We learned this from witnesses who emerged from the courtroom, complaining about how late it was to manage their shopping. Word spread that an 'interesting' trial was approaching its climax, and most people still in the building pushed into our corridor to await the verdict. I hated them for adding to the tension without understanding what was at stake.

Soviet law stipulates that even after a closed trial, the reading of the verdict must be open to the public. But when the court had apparently returned from deliberation, only witnesses were permitted inside the courtroom. The police lieutenant slammed the door shut again, like a blade across my throat.

Minutes later the door opened for the last time. The first policeman out had a pulpy vodka face. 'Five years, normal regimen,' he croaked. 'Clear the way there you—move aside.'

We did not believe him: real trials do not end this way. Soon the prosecutor emerged followed by Kuperman, sadly confirming the sentence. The spectators pressed closer, like the Paris rabble straining for a glimpse of the doomed. A police detachment cleared a passageway. When would the judge come to announce the reprieve?

Then Oktyabrina appeared, escorted by a wart-hog of a policewoman and two male colleagues. Her big eyes were pallid, but otherwise she looked healthy and inexplicably taller than before. When she made us out in the murkiness of the corridor, she broke into a grin of relief. It was her first sight of friends since her arrest. But she quickly reshaped the grin into a pout.

'Honestly, you big darlings,' she began. 'How many

276

times have I *told* you: gossip at the well lets the herd go to hell.'

Then she caught sight of the Minister in the corner and grinned again, despite herself. 'Aloha, my dear friend,' she cried. She waved as if from shipboard and blew him a kiss.

'For goodness sake, don't *fuss*,' she exclaimed. 'Read a novel called *Resurrection*: people who are sure about their inner selves thrive on pressures from without.'

All this took less than a minute. Angered by her exchange with non-prisoners, the police escort yanked her away—towards the basement cells, and from there back to jail. Her shoulders were slanted in a certain way which perhaps only I could interpret. I knew she was trying to concentrate on something. Half way down the corridor, she threw her head over her shoulder and her eyes instantly seeped to the depths of mine. It was the same look as when we first met at Kostya's—an obvious artifice to make me feel special. Except that the pretense was gone and more than I'd ever understood was added.

'Zhoe!' she called. 'I'm not walking this rocky road alone. Because I remember everything, understand everything. You simply *can't* leave me now.' The policewoman shoved her forward and she was gone.

The Minister made a move to follow, but stopped and looked at the ceiling. 'So she's finished too,' he stuttered. 'That sprig of youth. And many of our great people will savor its snapping. Oh yes, with somebody else's ass, it's fine to sit on a porcupine.'

He wiped his nose and stared at the handkerchief. 'G-good G-god, my l-language—I'm b-becoming one of *t-them*. Who w-wants some c-cognac, I can't go h-h-home.'

Gelda took his arm and pulled him to the first of many evenings together. At the last minute, the Minister kissed me and begged that I take his briefcase. He had no need of it, he said, and nothing better to give.

'T-try not t-to think about h-her,' he said quietly. 'T-try not to think of m-me. At least you were n-n-never the t-type to g-get r-romantically involved.'

Kostya and I walked the opposite way from the court-house into the needles of frozen mist. 'Listen, Zhoe buddy,' he said, 'hop on the next plane to Paris or some-where—you need a vacation. We all loved her, but the kid was the one in a million for you.'

## 25

☐ The five years are being served in a labor camp. After Stalin, they were renamed 'colonies', but the improvement is largely semantic. Sheer survival is not always at stake for the prisoners, but thanks to grueling physical labor on a deprived diet, it dominates their thoughts. Labor-camp policy makes even ordinary appetites groan; although Oktyabrina's 'normal regimen' gives her the maximum of 2,100 calories a day, she will never have a moment free from hunger.

Kuperman assumes she is in a women's colony of the Mordovian Autonomous Republic, a swampy region with a severe climate some four hundred miles east of Moscow. He does not know precisely which camp; this information is not revealed. Kuperman did not advise appealing against either the verdict or sentence: there was virtually no hope for either, and any commotion might lessen her chances for parole after three years. He is convinced that someone in the Moscow City Communist Party had fixed her sentence prior to the trial, and it is wiser not to oppose such decisions now but wait for an easing of the anti-hooligan campaign.

Four days after the trial, *Komsomolskaya Pravda* ran a second article about Oktyabrina. The author was the genial correspondent who'd shared our vigil.

*Following up the Iniatives of KOMSOMOLSKAYA PRAVDA:*

## THE FINALE OF LA DOLCE VITA

*Oktyabrina Matveyeva is being tried:*

*The same girl whom this newspaper described in abundant detail last month in the feuilleton 'Riff-Raff.' Today we can answer the storm of indignation and outrage that her behavior provoked among our readers. For the acts which soiled the dignity of the Soviet people, Matveyeva was brought to criminal justice.*

*Frankly, it's sad to see such a girl in the dock. She should be dashing to class with excited girl friends, discussing her infatuation with some newly-discovered poetry, turning the heads of happy young cavaliers—for nature has not shortchanged her.*

*In short, she should be living life to the hilt and growing up: learning to be a responsible adult.*

*But no, she's here—in the dock of a criminal court. None of her 'magnificent lovers' has managed to 'rescue' her—even bothered to visit the court for support. But this will not deter the court from its duty to administer justice in accordance with V. I. Lenin's teachings.*

*Matveyeva's guilt is spelled out in great detail. The facts are meticulously established and corroborated by documents and witnesses' testimony. Moreover, Matveyeva herself denies nothing. Nevertheless, the trial lasts many hours. With great tact and benevolence Judge Pyotr Vladimorovich Milutin tries to penetrate Matveyeva's soul. One senses that they see before them not primarily a criminal, but a person—one whose whole life still lies ahead. (Incidentally, it's a pity no one thought of televising the proceedings. They would have been extremely instructive.)*

*Step by step, sparing her vanity, the Judge lays bare her character. But nothing has changed. She still refuses to understand how she has poured filth on her Mother-*

land and people. On the contrary she demonstrates her contempt for society by insulting the Judge.

Question: *And now, Oktyabrina. Do you still see nothing wrong in being supported by one man after another?*

Matveyeva: *They never complained about not getting their money's worth. If you must know, some were in love with me.*

Question: *Have you ever thought about what you live for Oktyabrina? Ever thought about your relationship to the ideals, work and sacrifices taking place all around you for our common goals?*

Matveyeva: *Perhaps I have thought about my ideals, but I don't discuss intimacies with strangers. Anyway, you can't put into words who you are and what you live for. A fish moves towards where it's deeper, a person towards where it's better—perhaps you know the saying.*

Question: *Once again, the court asks you to consider your behavior. Don't you regret the way you live?*

Matveyeva: *I lived the way I wanted to. I don't see what's wrong with that. I mean, I never hurt anybody, did I?*

*She lived as she wanted to. Didn't hurt anyone. The words were painful. For Matveyeva refuses to recognize that Soviet society, itself, all its deeply humane Leninist principles and goals, is viciously undermined by her kind of gangrene.*

*Who craves this undermining? Our enemies of course: the enemies of Leninism, of everything progressive in mankind. Our enemies feed on the hope that riff-raff like Matveyeva, specially among our youth, will somehow weaken our socialist state. In this hysterical hope, they smuggle all the anti-Soviet drivel they can through our borders. Such as the tawdry and obscene 'magazines' that so delighted Matveyeva.*

*For many people the expression, 'the putrid influence*

281

*of the Western way of life', still hangs in mid-air. Oktya-*
*brina Matveyeva, has made it sickeningly graphic. She*
*'presented herself' to Moscow over a year ago. Since then*
*her life has been vulgar and ugly—rotten, like a swamp.*
*Like her 'answers' in court and her 'ideals'. Like every-*
*thing she represents.*

*What should be done with people who violate every-*
*thing we cherish? Who corrupt our youth, the inheritors*
*of our revolutionary Leninist ideals? The court reached*
*the only correct answer to this melancholy question.*
*Having searched deep into the defendant's soul and*
*found nothing sacred there, it sentenced her to five years'*
*deprivation of freedom.*

This was my last contact with Oktyabrina. I haven't
heard from her again; now there is no one from whom I
can expect to hear *of* her. Spring smells floating through
my window make it hard to focus on facts, but I have a
grip on them.

I probably won't hear from Oktyabrina for three
years, until her early release for good behavior. It will be
hard to see her even then, for she won't be permitted to
live in Moscow. In theory, visits of up to two weeks are
allowed. But any one of a dozen officials acquainted with
Oktyabrina's dossier may prevent her from coming to
the capital and its temptations. She'd risk too much, a
much more severe second conviction, by sneaking in
again, without a *propiska*. Most likely, she'll live out her
life in Nikolaiyevka. Or, if she's lucky—because she may
be kept on her collective farm—in the relative cosmopol-
itanism of Omsk.

When they are imaginary, stories like this sometimes
end with a letter from their heroines. I've thought of the
one Oktyabrina would send so often that I can write it
myself. It would be in her unevenly sloping script; the
text would be both breathless and full of imagery, which

means it could either have been dashed off on an impulse or carefully pondered.

> Darling Zhoe!
> When the moon comes up over the hills, the snow is somehow reddish, like a blanket of garnets. Only in my beloved Russian countryside have I come to understand a certain inner meaning of existence, the ecstasy not only of being alive, but of being *oneself* in an environment of obligations. This is why I haven't written sooner: I've been frantically busy exploring my depths. . . .

There would be an explanation—with much truth—of how camp life had ended her final, final silly phase. She would make sly hints about our 'devastating' love-making, and guarded references to my divorce, the causes of which genuinely interested her in our few 'man-and-wife' days before Vladimir's illness. She would pretend she hadn't needed my food parcels but couch her thanks in jokes; the p.s. would be an old Russian saying about separation not being alienation. No smudge of cosmetics would soil the notepaper: camp conditions would see to that.

But the note will never come. If the censorship of ordinary mail is fierce, what chance have prisoners' letters?

I'm not worried about spiritual damage to Oktyabrina in her camp. Most prisoners, if not debased on arrival, are hardened beyond recognition by the severe conditions and coarseness of guards and fellow convicts. Oktyabrina is immune to this—but she is surely thinner now: it is a question of pure hunger and cold.

I hope she's allowed to wear my sheepskin coat. But it's strange that I have more presents from her than she from me. The mass-produced *matrioshka* and splendid Birth of Christ icon adorn my living-room, together with the Minister's office plants. The Maxwell House can now holds my paper clips instead of hairpins or Gelda's worms.

And I have memories. Some well up so overwhelmingly that I suspect self-deception: it's not Oktyabrina I pity, but myself; not the injustice to her but the deprivation to me. Other memories are straightforward: the way she sipped a glass of tea.

The way she grimaced when it had too much lemon and smacked her lips in exultation after making it sweet. No one can understand the joy of her hundred hourly performances without actually seeing her mime's face. I liked her best when she was unaware that I was watching. Every gesture—the clutching of the glass, the pursing of her lips—was an event.

Hardly a day in our year lacks something to remember. A week before the heatwave, when she still had hopes for Alexander, she coaxed him to the ballet. The tickets required considerable hunting, and she seduced Alexander by pretending they were for a visiting African troupe with 'naked bosoms and all kinds of erotic rituals'. But once in the lobby Alexander spied the *Sleeping Beauty* poster and left. Whereupon Oktyabrina prowled the streets to procure a substitute escort: a corpulent colonel.

Of all the animals in the zoo, she loved a young chimpanzee best. He was named 'Cheetah', in honor of the Tarzan films, the *exotika* of Oktyabrina's schoolgirl generation. One day, a drunk teenager fractured Cheetah's skull with a rock. Oktyabrina's reaction was a characteristic mixture of cunning and fantasy: she sent a signed petition for 'recuperative' bananas to the Supreme Soviet. It came to nothing, but I hadn't realized until now that she risked discovery for this 'mercy mission' too.

I like to retrace those 'exploits'; the memory of more

284

personal moments leads too swiftly to self-pity. After our evening at Kostya's, she came home with me and entered the bedroom directly, saying only that all the lights should be off. At any time before this in our year, we would have been disastrous. That night, our nervousness lasted only until her feet were warm, after which she clung to me with more strength than should have resided in her skinny arms and her trembling legs. An hour later, I knew that more than nervousness kept her thin. She made 'Zhoe' into a hundred Russiant variants; she cried out in free delight—not quite the same as mine, for she was still too young to know how crazy it is, how truly exalted, to have passion with a friend.

The next morning, she stretched out on the davenport. 'I feel so contented somehow,' she said. 'Like a cow—is that absolutely inexcusable?'

I suppose it's obvious that I never see the davenport without thinking of her. Several places in the city have the same effect. The ice-cream café where she wolfed down sundaes with jam. And the Kropotkinskaya Quai, where one June evening, leathery truck drivers braked their rattling machines to contemplate her, strolling in a preposterous slouch hat. She waved to them like the dewy-eyed young heroine of third-rate Soviet films, re-marking about the maternal properties of the sun, then setting brilliantly on the river.

*Let there always be sunshine!* . . .

And there is Petrovka of course. It is more teeming than ever lately, even on sopping afternoons. The pedestrian railings have been moved further into the street, but the abstracted crowds spill beyond them as be-fore, oblivious to the traffic, the policemen's whistles and each other. The lines at stalls offering gloves, cigarettes, panties and postage stamps are as long as ever. Today there is an exceptional crush for pineapples, of which a shipload recently arrived. But lemons disappeared again almost two months ago, and tea without them isn't the same.

The Bolshoi Theatre's sagging roof is under repair; its makeshift tin drainpipes are as crooked as ever. Behind the theater, an establishment called Café Friendship has greedily absorbed a coat of spring paint. It is an outdoor eatery featuring frankfurters, inedible green peas and chipped glasses of muddy coffee. Across the street, Wanda, the Polish shop, has put a lustrous lipstick on sale, and a thousand women materialize instantly to besiege the counters.

Bookstore No 44 carries on as before, several doors above Wanda; the Minister's request for appointment as the new manager has been denied. In the struggling crowd, a middle-aged woman with rimless glasses and a tight bun, nothing more or less than a Chekhov character, is looking for a volume of Chekhov stories. When she leaves, it is to fight her way into a fish store for supper's salted cod, but she loses no dignity in doing it.

The fish store, a pathetic butcher's, a pharmacy from a silent movie set. . . . A cluster of red kerchiefs on school children stands out in the ceaseless stream of bodies pushing along the street and in and out of these establishments. Then three bantan Asian soldiers strolling arm in arm, followed by a hulking muzhik with a full beard holding tight to his grandson, who in turn is clutching a white toy horse.

A grizzled taxi driver slows down to allow a neatly-dressed man to beg for a ride. A handsome girl is giving an impatient stranger her telephone number, knowing they'll be in bed together in several hours. A schoolboy in uniform checks to see whether he still has his wrist watch. A hundred peasant grandmothers trudge onward with their sacks. . . . What makes these scenes seem so memorable? Perhaps no more than a perception that we have little say in who we are and what we do. Something in this old street makes truism about fate and mortality especially real.

Petrovka is what Petrovka was; even the changes seem to speak of the continuity of Russian life—and of the human condition. I can't say I love it any longer, but it's her street and I want to stay. What would I do in Chicago?

'*You* can't *leave me now*,' she called in the courthouse. Surely this was meant to imply that I'm with her, 'inside' forever. But we both know enough about her use of ambiguity to recognize its other meaning. The problem is to keep my stories neutral enough to deter expulsion. This is progressively harder; now even Esenin is under attack in vengeful tirades. The retreat towards Stalinism wasn't temporary, as optimists hoped; we've settled into another age of hard times, seemingly more natural to Russia than its occasional liberalizing spurts.

To ease this pressure, I walk down Petrovka in the early afternoon. The familiar ache of being alone is also a comfort, and a bond with the missing person. I indulge myself in the old game of seeing her reflection in a shop window and postponing the moment of discovering that the girl is a pale imitation. I can't imagine that I'll never see her again.

978-0-595-47602-2
0-595-47602-3

Printed in the United States
93574LV00003B/220-237/A

9 780595 476022